Tales of the Alhambra

Tales of the Alhambra

by Washington Irving

©2011 SMK Books

Wilder Publications, LLC.
PO Box 3005
Radford VA 24143-3005

ISBN 10: 1-61720-462-5
ISBN 13: 978-1-61720-462-3

Table of Contents:

The Journey

In the spring of 1829, the author of this work, whom curiosity had brought into Spain, made a rambling expedition from Seville to Granada in company with a friend, a member of the Russian Embassy at Madrid.

Many are apt to picture Spain to their imaginations as a soft southern region, decked out with the luxuriant charms of voluptuous Italy. On the contrary, though there are exceptions in some of the maritime provinces, yet, for the greater part, it is a stern, melancholy country, with rugged mountains, and long sweeping plains, destitute of trees, and indescribably silent and lonesome, partaking of the savage and solitary character of Africa. What adds to this silence and loneliness, is the absence of singing-birds, a natural consequence of the want of groves and hedges. The vulture and the eagle are seen wheeling about the mountain-cliffs, and soaring over the plains, and groups of shy bustards stalk about the heaths, but the myriads of smaller birds, which animate the whole face of other countries are met with but in few provinces in Spain, and in those chiefly among the orchards and gardens which surround the habitations of man.

In the interior provinces the traveller occasionally traverses great tracts cultivated with grain as far as the eye can reach, waving at times with verdure, at other times naked and sunburnt, but he looks around in vain for the hand that has tilled the soil. At length he perceives some village on a steep hill, or rugged crag, with mouldering battlements and ruined watch-tower: a stronghold, in old times against civil war or Moorish inroad; for the custom among the peasantry of congregating together for mutual protection is still kept up in most parts of Spain, in consequence of the maraudings of roving freebooters.

But though a great part of Spain is deficient in the garniture of groves and forests, and the softer charms of ornamental cultivation, yet its scenery is noble in its severity and in unison with the attributes of its people; and I think that I better understand the proud, hardy, frugal, and abstemious Spaniard, his manly defiance of hardships, and contempt of effeminate indulgences, since I have seen the country he inhabits.

There is something, too, in the sternly simple features of the Spanish landscape, that impresses on the soul a feeling of sublimity. The immense plains of the Castiles and of La Mancha, extending as far as the eye can reach, derive an interest from their very nakedness and immensity, and possess, in some degree, the solemn grandeur of the ocean. In ranging over these boundless wastes the eye catches sight here and there of a struggling herd of cattle attended by a lonely herdsman, motionless as a statue, with his long slender pike tapering up like a lance into the air; or beholds a long train of mules slowly moving along the waste like a train of camels in the desert; or a single horseman, armed with blunderbuss and stiletto, and prowling over the plain. Thus the country, the habits; the very looks of the people, have something of the Arabian character. The general insecurity of the country is evinced in the universal use of weapons. The herdsman in the field, the shepherd in the plain, has his musket and his knife. The wealthy villager rarely ventures to the market-town without his gun, and, perhaps, a servant on foot with a blunderbuss on his shoulder; and the most petty journey is undertaken with the preparation of a war-like enterprise.

The dangers of the road produce also a mode of traveling resembling, on a diminutive scale, the caravans of the East. The carriers congregate in convoys, and set off in large and well-armed trains on appointed days; while additional travelers swell their number and contribute to their strength. In this primitive way is the commerce of the country carried on. The muleteer is the general medium of traffic, and the legitimate traverser of the land, crossing the peninsula from the Pyrenees and the Asturias to the Alpuxarras, and even to the gates of Gibraltar. He lives frugally and hardily: his saddle-bags of coarse cloth hold his scanty stock of provisions; a leathern bottle, hanging at his saddle-bow, contains wine or water, for a supply across barren mountains and thirsty plains; a mule-cloth spread upon the ground is his bed at night, and his pack-saddle his pillow. His low, but clean-limbed and sinewy form betokens strength; his complexion is dark and sunburnt; his eye resolute, but quiet in its expression, except when kindled by sudden emotion; his demeanor is frank, manly, and courteous, and he never passes you without a grave salutation: "God guard you!" "God be with you, Sir!"

As these men have often their whole fortune at stake upon the burden of their mules, they have their weapons at hand, slung to their saddles, and ready to be snatched out for desperate defence; but their united numbers render them secure against petty bands of marauders, and the solitary robber, armed to the teeth, and mounted on his Andalusian steed, hovers about them, like a pirate about a merchant convoy, without daring to assault.

The Spanish muleteer has an inexhaustible stock of songs and ballads, with which to beguile his incessant wayfaring. These he chants forth with a loud voice, and long, drawling cadence, seated sideways on his mule, who seems to listen with infinite gravity, and to keep time, with his paces, to the tune. The couplets thus chanted are often old traditional romances about the Moors, or some legend of a saint, or some love-ditty; or, what is still more frequent, some ballad about a bold smuggler, or hardy robber, for both are poetical heroes among the common people of Spain.

The ancient kingdom of Granada is one of the most mountainous regions of Spain. Vast sierras, or chains of mountains, destitute of shrub or tree, and mottled with variegated marbles and granites, elevate their sunburnt summits against a deep-blue sky; yet in their rugged bosoms lie engulfed verdant and fertile valleys, where the desert and the garden strive for mastery, and the very rock is, as it were, compelled to yield the fig, the orange, and the citron, and to blossom with the myrtle and the rose.

In the wild passes of these mountains the sight of walled towns and villages, built like eagles' nests among the cliffs, and surrounded by Moorish battlements, or of ruined watch-towers perched on lofty peaks, carries the mind back to the chivalric days of Christian and Moslem warfare, and to the romantic struggle for the conquest of Granada. In traversing these lofty sierras the traveller is often obliged to alight, and lead his horse up and down; the steep and jagged ascents and descents, resembling the broken steps of a staircase. Sometimes the road winds along dizzy precipices, without parapet to guard him from the gulfs below, and then will plunge down steep and dark and dangerous declivities. Sometimes it struggles through rigged ravines, worn by winter torrents, the obscure path of the smuggler; while, ever and anon, the ominous cross, the monument of robbery and murder, erected on a mound of stones at some lonely part of the road, admonishes the traveller that he is among the haunts of banditti, perhaps at that very moment under the eye of some lurking outlaw. Sometimes, in winding through the narrow valleys, he is startled by a hoarse bellowing, and beholds above him on some green fold of the mountain a herd of fierce Andalusian bulls, destined for the combat of the arena. I have felt, if I may so express it, an agreeable horror in thus contemplating, near at hand, these terrific animals, clothed with tremendous strength, and ranging their native pastures in untamed wildness, strangers almost to the face of man: they know no one but the solitary herdsman who attends upon them, and even he at times dares not venture to approach them. The low bellowing of these bulls, and their menacing aspect as they look down from their rocky height, give additional wildness to the savage scenery.

As our proposed route to Granada lay through mountainous regions, where the roads are little better than mule-paths, and said to be frequently beset by robbers, we took due travelling precautions. Forwarding the most valuable part of our luggage a day or two in advance by the carriers, we retained merely clothing and necessaries for the journey and money for the expenses of the road; with a little surplus of hard dollars by way of robber purse, to satisfy the gentlemen of the road should we be assailed. Unlucky is the too wary traveller who, having grudged this precaution, falls into their clutches empty-handed; they are apt to give him a sound rib-roasting for cheating them out of their dues.

A couple of stout steeds were provided for our own mounting, and a third for our scanty luggage and the conveyance of a sturdy Biscayan lad, about twenty years of age, who was to be our guide, our groom, our valet, and at all times our guard. For the latter office he was provided with a formidable gun, with which he promised to defend us against solitary footpads. He made much vain-glorious boast about his weapon at the outset of the journey; though, to the discredit of his generalship, it was suffered to hang unloaded behind his saddle. He was a faithful, cheery, kind-hearted creature, as full of saws and proverbs as that miracle of squires, the renowned Sancho himself, whose name, by the by, we bestowed upon him, and, like a true Spaniard, though treated by us with companionable familiarity, he never for a moment, in his utmost hilarity, overstepped the bounds of respectful decorum.

Such were our minor preparations for the journey, but above all we laid in an ample-stock of good-humor, and a genuine disposition to be pleased; determining to take things as we found them, rough or smooth, and mingle with all classes and conditions in a kind of vagabond companionship. It is the true way to travel in Spain. With such disposition and determination, what a country is it for a traveller, where the most miserable inn is as full of adventure as an enchanted castle, and every meal is in itself an achievement! Let others repine at the lack of turnpike roads and sumptuous hotels, and all the elaborate comforts of a country cultivated and civilized into tameness and commonplace; but give me the rude mountain scramble; the roving, hap-hazard wayfaring; the half wild, yet frank and hospitable manners, which impart such a true game-flavor to dear old romantic Spain!

Shortly after sunset on our first day's journey we arrived at Arahal, a little town among the hills. We found it in a bustle with a party of mountain soldiers, who were patrolling the country to ferret out robbers. The appearance of foreigners like ourselves was an unusual circumstance in an interior country town; and little Spanish towns of the kind are easily put in a state of gossip and wonderment by such an occurrence. Mine host, with two or three old wiseacre comrades in brown cloaks, studied our passports in a corner of the inn, while a constable took notes by the dim light of a lamp. The passports were in foreign, languages and perplexed them, but our Squire Sancho assisted them in their studies, and magnified our importance with the grandiloquence of a Spaniard. In the meantime the magnificent distribution of a few cigars had won the hearts of all around us; in a little while the whole community seemed put in agitation to make us welcome. The mayor himself waited upon us, and a great rush-bottomed arm-chair was ostentatiously bolstered into our room by our landlady, for the accommodation of that important personage. The commander of the patrol took supper with us: a lively, talking, laughing Andaluz, who had made a campaign in South America, and recounted his exploits in love and war with much pomp of phrase, vehemence of gesticulation, and mysterious rolling of the eye. He told us that he had a list of all the robbers in the country, and meant to ferret out every mother's son of them; he offered us at the same time some of his soldiers as an escort. "One is enough to protect you, señors; the robbers know me, and know my men; the sight of one is enough to spread terror through a whole sierra." We thanked him for his offer, but assured him, in his own strain, that with the protection of our redoubtable squire, Sancho, we were not afraid of all the rascals of Andalusia.

While we were supping with our braggart friend, we heard the notes of a guitar, and the click of castanets, and presently a chorus of voices singing a popular air. In fact, mine host had gathered together the amateur singers and musicians, and the rustic belles of the neighborhood, and, on going forth, the court-yard of the inn presented a scene of true Spanish festivity. We took our seats with mine host and hostess and the commander of the patrol, under an archway opening into the court; the guitar passed from hand to hand, but a jovial shoe-maker was the Orpheus of the place. He was a pleasant-looking fellow, with huge black whiskers; his sleeves were rolled up to his elbows. He touched the guitar with masterly skill, and afterwards danced a fandango with a buxom Andalusian damsel, to the great delight of the spectators. But none of the females present could compare with mine host's pretty daughter, Pepita, who had slipped away and made her toilette for the occasion, and had covered her head with roses; and who distinguished herself in a dance with a handsome young dragoon. We ordered our host to let wine and refreshments circulate freely among the company, yet, though there was a motley assembly of soldiers, muleteers, and villagers, no one exceeded the bounds of sober enjoyment. The scene was a study for a painter: the picturesque group of dancers, the troopers in their half military dresses, the peasantry wrapped in their brown cloaks; nor must I omit to mention the old meagre constable, in short black cloak, who took no notice of anything going on, but sat in a corner diligently writing by the dim light of a huge copper lamp, that might have figured in the days of Don Quixote.

The following morning was bright and balmy, as a May morning ought to be, according to the poets. Leaving Arahal at seven o'clock, with all the people of the inn at the door to cheer us off, we pursued our way through a fertile country, covered with grain and beautifully verdant; but which in summer, when the harvest is over and the fields parched and brown, must be monotonous and lonely; for, as in our ride of yesterday, there were neither houses nor people to be seen. The latter all congregate in villages and strongholds among the hills, as if these fertile plains were still subject to the ravages of the Moor.

At noon we came to where there was a group of trees, beside a brook in a rich meadow. Here we alighted to make our mid-day meal. Knowing the scanty larders of Spanish inns, and the houseless tracts we might have to traverse, we had taken care to have the saddle-bags of our squire well stocked with cold provisions, and his leathern bottle, which might hold a gallon, filled to the neck with choice wine.

Our repast being finished, we spread our cloaks on the greensward under the tree, and took a luxurious siesta, in the Spanish fashion. The clouding up of the weather, however, warned us to depart, and a harsh wind sprang up from the southeast. Towards five o'clock we arrived at Osuna, a town of fifteen thousand inhabitants, situated on the side of a hill, with a church and a ruined castle. The inn was outside of the walls; it had a cheerless look. The evening being cold, the inhabitants were crowded round a pan of coals in a chimney-corner; and the hostess was a dry old woman, who looked like a mummy. Every one eyed us askance as we entered, as Spaniards are apt to regard strangers; a cheery, respectful salutation on our part, touching our sombreros, set Spanish pride at ease; and when we took our seats among them, lit our cigars, and passed the cigar-box round among them, our victory was complete. I have never known a Spaniard, whatever his rank or condition, who would suffer himself to be outdone in courtesy; and to the common Spaniard the present of a cigar is irresistible. Care, however, must be taken never to offer him a present with an air of superiority and condescension; he is too much of a gentleman to receive favors at the cost of his dignity.

Leaving Osuna at an early hour the next morning, we entered the sierra or range of mountains. The road wound through picturesque scenery, but lonely; and a cross here and there by the roadside, the sign of a murder, showed that we were now coming among the "robber haunts." This wild and intricate country, with its silent plains and valleys intersected by mountains, has ever been famous for banditti. About nightfall we arrived at the gates of Antiquera, that old city of warlike reputation, lying, in the lap of the great sierra which runs through Andalusia.

Everything in this venerable city has a decidedly Spanish stamp. It lies too much out of the frequented track of foreign travel to have its old usages trampled out. Here I observed old men still wearing the ancient hunting-cap, once common throughout Spain; while the young men wore the little round-crowned hat, with brim turned up all round, like a cup turned down in its saucer; while the brim was set off with little black tufts like cockades. The women, too, were all in mantillas and basquinas. As Antiquera, though a considerable city, is, as I observed, somewhat out of the track of travel, I had anticipated bad quarters and poor fare at the inn. I was agreeably disappointed, therefore, by a supper-table amply supplied, and what was still more acceptable, good clean rooms and comfortable beds.

Early in the morning I strolled to the ruins of the old Moorish castle, which itself had been reared on the ruins of a Roman fortress. Here, taking my seat on the remains of a crumbling tower, I enjoyed a grand and varied landscape, beautiful in itself, and full of storied and romantic associations; for I was now in the very heart of the country famous for the chivalrous contests between Moor and Christian.

On returning to the inn I found our man Sancho in high gossip with the landlord and two or three of his hangers-on. He had just been telling some marvellous story about Seville, which mine host seemed piqued to match with one equally marvellous about Antiquera. There was once a fountain, he said, in one of the public squares called The fountain of the bull, because the water gushed from the mouth of a bull's head, carved of stone. Underneath the head was inscribed: In front of the bull there is treasure. Many digged in front of the fountain, but lost their labor and found no money. At last one knowing fellow construed the motto a different way. It is in the forehead of the bull that the treasure is to be found, said he to himself, and I am the man to find it. Accordingly he came, late at night, with a mallet, and knocked the head to pieces; and what do you think he found?

"Plenty of gold and diamonds!" cried Sancho, eagerly. "He found nothing," rejoined mine host, dryly, and he ruined the fountain."

Here a great laugh was set up by the landlord's hangers-on; who considered Sancho completely taken in by what I presume was one of mine host's standing jokes.

Leaving Antiquera at eight o'clock, we had a delightful ride along the little river, and by gardens and orchards fragrant with the odors of spring and vocal with the nightingale.

At noon we halted in sight of Archidona, in a pleasant little meadow among hills covered with olive-trees, and Sancho was told to produce his saddle-bags. He had been unusually silent this morning ever since the laugh raised at his expense, but now his countenance brightened, and he produced his saddle-bags with an air of triumph. They contained the contributions of four days' journeying, but had been signally enriched by the foraging of the previous evening in the plenteous inn at Antiquera; and this seemed to furnish him with a set-off to the banter of mine host.

In front of the bull there is treasure

would he exclaim, with a chuckling laugh, as he drew forth the heterogeneous contents one by one, in a series which seemed to have no end. First came forth a shoulder of roasted kid, very little the worse for wear; then an entire partridge; then a great morsel of salted codfish wrapped in paper; then the residue of a ham; then the half of a pullet, together with several rolls of bread, and a rabble rout of oranges, figs, raisins, and walnuts. His leathern bottle also had been recruited with some excellent wine of Malaga. At every fresh apparition from his larder, he would enjoy our ludicrous surprise, throwing himself back on the grass, shouting with laughter, and exclaiming, "Front of the bull!—front of the bull! Ah, señors, they thought Sancho a simpleton at Antiquera; but Sancho knew where to find the treasure."

While we were diverting ourselves with his simple drollery, a solitary beggar approached, who had almost the look of a pilgrim. He had a venerable gray beard, and was evidently very old, supporting himself on a staff, yet age had not bowed him down; he was tall and erect, and had the wreck of a fine form. He wore a round Andalusian hat, a sheep-skin jacket, and leathern breeches, gaiters, and sandals. His dress, though old and patched, was decent, his demeanor manly, and he addressed us with the grave courtesy that is to be remarked in the lowest Spaniard. We were in a favorable mood for such a visitor; and in a freak of capricious charity gave him some silver, a loaf of fine wheaten bread, and a goblet of our choice wine of Malaga. He received them thankfully, but without any groveling tribute of gratitude. Tasting the wine, he held it up to the light, with a slight beam of surprise in his eye; then quaffing it off at a draught, "It is many years," said he, "since I have tasted such wine. It is a cordial to an old man's heart." Then, looking at the beautiful wheaten loaf, "blessed be such bread!" So saying, he put it in his wallet. We urged him to eat it on the spot. "No, señors," replied he, "the wine I had either to drink or leave; but the bread I may take home to share with my family."

Our man Sancho sought our eye, and reading permission there, gave the old man some of the ample fragments of our repast, on condition, however, that he should sit down and make a meal.

He accordingly took his seat at some little distance from us, and began to eat slowly, and with a sobriety and decorum that would have become a hidalgo. There was altogether a measured manner and a quiet self-possession about the old man, that made me think that he had seen better days: his language, too, though simple, had occasionally something picturesque and almost poetical in the phraseology. I set him down for some broken-down noble-man. I was mistaken; it was nothing but the innate courtesy of a Spaniard, and the poetical turn of thought and language often to be found in the lowest classes of this clear-witted people. For fifty years, he told us, he had been a shepherd, but now he was out of employ and destitute. "When I was a young man," said he, "nothing could harm or trouble me; I was always well, always gay; but now I am seventy-nine years of age, and a beggar, and my heart begins to fail me."

Still he was not a regular mendicant: it was not until recently that want had driven him to this degradation; and he gave a touching picture of the struggle between hunger and pride, when abject destitution first came upon him. He was returning from Malaga without money; he had not tasted food for some time, and was crossing one of the great plains of Spain, where there were but few habitations. When almost dead with hunger, he applied at the door of a country inn. "Excuse us, brother, for God's sake!" was the reply—the usual mode in Spain of refusing a beggar. "I turned away," said he, "with shame greater than my hunger, for my heart was yet too proud. I came to a river with high banks, and deep, rapid current, and felt tempted to throw myself in: 'What should such an old, worthless, wretched man as I live for?' But when I was on the brink of the current, I turned away. I traveled on until I saw a country-seat at a little distance from the road, and entered the outer gate of the court-yard. The door was shut, but there were two young ladies at a window. I approached and begged;—'Excuse us, brother, for God's sake!'—and the window was closed. I crept out of the court-yard, but hunger overcame me, and my heart gave way: I thought my hour at hand, so I laid myself down at the gate, and covered my head to die. In a little while afterwards the master of the house came home: seeing me lying at his gate, he uncovered my head, had pity on my gray hairs, took me into his house, and gave me food."

The old man was on his way to his native place, Archidona, which was in full view on the steep and rugged mountain. He pointed to the ruins of its castle. As his heart warmed with wine he went on to tell us a story of the buried treasure left under the castle by the Moorish king. His own house was next to the foundation of the castle. The curate and notary dreamed three times of the treasure, and went to work at the place pointed out in their dreams. His own son-in-law heard the sound of their pickaxes and spades at night. What they found nobody knows; they became suddenly rich, but kept their own secret. Thus the old man had once been next door to fortune, but was doomed never to get under the same roof.

I have remarked that the stories of treasure buried by the Moors, so popular throughout Spain, are most current among the poorest people. Kind nature consoles with shadows for the lack of substantials. The thirsty man dreams of fountains and running streams; the hungry man of banquets; and the poor man of heaps of hidden gold: nothing certainly is more opulent than the imagination of a beggar.

Our afternoon's ride took us through a steep and rugged defile of the mountains, called the Pass of the King; being one of the great passes into the territories of Granada, and the one by which King Ferdinand conducted his army. Towards sunset the road, winding round a hill, brought us in sight of the famous little frontier city of Loxa, which repulsed Ferdinand from its walls. It was the stronghold of that fiery veteran, old Ali Atar, father-in-law of Boabdil; and here it was that the latter collected his troops, and sallied forth on that disastrous foray which ended in the death of the old governor of the castle, and his own captivity. From its commanding position at the gate, as it were, of this mountain-pass, Loxa has not unaptly been termed the key of Granada. It is wildly picturesque; built along the face of a rugged mountain. The ruins of a Moorish citadel crown a rocky mound which rises out of the centre of the town. The river Xenil washes its base, winding among rocks and groves, and gardens, and meadows, and crossed by a Moorish bridge. Above the city all is savage and sterile, below is the richest vegetation and the freshest verdure. A similar contrast is presented by the river: above the bridge it is placid and grassy, reflecting groves and gardens; below it is rapid, noisy, and tumultuous. The Sierra Nevada, the royal mountains of Granada, crowned with perpetual snow, form the distant boundary to this varied landscape, one of the most characteristic of romantic Spain.

Alighting at the entrance to the city, we gave our horses to Sancho to lead them to the inn, while we strolled about to enjoy the singular beauty of the environs. As we crossed the bridge to a fine public walk, the bells tolled the hour of orison. At the sound the wayfarers, whether on business or pleasure, paused, took off their hats, crossed themselves, and repeated their evening prayer: a pious custom still rigidly observed in retired parts of Spain. Altogether it was a solemn and beautiful evening scene, and we wandered on as the evening gradually closed, and the new moon began to glitter between the high elms of the public walk. We were roused from this quiet state of enjoyment by the voice of our trusty squire hailing us from a distance.

The inn to which he conducted us was called the Crown, and we found it quite in keeping with the character of the place, the inhabitants of which seem still to retain the bold, fiery spirit of the olden time. The hostess was a young and handsome Andalusian widow, whose trim petticoat of black silk, fringed with bugles, set off the play of a graceful form and round pliant limbs. Her step was firm and elastic; her dark eye was full of fire; and the coquetry of her air, and varied ornaments of her person, showed that she was accustomed to be admired.

She was well matched by her brother, nearly about her own age. He was tall, vigorous, and well-formed, with a clear olive complexion, a dark beaming eye, and curling chestnut whiskers that met under his chin. He was gallantly dressed in a short green velvet jacket, fitted to his shape, profusely decorated with silver buttons, with a white handkerchief in each pocket. He had breeches of the same, with rows of buttons from the hips to the knees; a pink silk handkerchief round his neck, gathered through a ring, on the bosom of a neatly plaited shirt; a sash round the waist to match; high gaiters of the finest russet-leather, elegantly worked, and open at the calf to show his stocking; and russet shoes, setting off a well-shaped foot.

As he was standing at the door, a horseman rode up and entered into a low and earnest conversation with him. He was dressed in a similar style, and almost with equal finery; a man about thirty, square-built, with strong Roman features, handsome, though slightly pitted with small-pox; with a free, bold, and somewhat daring air. His powerful black horse was decorated with, tassels and fanciful trappings, and a couple of broad-mouthed blunderbusses hung behind the saddle. He had the air of one of those smugglers I have seen in the mountains of Ronda, and evidently had a good understanding with the brother of mine hostess; nay, if I mistake not, he was a favored admirer of the widow. In fact, the whole inn and its inmates had something of a suspicious aspect, and a blunderbuss stood in a corner beside the guitar. The horseman I have mentioned passed his evening in the inn, and sang several bold mountain romances with great spirit. As we were at supper, two poor Asturians put in, in distress, begging food and a night's lodging. They had been waylaid by robbers as they came from a fair among the mountains, robbed of a horse which carried all their stock in trade, stripped of their money, and most of their apparel, beaten for having offered resistance, and left almost naked on the road. My companion, with a prompt generosity natural to him, ordered them a supper and a bed, and gave them a sum of money to help them forward towards their home.

As the evening advanced, the dramatis personæ thickened. A large man, about sixty years of age, of powerful frame, came strolling in, to gossip with mine hostess. He was dressed in the ordinary Andalusian costume, but had a huge sabre tucked under his arm; wore large moustaches, and had something of a lofty swaggering air. Every one seemed to regard him with great deference.

Our man Sancho whispered to us that he was Don Ventura Rodriguez, the hero and champion of Loxa, famous for his prowess and the strength of his arm. In the time of the French invasion he surprised six troopers who were asleep; he first secured their horses, then attacked them with his sabre, killed some, and took the rest prisoners. For this exploit the king allows him the fifth of a Spanish dollar per day, and has dignified him with the title of Don.

I sat until a late hour listening to the varied themes of this motley group, who mingled together with the unreserve of a Spanish inn. We had smuggler songs, stories of robbers, guerilla exploits, and Moorish legends. The last were from our handsome landlady, who gave a poetical account of the Infiernos, or infernal regions of Loxa,—dark caverns, in which subterranean streams and waterfalls make a mysterious sound. The common people say that there are money-coiners shut up there from the time of the Moors; and that the Moorish kings kept their treasures in those caverns.

I retired to bed with my imagination excited by all that I had seen and heard in this old warrior city, but slept soundly until morning.

On leaving Loxa we were joined by a horseman, well mounted and well armed, and followed on foot by a musketeer. He saluted us courteously, and soon let us into his quality. He was the chief of the customs, or rather, I should suppose, chief of an armed company whose business it is to patrol the roads and look out for smugglers. In the course of our morning's ride I drew from him some particulars concerning the smugglers, who have risen to be a kind of mongrel chivalry in Spain. They come into Andalusia, he said, from various parts, but, especially from La Mancha; sometimes to receive goods, to be smuggled on an appointed night across the line at the strand of Gibraltar; sometimes to meet a vessel, which is to hover on a given night off a certain part of the coast. They keep together and travel in the night. In the day-time they lie quiet in gullies of the mountains, or lonely farm-houses; where they are generally well received, as they make the family liberal presents of their smuggled wares. Indeed, much of the finery and trinkets worn by the wives and daughters of the mountain hamlets and farm-houses are presents from the gay and open-handed smugglers.

Arrived at the part of the coast where a vessel is to meet them, they look out at night from some rocky point or headland. If they descry a sail near the shore they make a concerted signal; sometimes it consists in suddenly displaying a lantern three times from beneath the folds of the cloak. If the signal is answered, they descend to the shore and prepare for quick work. The vessel runs close in; all her boats are busy landing the smuggled goods, made up into snug packages for transportation on horseback. These are hastily thrown on the beach, as hastily gathered up and packed on the horses, and then their riders clatter off to the mountains. They travel by the roughest, wildest, and most solitary roads, where it is almost fruitless to pursue them. The custom-house guards do not attempt it: they take a different course. When they hear of one of these bands returning full freighted through the mountains, they go out in force, sometimes twelve infantry and eight horsemen, and take their station where the mountain defile opens into the plain. The infantry, who lie in ambush some distance within the defile, suffer the band to pass, then rise and fire upon them. The smugglers dash forward, but are met in front by the horsemen. A wild skirmish ensues. The smugglers, if hard pressed, become desperate. Some dismount, use their horses as breastworks, and fire over their backs; others cut the cords, let the packs fall off to delay the enemy, and endeavor to escape with their steeds. Some get off in this way with the loss of their packages; some are taken, horses, packages, and all; others abandon everything, and make their escape by scrambling up the mountains. "And then," cried Sancho, who had been listening with a greedy ear, "and then they become legitimate robbers."

I could not help laughing at Sancho's idea of a legitimate calling of the kind; but the chief of customs told me it was really the case that the smugglers, when thus reduced to extremity, thought they had a kind of right to take the road, and lay travellers under contribution, until they had collected funds enough to mount and equip themselves in their former style.

Towards noon our wayfaring companion took leave of us and turned up a steep defile, and shortly afterwards we emerged from the mountains, and entered upon the far-famed Vega of Granada.

Our last mid-day's repast was taken under a grove of olive-trees on the border of a rivulet. The day was without a cloud. The heat of the sun was tempered by cool breezes from the mountains. Before us extended the glorious Vega. In the distance was romantic Granada surmounted by the ruddy towers of the Alhambra, while far above it the snowy summits of the Sierra Nevada shone like silver.

Our repast finished, we spread our cloaks and took our last nap in the open air, lulled by the humming of bees among the flowers and the notes of doves among the olive-trees. When the sultry hours were passed we resumed our journey, and arrived about sunset at the gates of Granada.

Palace of the Alhambra

To the traveler imbued with a feeling for the historical and poetical, so inseparably, intertwined in the annals of romantic Spain, the Alhambra is as much an object of devotion as is the Caaba to all true Moslems. How many legends and traditions, true and fabulous,—how many songs and ballads, Arabian and Spanish, of love and war and chivalry, are associated with this Oriental pile! It was the royal abode of the Moorish kings, where, surrounded with the splendors and refinements of Asiatic luxury, they held dominion over what they vaunted as a terrestrial paradise, and made their last stand for empire in Spain. The royal palace forms but part of a fortress, the walls of which, studded with towers, stretch irregularly round the whole crept of a hill, a spur of the Sierra Nevada or Snowy Mountains, and overlook the city; externally it is a rude congregation of towers and battlements, with no regularity of plan or grace of architecture, and giving little promise of the grace and beauty which prevail within.

In the time of the Moors the fortress was capable of containing within its outward precincts an army of forty thousand men, and served occasionally as a stronghold of the sovereigns against their rebellious subjects. After the kingdom had passed into the hands of the Christians, the Alhambra continued to be a royal demesne, and was occasionally inhabited by the Castilian monarchs. The emperor Charles V. commenced a sumptuous palace within its walls, but was deterred from completing it by repeated shocks of earthquakes. The last royal residents were Philip V. and his beautiful queen, Elizabeth of Parma, early in the eighteenth century. The sojourn of the sovereigns was transient, and after their departure the palace once more became desolate. Still the place was maintained with some military state. The governor held it immediately from the crown, and was independent of the captain-general of Granada. A considerable garrison was kept up; the governor had his apartments in the front of the old Moorish palace, and never descended into Granada without some military parade. The fortress, in fact, was a little town of itself, having several streets of houses within its walls, together with a convent and a parochial church.

The desertion of the court, however, was a fatal blow to the Alhambra. Its beautiful halls became desolate, and some of them fell to ruin; the gardens were destroyed, and the fountains ceased to play. By degrees the dwellings became filled with a loose and lawless population; smugglers, who availed themselves of its independent jurisdiction to carry on a wide and daring course of smuggling, and thieves and rogues of all sorts, who made this their place of refuge whence they might depredate upon Granada and its vicinity. The strong arm of government at length interfered; the whole community was thoroughly sifted; none were suffered to remain but such as were of honest character, and had legitimate right to a residence; the greater part of the houses were demolished and a mere hamlet left, with the parochial church and the convent. During the troubles in Spain, when Granada was in the hands of the French, the Alhambra was garrisoned by their troops, and the palace was occasionally inhabited by the French commander. With that enlightened taste which has ever distinguished the French nation in their conquests, this monument of Moorish elegance and grandeur was rescued from the absolute ruin and desolation that were overwhelming it. The roofs were repaired, and the saloons and galleries protected from the weather, the gardens cultivated, the watercourses restored, the fountains once mire made to throw up their sparkling showers; and Spain may thank her invaders for having preserved to her the most beautiful and interesting of her historical monuments.

On the departure of the French they blew up several towers of the outer wall, and left the fortifications scarcely tenable. Since that time the military importance of the post is at an end. The garrison is a handful of invalid soldiers, whose principal duty is to guard some of the outer towers, which serve occasionally as a prison of state; and the governor, abandoning the lofty hill of the Alhambra, resides in the centre of Granada, for the more convenient dispatch of his official duties.

Our first object of course, oft the morning after our arrival, was a visit to this time-honored edifice. Leaving our inn, and traversing the renowned square of the Vivarrambla, once the scene of Moorish jousts and tournaments, now a crowded market-place, we proceeded along the main street of what, in the time of the Moors, was the Great Bazaar, and where small shops and narrow alleys still retain the Oriental character. Crossing an open place in front of the palace of the captain-general, we ascended a confined and winding street, the name of which reminded us of the chivalric days of Granada. It is called the street of the Gomeres, from a Moorish family famous in chronicle and song. This street led up to a massive gateway of Grecian architecture, built by Charles V., forming the entrance to the domain of the Alhambra.

At the gate were two or three ragged superannuated soldiers, dozing on a stone bench, while a tall, meagre varlet, whose rusty-brown cloak was evidently intended to conceal the ragged state of his nether garments, was lounging in the sunshine and gossiping with an ancient sentinel on duty. He joined us as we entered the gate, and offered his services to show us the fortress.

I have a traveller's dislike to officious ciceroni, and did not altogether like the garb of the applicant.

"You are well acquainted with the place, I presume?"

"Nobody better; in fact, sir, I am a son of the Alhambra!"

The common Spaniards have certainly a most poetical way of expressing themselves. "A son of the Alhambra!" the appellation caught me at once; the very tattered garb of my new acquaintance assumed a dignity in my eyes. It was emblematic of the fortunes of the place, and befitted the progeny of a ruin.

I put some further questions to him and found that his title was legitimate. His family had lived in the fortress from generation to generation ever since the time of the Conquest. His name was Mateo Ximenes. The first title of this ragged worthy, however, had completely captivated me; so I gladly accepted the services of the "son of the Alhambra."

We now found ourselves in a deep narrow ravine, filled with beautiful, groves, with a steep avenue, and various footpaths winding through it, bordered with stone seats and ornamented with fountains. To our left we beheld the towers of the Alhambra above us; to our right, on the opposite side of the ravine, we were equally dominated by rival towers on a rocky eminence. These, we were told, were the Vermilion Towers, so called from their ruddy hue. No one knows their origin. They are of a date much anterior to the Alhambra; some suppose them to have been built by the Romans; others, by some wandering colony of Phœnicians. Ascending the steep and shady avenue, we arrived at the foot of a huge square Moorish tower, forming a kind of barbican, through which passed the main entrance to the fortress. This portal is called the Gate of Justice, from the tribunal held within its porch during the Moslem domination for the immediate trial of petty causes: a custom common to the Oriental nations, and occasionally alluded to in the Sacred Scriptures. "Judges and officers shalt thou make thee in all thy gates, and they shall judge the people with just judgment."

The great vestibule, or porch of the gate, is formed by an immense Arabian arch, of the horseshoe form, which springs to half the height of the tower. On the keystone of this arch is engraven a gigantic hand. Within the vestibule, on the keystone of the portal, is sculptured, in like manner, a gigantic key. Those who pretend to some knowledge of the Mohammedan symbols, affirm that the hand is the emblem of doctrine; the five fingers designating the five principal commandments of the creed of Islam, fasting, pilgrimage, alms-giving, ablution, and war against infidels. The key, they say, is the emblem of the faith or of power; the key of David, transmitted to the prophet. "And the key of the house of David will I lay upon his shoulder; so he shall open and none shall shut, and he shall shut and none shall open." (Isa. xxii. 22.) The key, we are told, was emblazoned on the standard of the Moslems in opposition to the Christian emblem of the cross, when they subdued Spain or Andalusia. It betokened the conquering power invested in the prophet. "He that hath the key of David, he that openeth and no man shutteth; and shutteth and no man openeth." (Rev. iii. 7.)

A different explanation of these emblems, however, was given by the legitimate son of the Alhambra, and one more in unison with the notions of the common people, who attach something of mystery and magic to everything Moorish, and have all, kinds of superstitions connected with this old Moslem fortress. According to Mateo, it was a tradition handed down from the oldest inhabitants, and which he had from his father and grandfather, that the hand and key were magical devices on which the fate of the Alhambra depended. The Moorish king who built it was a great magician, or, as some believed, had sold himself to the devil, and had laid the whole fortress under a magic spell. By this means it had remained standing for several years, in defiance of storms and earthquakes, while almost all other buildings of the Moors had fallen to ruin and disappeared. This spell, the tradition went on to say, would last until the hand on the outer arch should reach down and grasp the key, when the whole pile would tumble to pieces, and all the treasures buried beneath it by the Moors would be revealed.

After passing through the barbican, we ascended a narrow lane, winding between walls, and came on an open esplanade within the fortress, called the Place of the Cisterns, from great reservoirs which undermine it, cut in the living rock by the Moors to receive the water brought by conduits from the Darro, for the supply of the fortress. Here, also, is a well of immense depth, furnishing the purest and coldest of water,—another monument of the delicate taste of the Moors, who were indefatigable in their exertions to obtain that element in its crystal purity.

In front of this esplanade is the splendid pile commenced by Charles V., and intended, it is said, to eclipse the residence of the Moorish kings. Much of the Oriental edifice intended for the winter season was demolished to make way for this massive pile. The grand entrance was blocked up so that the present entrance to the Moorish palace is through a simple and almost humble portal in a corner. With all the massive grandeur and architectural merit of the palace of Charles V., we regarded it as an arrogant intruder, and passing by it with a feeling almost of scorn, rang, at the Moslem portal.

While waiting for admittance, our self-imposed cicerone, Mateo Ximenes, informed us that the royal palace was intrusted to the care of a worthy old maiden dame who, according to Spanish custom, went by the neighborly appellation, of Tia Antonia (Aunt Antonia), who maintained the Moorish halls and gardens in order and showed them to strangers. While we were talking, the door was opened by a plump little black-eyed Andalusian damsel, whom Mateo addressed as Dolores, but who from her bright looks and cheerful disposition evidently merited a merrier name. Mateo informed me in a whisper that she was the niece of Tia Antonia, and I found she was the good fairy who was to conduct us through the enchanted palace. Under her guidance we crossed the threshold, and were at once transported, as if by magic wand, into other times and an Oriental realm, and were treading the scenes of Arabian story. Nothing could be in greater contrast than the unpromising exterior of the pile with the scene now before us. We found ourselves in a vast court, paved with white marble. Along the mouldings of the cornices and on various parts of the walls were escutcheons and ciphers, and Cufic and Arabic characters, repeating the pious mottoes of the Moslem monarchs, the builders of the Alhambra, or extolling their grandeur and munificence. Along the centre of the court extended an immense basin or tank receiving its water from two marble vases. Great numbers of gold-fish were to be seen gleaming through the waters of the basin, and it was bordered by hedges of roses.

Passing from the court of the Alberca under a Moorish archway, we entered the renowned Court of Lions. No part of the edifice gives a more complete idea of its original beauty than this, for none has suffered so little from the ravages of time. In the centre stands the fountain famous in song and story. The alabaster basins still shed their diamond drops; the twelve lions which support them, and give the court its name, still cast forth crystal streams as in the days of Boabdil. Round the four sides of the court are light Arabian arcades of open filigree work, supported by slender pillars of white marble, which it is supposed were originally gilded. The architecture, like that in most parts of the interior of the palace, is characterized by elegance rather than grandeur, bespeaking a delicate and graceful taste, and a disposition to indolent enjoyment. When one looks upon the apparently fragile fretwork of the walls, it is difficult to believe that so much has survived the wear and tear of centuries, the shock of earthquakes, the violence of war, and the quiet, though no less baneful, pilferings of the tasteful traveller: it is almost sufficient to excuse the popular tradition, that the whole is protected by a magic charm.

On one side of the court a rich portal opens into the Hall of the Abencerrages: so called from the gallant cavaliers of that illustrious line who were here perfidiously massacred. There are some who doubt the whole story, but our humble cicerone Mateo pointed out the very wicket of the portal through which they were introduced one by one into the Court of Lions, and the white marble fountain in the centre of the hall beside which they were beheaded. He showed us also certain broad ruddy stains on the pavement, traces of their blood, which, according to popular belief, can never be effaced.

Finding we listened to him apparently with easy faith, he added, that there was often heard at night, in the Court of Lions, a low confused sound, resembling the murmuring of a multitude, and now and then a faint tinkling, like the distant clank of chains. These sounds were made by the spirits of the murdered Abencerrages; who nightly haunt the scene of their suffering and invoke the vengeance of Heaven on their destroyer.

The sounds in question had no doubt been produced, as I had afterwards an opportunity of ascertaining, by the bubbling currents and tinkling falls of water conducted under the pavement through pipes and channels to supply the fountains; but I was too considerate to intimate such an idea to the humble chronicler of the Alhambra.

Encouraged by my easy credulity, Mateo gave me the following as an undoubted fact, which he had from his grandfather:—

There was once an invalid soldier, who had charge of the Alhambra to show it to strangers; as he was one evening, about twilight, passing through the Court of Lions, he heard footsteps on the Hall of the Abencerrages; supposing some strangers to be lingering there, he advanced to attend to them, when to his astonishment he beheld four Moors richly dressed, with gilded cuirasses and cimeters, and poniards glittering with precious stones. They were walking to and fro, with solemn pace; but paused and beckoned to him. The old soldier, however, took to flight, and could never afterwards be prevailed upon to enter the Alhambra. Thus it is that men sometimes turn their backs upon fortune; for it is the firm opinion of Mateo, that the Moors intended to reveal the place where their treasures lay buried. A successor to the invalid soldier was more knowing; he came to the Alhambra poor; but at the end of a year went off to Malaga, bought houses, set up a carriage, and still lives there, one of the richest as well as oldest men of the place; all which, Mateo sagely surmised, was in consequence of his finding out the golden secret of these phantom Moors.

I now perceived I had made an invaluable acquaintance in this son of the Alhambra, one who knew all the apocryphal history of the place, and firmly believed in it, and whose memory was stuffed with a kind of knowledge for which I have a lurking fancy, but which is too apt to be considered rubbish by less indulgent philosophers.

Immediately opposite the Hall of the Abencerrages, a portal, richly adorned, leads into a hall of less tragical associations. It is light and lofty, exquisitely graceful in its architecture, paved with white marble, and bears the name of the Hall of the Two Sisters.

On each side of this hall are recesses or alcoves for ottomans and couches, on which the lords of the Alhambra indulged in that dreamy repose so dear to the Orientalists. A cupola or lantern admits a tempered light from above and a free circulation of air; while on one side is heard the refreshing sound of waters from the fountain of the lions, and on the other side the soft plash from the basin in the garden of Lindaraxa.

An abundant supply of water, brought from the mountains by old Moorish aqueducts, circulates throughout the palace, supplying its baths and fish-pools, sparkling in jets within its halls or murmuring in channels along the marble pavements. When it has paid its tribute to the royal pile, and visited its gardens and parterres, it flows down the long avenue leading to the city, tinkling in rills, gushing in fountains, and maintaining a perpetual verdure in those groves that embower and beautify the whole hill of the Alhambra.

Those only who have sojourned in the ardent climates of the South can appreciate the delights of an abode combining the breezy coolness of the mountain with the freshness and verdure of the valley. While the city below pants with the noontide heat, and the parched Vega trembles to the eye, the delicate airs from the Sierra Nevada play through these lofty halls, bringing with them the sweetness of the surrounding gardens.

Important Negotiations.

The day was nearly spent before we could tear ourself from this region of poetry and romance to descend to the city and return to the forlorn realities of a Spanish inn. In a visit of ceremony to the Governor of the Alhambra to whom we had brought letters, we dwelt with enthusiasm on the scenes we had witnessed, and could not but express surprise that he should reside in the city when he had such a paradise at his command. He pleaded the inconvenience of a residence in the palace from its situation on the crest of a hill, distant from the seat of business and the resorts of social intercourse. It did very well for monarchs, who often had need of castle walls to defend o them from their own subjects. "But señors," added he, smiling, if you think a residence there so desirable, my apartments in the Alhambra are at your service."

It is a common and almost indispensable point of politeness in a Spaniard to tell you his house is yours. "This house is always at the command of your Grace." In fact anything of his which you admire is immediately offered to you. It is equally a mark of good breeding in you not to accept it; so we merely bowed our acknowledgments of the courtesy of the Governor in offering us a royal palace. We were mistaken however. The Governor was in earnest. "You will find a rambling set of empty, unfurnished rooms," said he; "but Tia Antonia, who has charge of the palace, may be able to put them in some kind of order, and to take care of you while you are there. If you can make any arrangement with her for your accommodation, and are content with scanty fare in a royal abode, the palace is at your service."

We took the Governor at his word, and hastened up the steep street of Gomeres, and through the Great Gate of Justice, to negotiate with Dame Antonia. All went smoothly. The good Tia Antonia had a little furniture to put in the rooms, but it was of the commonest kind. We assured her we could bivouac on the floor. She could supply our table, but only in her own simple way;—we wanted nothing better. Her niece, Dolores, would wait upon us; and at the word we threw up our hats and the bargain was complete.

The very next day we took up our abode in the palace, and never did sovereigns share a divided throne with more perfect harmony. Several days passed by like a dream, when my worthy associate, being summoned to Madrid, was compelled to abdicate, leaving me sole monarch of this shadowy realm. For myself, being in a manner a haphazard loiterer about the world, and prone to linger in its pleasant places, here have I been suffering day by day to steal away unheeded, spell-bound, for aught I know, in this old enchanted pile. Having always a companionable feeling for my reader, and being prone to live with him on confidential terms, I shall make it a point to communicate to him my reveries and researches during this state of delicious thraldom. If they have the power of imparting to his imagination any of the witching charms of the place, he will not repine at lingering with me for a season in the legendary halls of the Alhambra.

And first it is proper to give him some idea of my domestic arrangements: they are rather of a simple kind for the occupant of a regal palace; but I trust they will be less liable to disastrous reverses than those of my royal predecessors.

My quarters are at one end of the' Governor's apartment, a suite of chambers, in front of the palace, looking out upon the great esplanade; the apartment is modern, but the end opposite to my sleeping-room communicates with a cluster of little chambers, partly Moorish, partly Spanish, allotted to Tia Antonia and her family. In consideration of keeping the palace in order, the good dame is allowed all the perquisites received from visitors, and all the produce of the gardens; excepting that she is expected to pay an occasional tribute of fruits and flowers to the Governor. Her family consists of a nephew and niece, the children of two different brothers. The nephew, Manuel Molina, is a young man of sterling worth and Spanish gravity. He had served in the army, both in Spain and the West Indies, but is now studying medicine in the hope of one day or other becoming physician to the fortress, a post worth at least one hundred and forty dollars a year. The niece is the plump little black-eyed Dolores already mentioned; and who, it is said, will one day inherit all her aunt's possessions, consisting of certain petty tenements in the fortress, in a somewhat ruinous condition it is true, but which, I am privately assured by Mateo Ximenes, yield a revenue of nearly one hundred and fifty dollars; so that she is quite an heiress in the eyes of the ragged son of the Alhambra.

The good dame Antonia fulfils faithfully her contract in regard to my board and lodging; and as I am easily pleased, I find my fare excellent; while the merry-hearted little Dolores keeps my apartment in order, and officiates as handmaid at mealtimes. I have also at my command a tall, stuttering, yellow-haired lad, named Pépe, who works in the gardens, and would fain have acted as valet; but in this he was forestalled by Mateo Ximenes, the "son of the Alhambra." This alert and officious wight has managed, somehow or other, to stick by me ever since I first encountered him at the outer gate of the fortress, and to weave himself into all my plans, until he has fairly appointed and installed himself my valet, cicerone, guide, guard, and historiographic squire; and I have been obliged to improve the state of his wardrobe, that he may not disgrace his various functions; so that he has cast his old brown mantle, as a snake does his skin, and now appears about the fortress with a smart Andalusian hat and jacket, to his infinite satisfaction, and the great astonishment of his comrades. The chief fault of honest Mateo is an over-anxiety to be useful. I am in a manner the victim of his officiousness; I cannot put my foot over the threshold of the palace, to stroll about the fortress, but he is at my elbow, to explain everything I see; and if I venture to ramble among the surrounding hills, he insists upon attending me as a guard, though I vehemently suspect he would be more apt to trust to the length of his legs than the strength of his arms, in case of attack. After all, however, the poor fellow is at times an amusing companion; what he chiefly values himself on, is his stock of local information, having the most marvellous stories to relate of every tower, and vault, and gateway of the fortress, in all of which he places the most implicit faith.

Most of these he has derived, according to his own account, from his grandfather, a little legendary tailor, who lived to the age of nearly a hundred years, during which he made but two migrations beyond the precincts of the fortress. His shop, for the greater part of a century, was the resort of a knot of venerable gossips, where they would pass half the night talking about old times, and the wonderful events and hidden secrets of the place. The whole living, moving, thinking, and acting of this historical little tailor had thus been bounded by the walls of the Alhambra; within them he had been born, within them he lived, breathed, and had his being; within them he died and was buried. Fortunately for posterity his traditionary lore died not with him. The authentic Mateo, when an urchin, used to be an attentive listener to the narratives of his grandfather, and of the gossiping group assembled round the shopboard, and is thus possessed of a stock of valuable knowledge concerning the Alhambra, not to be found in books, and well worthy the attention of every curious traveler.

Such are the personages that constitute my regal house-hold; and I question whether any of the potentates, Moslem or Christian, who have preceded me in the palace, have been waited upon with greater fidelity, or enjoyed a serener sway.

When I rise in the morning, Pépe, the stuttering lad from the gardens, brings me a tribute of fresh-culled flowers, which are afterwards arranged in vases by the skillful hand of Dolores. My meals are made wherever caprice dictates; sometimes in one of the Moorish halls, sometimes under the arcades of the court of Lions, surrounded by flowers and fountains: and when I walk out, I am conducted by the assiduous Mateo to the most romantic retreats of the mountains, and delicious haunts of the adjacent valleys, not one of which but is the scene of some wonderful tale.

Inhabitants of the Alhambra

I have often observed that the more proudly a mansion has been tenanted in the day of its prosperity, the humbler are its inhabitants in the day of its decline, and that the palace of a king commonly ends in being the nestling-place of the beggar.

The Alhambra is in a rapid state of similar transition. Whenever a tower falls to decay, it is seized upon by some tatterdemalion family, who become joint-tenants with the bats and owls, of its gilded halls; and hang their rags, those standards of poverty, out of its windows and loopholes.

I have amused myself with remarking some of the motley characters that have thus usurped the ancient abode of royalty, and who seem as if placed here to give a farcical termination to the drama of human pride. One of these even bears the mockery of a regal title. It is a little old woman named Maria Antonia Sabonea, but who goes by the appellation of the Cockle-queen. She is small enough to be a fairy; and a fairy she may be for aught I can find out, for no one seems to know her origin. Her habitation is in a kind of closet under the outer staircase of the palace, and she sits in the cool stone corridor, plying her needle and singing from morning till night, with a ready joke for every one that passes; for though one of the poorest, she is one of the merriest little women breathing. Her great merit is a gift for story-telling, having, I verily believe, as many stories at her command as the inexhaustible Scheherezade of the Thousand and One Nights.

A rival personage to this little fairy queen is a portly old fellow with a bottle-nose, who goes about in a rusty garb, with a cocked hat of oil-skin and a red Cockade. He is one of the legitimate sons of the Alhambra, and has lived here all his life, filling various offices, such as deputy constable, sexton of the parochial church, and marker of a fives-court, established at the foot of one of the towers. He is as poor as a rat, but as proud as he is ragged, boasting of his descent from the illustrious house of Aguilar.

Of this motley community, I find the family of my gossiping squire, Mateo Ximenes, to form, from their number at least, a very important part. His boast of being a soil of the Alhambra is not unfounded. His family has inhabited the fortress ever since the time of the Conquest, handing down an hereditary poverty from father to son; not one of them having ever been known to be worth a maravedi. His father, by trade a ribbon-weaver, and who succeeded the historical tailor as the head of the family, is now near seventy years of age, and lives in a hovel of reeds and plaster, built by his own hands, just above the iron gate. The furniture consists of a crazy bed, a table, and two or three chairs; a wooden chest, containing, besides his scanty clothing, the "archives of the family." These are nothing more or less than the papers of various lawsuits sustained by different generations; by which it would seem that, with all their apparent carelessness and good-humor, they are a litigious brood. Most of the suits have been brought against gossiping neighbors for questioning the purity of their blood, and denying their being old Christians, without Jewish or Moorish taint. In fact, I doubt whether this jealousy about their blood has not kept them so poor in purse: spending all their earnings on lawyers and constables. The pride of the hovel is an escutcheon suspended against the wall, in which are emblazoned quarterings of various noble houses, with which this poverty-stricken brood claim affinity.

There are two classes of people to whom life seems one long holiday,—the very rich and the very poor; one, because they need do nothing; the other, because they have nothing to do; but there are none who understand the art of doing nothing and living upon nothing, better than the poor classes of Spain. Climate does one-half, and temperament the rest. Give a Spaniard the shade in summer and the sun in winter, a little bread, garlic, pease, oil, and an old brown cloak and a guitar, and let the world roll on as it pleases. Talk of poverty! with him it has no disgrace. It sits upon him with a grandiose style, like his ragged cloak. He is a hidalgo, even when in rags.

Before concluding these remarks, I must mention one of the amusements of the place, which has particularly struck me. I had repeatedly observed a long, lean fellow perched on the top of one of the towers, manœuvring two or three fishing-rods, as though he were angling for the stars. I was for some time perplexed by the evolutions of this aerial fisherman, and my perplexity increased on observing others employed in like manner on different parts of the battlements and bastions; it was not until I consulted Mateo Ximenes that I solved the mystery.

It seems that the pure and airy situation of this fortress has rendered it a prolific breeding-place for swallows and martlets, who sport about its towers in myriads, with the holiday glee of urchins just let loose from school. To entrap these birds in their giddy circlings, with hooks baited with flies, is one of the favorite amusements of the ragged "sons of the Alhambra," who, with the good-for-nothing ingenuity of arrant idlers, have thus invented the art of angling in the sky.

The Hall of Ambassadors

In one of my visits to the old Moorish chamber where the good Tia Antonia cooks her dinner and receives her company, I observed a mysterious door in one corner, leading apparently into the ancient part of the edifice. My curiosity being aroused, I opened it, and found myself in a narrow, blind corridor, groping along which I came to the head of a dark winding staircase, leading down an angle of the Tower of Comares. Down this staircase I descended darkling, guiding myself by the wall until I came to a small door at the bottom, throwing which open, I was suddenly dazzled by emerging into the brilliant antechamber of the Hall of Ambassadors; with the fountain of the court of the Alberca sparkling before me. The antechamber is separated from the court by an elegant gallery, supported by slender columns. At each end of the antechamber are alcoves, and its ceiling is richly stuccoed and painted. Passing through a magnificent portal, I found myself in the far-famed Hall of Ambassadors, the audience chamber of the Moslem monarchs. It is said to be thirty-seven feet square, and sixty feet high; occupies the whole interior of the Tower of Comares; and still bears the traces of past magnificence. The walls are beautifully stuccoed and decorated with Morisco fancifulness; the lofty ceiling was originally of the same favorite material, with the usual frostwork and pensile ornaments; which, with the embellishments of vivid coloring and gilding, must have been gorgeous in the extreme. Unfortunately it gave way during an earthquake, and brought down with it an immense arch which traversed the hall. It was replaced by the present vault or dome of larch or cedar, with, intersecting ribs, the whole curiously wrought and richly colored; still Oriental in its character, reminding one of those ceilings of cedar and vermilion that we read of in the Prophets and the Arabian Nights."

From the great height of the vault above the windows, the upper part of the hall is almost lost in obscurity; yet there is a magnificence as well as solemnity in the gloom, as through it we have gleams of rich gilding and the brilliant tints of the Moorish pencil.

The royal throne was placed opposite the entrance in a recess, which still bears an inscription intimating that Yusef I. (the monarch who completed the Alhambra) made this the throne of his empire. Everything in this noble hall seems to have been calculated to surround the throne with impressive dignity and splendor; there was none of the elegant voluptuousness which reigns in other parts of the palace. The tower is of massive strength, domineering, over the whole edifice and overhanging the steep hillside. On three sides of the Hall of Ambassadors are windows cut through the immense thickness of the walls and commanding extensive prospects. The balcony of the central window especially looks down upon the verdant valley of the Darro, with its walks, its groves, and gardens. To the left it enjoys a distant prospect of the Vega; while directly in front rises the rival height of the Albaycin, with its medley of streets, and terraces, and gardens, and once crowned by a fortress that vied in power with the Alhambra. "Ill fated the man who lost all this!" exclaimed Charles V., as he looked forth from this window upon the enchanting scenery it commands.

The balcony of the window where this royal exclamation was made, has of late become one of my favorite resorts. I have just been seated there, enjoying the close of a long, brilliant day. The sun, as he sank behind the purple mountains of Alhama, sent a stream of effulgence up the valley of the Darro, that spread a melancholy pomp over the ruddy towers of the Alhambra; while the Vega, covered with a slight sultry vapor that caught the setting ray, seemed spread out in the distance like a golden sea. Not a breath of air disturbed the stillness of the hour, and though the faint sound of music and merriment now and then rose from the gardens of the Darro, it but rendered more impressive the monumental silence of the pile which overshadowed me. It was one of those hours and scenes in which memory asserts an almost magical power: and, like the evening sun beaming on these mouldering towers, sends back her retrospective rays to light up the glories of the past.

As I sat watching the effect of the declining daylight upon this Moorish pile, I was led into a consideration of the light, elegant, and voluptuous character prevalent throughout its internal architecture, and to contrast it with the grand but gloomy solemnity of the Gothic edifices reared by the Spanish conquerors. The very architecture thus bespeaks the opposite and irreconcilable natures of the two warlike people who so long battled here for the mastery of the Peninsula. By degrees I fell into a course of musing upon the singular fortunes of the Arabian or Morisco-Spaniards, whose whole existence is as a tale that is told, and certainly forms one of the most anomalous yet splendid episodes in history. Potent and durable as was their dominion, we scarcely knew how to call them. They were a nation without a legitimate country or name. A remote wave of the great Arabian inundation, cast upon the shores of Europe, they seem to have all the impetus of the first rush of the torrent. Their career of conquest, from the rock of Gibraltar to the cliffs of the Pyrenees, was as rapid and brilliant as the Moslem victories of Syria and Egypt. Nay, had they not been checked on the plains of Tours, all France, all Europe, might have been overrun with the same facility as the empires of the East, and the Crescent at this day have glittered on the fanes of Paris and London.

Repelled within the limits of the Pyrenees, the mixed hordes of Asia and Africa, that formed this great irruption, gave up the Moslem principle of conquest, and sought to establish in Spain a peaceful and permanent dominion. As conquerors, their heroism was only equaled by their moderation; and in both, for a time, they excelled the nations with whom they contended. Severed from their native homes, they loved the land given them as they supposed by Allah, and strove to embellish it with everything that could administer to the happiness of man. Laying the foundations of their power in a system of wise and equitable laws, diligently cultivating the arts and sciences, and promoting agriculture, manufactures, and commerce, they gradually formed an empire unrivalled for its prosperity by any of the empires of Christendom; and diligently drawing round them the graces and refinements which marked the Arabian empire in the East, at the time of its greatest civilization, they diffused the light of Oriental knowledge through the western regions of benighted Europe.

The cities of Arabian Spain became the resort of Christian artisans, to instruct themselves in the useful arts. The universities of Toledo, Cordova, Seville, and Granada were sought by the pale student from other lands to acquaint himself with the sciences of the Arabs and the treasured lore of antiquity; the lovers of the gay science resorted to Cordova and Granada, to imbibe the poetry and music of the East; and the steel-clad warriors of the North hastened thither to accomplish themselves in the graceful exercises and courteous usages of chivalry.

If the Moslem monuments in Spain, if the Mosque of Cordova, the Alcazar of Seville, and the Alhambra of Granada, still bear inscriptions boasting of the power and permanency of their dominion, can the boast be derided as arrogant and vain? Generation after generation, century after century, passed away, and still they maintained possession of the land. A period elapsed longer than that which has passed since England was subjugated by the Norman Conqueror, and the descendants of Musa and Taric might as little anticipate being driven into exile across the same straits, traversed by their triumphant ancestors, as the descendants of Rollo and William, and their veteran peers, may dream of being driven back to the shores of Normandy.

With all this, however, the Moslem empire in Spain was but a brilliant exotic, that took no permanent root in the soil it embellished. Severed from all their neighbors in the West by impassable barriers of faith and manners, and separated by seas and deserts from their kindred of the East, the Morisco-Spaniards were an isolated people. Their whole existence was a prolonged, though gallant and chivalric struggle for a foothold in a usurped land.

They were the outposts and frontiers of Islamism. The Peninsula was the great battle-ground where the Gothic conquerors of the North and the Moslem conquerors of the East met and strove for mastery; and the fiery courage of the Arab was at length subdued by the obstinate and persevering valor of the Goth.

Never was the annihilation of a people more complete than that of the Morisco-Spaniards. Where are they? Ask the shores of Barbary and its desert places. The exiled remnant of their once powerful empire disappeared among the barbarians of Africa, and ceased to be a nation. They have not even left a distinct name behind them, though for nearly eight centuries they were a distinct people. The home of their adoption, and of their occupation for ages, refuses to acknowledge them, except as invaders and usurpers. A few broken monuments are all that remain to bear witness to their power and dominion, as solitary rocks, left far in the interior, bear testimony to the extent of some vast inundation. Such is the Alhambra;—a Moslem pile in the midst of a Christian land; an Oriental palace amidst the Gothic edifices of the West; an elegant memento of a brave, intelligent, and graceful people, who conquered, ruled, flourished, and passed away.

Alhamar, the Founder of the Alhambra

The Moors of Granada regarded the Alhambra as a miracle of art, and had a tradition that the king who founded it dealt in magic, or at least in alchemy, by means whereof he procured the immense sums of gold expended in its erection. A brief view of his reign will show the secret of his wealth. His name, Alhamar, was given to him, we are told, on account of his ruddy complexion.

He was of the noble and opulent line of the Beni Nasar, or tribe of Nasar, and was born in Arjona, in the year of the Hegira 592 (A.D. 1195.) At his birth the astrologers, we are told, cast his horoscope according to Oriental custom, and pronounced it highly auspicious; and a santon predicted for him a glorious career. No expense was spared in fitting him for the high destinies prognosticated. Before he attained the full years of manhood, the famous battle of the Navas (or plains) of Tolosa shattered the Moorish empire, and eventually severed the Moslems of Spain from the Moslems of Africa. Factions soon arose among the former, headed by warlike chiefs ambitious of grasping the sovereignty of the Peninsula. Alhamar became engaged in these wars; he was the general and leader of the Beni Nasar, and, as such, he opposed and thwarted the ambition of Aben Hud, who had raised his standard among the warlike mountains of the Alpuxarras, and been proclaimed king of Murcia and Granada. Many conflicts took place between these warring chieftains; Alhamar dispossessed his rival of several important places, and was proclaimed king of Jaen by his soldiery; but he aspired to the sovereignty of the whole of Andalusia, for he was of a sanguine spirit and lofty ambition. His valor and generosity went hand in hand; what he gained, by the one he secured by the other; and at the death of Aben Hud (A.D.1238) he became sovereign of all the territories, which owed allegiance to that powerful chief. He made his formal entry into Granada in the same year, amid the enthusiastic shouts of the multitude, who hailed him as the only one capable of uniting the various factions which prevailed, and which threatened to lay the empire at the mercy of the Christian princes.

Alhamar established his court in Granada; he was the first of the illustrious line of Nasar that sat upon a throne. He took immediate measures to put his little kingdom in a posture of defence against the assaults to be expected from his Christian neighbors, repairing and strengthening the frontier posts and fortifying the capital. Not content with the provisions of the Moslem law, by which every man is made a soldier, he raised a regular army to garrison his strongholds, allowing every soldier stationed on the frontier a portion of land for the support of himself, his horse, and his family,—thus interesting him in the defence of the soil in which he had a property. These wise precautions were justified by events. The Christians, profiting by the dismemberment of the Moslem power, were rapidly regaining their ancient territories. James the Conqueror had subjected all Valencia, and Ferdinand the Saint encamped in person before Jaen, the bulwark of Granada. Alhamar ventured to oppose him in the open field, but met with a signal defeat, and retired discomfited to his capital. Jaen still held out, and kept the enemy at bay during an entire winter, but Ferdinand swore not to raise his camp until he had gained possession of the place. Alhamar found it impossible to throw reinforcements into the besieged city; and was conscious of the insufficiency of his means to cope with the potent sovereign of Castile. Taking a sudden resolution, therefore, he repaired privately to the Christian camp, made his unexpected appearance in the presence of King Ferdinand, and frankly announced himself as the king of Granada. "I come," said he, "confiding in your good faith, to put myself under your protection. Take all I possess and receive me as your vassal"; so saying, he knelt and kissed the king's hand in token of allegiance.

Ferdinand was won by this instance of confiding faith, and determined not to be outdone in generosity. He raised his late enemy from the earth, embraced him as a friend, and, refusing the wealth he offered, left him sovereign of his dominions, under the feudal tenure of a yearly tribute, attendance at the Cortes as one of the nobles of the empire, and service in war with a certain number of horsemen. He moreover conferred on him the honor of knighthood, and armed him with his own hands.

It was not long after this that Alhamar was called upon for his military services, to aid King Ferdinand in his famous siege of Seville. The Moorish king sallied forth with five hundred chosen horsemen of Granada, than whom none in the world knew better how to manage the steed or wield the lance. It was a humiliating service, however, for they had to draw the sword against their brethren of the faith.

Alhamar gained a melancholy distinction by his prowess in this renowned conquest, but more true honor by the humanity which he prevailed upon Ferdinand to introduce into the usages of war. When in 1248 the famous city of Seville surrendered to the Castilian monarch, Alhamar returned sad and full of care to his dominions. He saw the gathering ills that menaced the Moslem cause; and uttered an ejaculation often used by him in moments of anxiety and trouble,—"How straitened and wretched would be our life, if our hope were not so spacious and extensive!"

As he approached Granada on his return he beheld arches of triumph which had been erected in honor of his martial exploits. The people thronged forth to see him with impatient joy, for his benignant rule had won all hearts. Wherever he passed he was hailed with acclamations as "The Conqueror." Alhamar gave a melancholy shake of the head on hearing the appellation. "There is no conqueror but God!" exclaimed he. From that time forward this exclamation became his motto, and the motto of his descendants, and appears to this day emblazoned on his escutcheons in the halls of the Alhambra.

Alhamar had purchased peace by submission to the Christian yoke; but he was conscious that, with elements so discordant and motives for hostility so deep and ancient, it could not be permanent. Acting, therefore, upon the old maxim, "Arm thyself in peace and clothe thyself in summer," he improved the present interval of tranquillity by fortifying his dominions, replenishing his arsenals, and promoting those useful arts which give wealth and real power. He confided the command of his various cities to such as had distinguished themselves by valor and prudence, and who seemed most acceptable to the people. He organized a vigilant police, and established rigid rules for the administration of justice. The poor and the distressed always found ready admission to his presence, and he attended personally to their assistance and redress. He erected hospitals for the blind, the aged, and infirm, and all those incapable of labor, and visited them frequently; not on set days with pomp and form, so as to give time for everything to be put in order, and every abuse concealed, but suddenly, and unexpectedly, informing himself, by actual observation and close inquiry, of the treatment of the sick, and the conduct of those appointed to administer to their relief. He founded schools and colleges, which he visited in the same manner, inspecting personally the instruction of the youth. He established butcheries and public ovens, that the people might be furnished with wholesome provisions at just and regular prices. He introduced abundant streams of water into the city, erecting baths and fountains, and constructing aqueducts and canals to irrigate and fertilize the Vega. By these means prosperity and abundance prevailed in this beautiful city; its gates were thronged with commerce, and its warehouses filled with luxuries and merchandise of every clime and country.

He moreover gave premiums and privileges to the best artisans; improved the breed of horses and other domestic animals; encouraged husbandry; and increased the natural fertility of the soil twofold by his protection, making the lovely valleys of his kingdom to bloom like gardens. He fostered also the growth and fabrication of silk, until the looms of Granada surpassed even those of Syria in the fineness and beauty of their productions. He moreover caused the mines of gold and silver and other metals, found in the mountainous regions of his dominions, to be diligently worked, and was the first king of Granada who struck money of gold and silver with his name, taking great care that the coins should be skillfully executed.

It was towards the middle of the thirteenth century, and just after his return from the siege of Seville, that he commenced the splendid palace of the Alhambra; superintending the building of it in person; mingling frequently among the artists and workmen, and directing their labors.

Though thus magnificent in his works and great in his enterprises, he was simple in his person and moderate in his enjoyments. His dress was not merely void of splendor, but so plain as not to distinguish him from his subjects. His wives were daughters of the principal nobles, and were treated by him as friends and rational companions. He passed much of his time in his gardens; especially in those of the Alhambra, which he had stored with the rarest plants and the most beautiful and aromatic flowers. Here he delighted himself in reading histories, or in causing them to be read and related to him; and sometimes in intervals of leisure, employed himself in the instruction of his three sons, for whom he had provided the most learned and virtuous masters.

As he had frankly and voluntarily offered himself a tributary vassal to Ferdinand, so he always remained loyal to his word, giving him repeated proofs of fidelity and attachment. When that renowned monarch died in Seville in 1254, Alhamar sent ambassadors to condole with his successor, Alonzo X., and with them a gallant train of a hundred Moorish cavaliers of distinguished rank, who were to attend round the royal bier during the funeral ceremonies, each bearing a lighted taper!

Alhamar retained his faculties and vigor to an advanced age. In his seventy-ninth year (A.D.1272) he took the field on horseback, accompanied by the flower of his chivalry, to resist an invasion of his territories. As the army sallied forth from Granada, one of the principal guides, who rode in the advance, accidentally broke his lance against the arch of the gate. The counsellors of the king, alarmed by this circumstance, which was considered an evil omen, entreated him to return. Their supplications were in vain. The king persisted, and at noontide the omen, say the Moorish chroniclers, was fatally fulfilled. Alhamar was suddenly struck with illness, and had nearly fallen from his horse. He was placed on a litter, and borne back towards

Granada, but his illness increased to such a degree that they were obliged to pitch his tent in the Vega. His physicians were filled with consternation, not knowing what remedy to prescribe. In a few hours he died, vomiting blood and in violent convulsions. The Castilian prince, Don Philip, brother of Alonzo X., was by his side when he expired. His body was embalmed, enclosed in a silver coffin, and buried in the Alhambra in a sepulchre of precious marble, amidst the unfeigned lamentations of his subjects, who bewailed him as a parent.

I have said that he was the first of the illustrious line of Nasar that sat upon a throne. I may add that he was the founder of a brilliant kingdom which will ever be famous in history and romance as the last rallying-place of Moslem power and splendor in the Peninsula.

The Mysterious Chambers

As I was rambling one day about the Moorish halls, my attention was, for the first time, attracted to a door in a remote gallery, communicating apparently with some part of the Alhambra which I had not yet explored. I attempted to open it, but it was locked. I knocked, but no one answered, and the sound seemed to reverberate through empty chambers. Here then was a mystery. Here was the haunted wing of the castle. How was I to get at the dark secrets here shut up from the public eye? Should I come privately at night with lamp and sword, according to the prying custom of heroes of romance; or should I endeavor to draw the secret from Pépe the stuttering gardener; or the ingenuous Dolores, or the loquacious Mateo? Or should I go frankly and openly to Dame Antonia and ask her all about it? I chose the latter course, as being the simplest though the least romantic; and found, somewhat to my disappointment, that there was no mystery in the case. I was welcome to explore the apartment, and there was the key.

Thus provided, I returned forthwith to the door. It opened, as I had surmised, to a range of vacant chambers; but they were quite different from the rest of the palace. The architecture, though rich and antiquated, was European. There was nothing Moorish about it. The first two rooms were lofty; the ceilings, broken in many places, were of cedar, deeply paneled and skillfully carved with fruits and flowers, intermingled with grotesque masks or faces.

The walls had evidently in ancient times been hung with damask; but now were naked, and scrawled over by that class of aspiring travellers who defile noble monuments with their worthless names. The windows, dismantled, and open to wind and weather, looked out into a charming little secluded garden, where an alabaster fountain sparkled among roses and myrtles, and was surrounded by orange and citron trees, some of which flung their branches into the chambers. Beyond these rooms were two saloons, longer but less lofty, looking also into the garden. In the compartments of the paneled ceilings were baskets of fruit and garlands of flowers, painted by no mean hand, and in tolerable preservation. The walls also had been painted in fresco in the Italian style, but the paintings were nearly obliterated; the windows were in the same shattered state with those of the other chambers. This fanciful suite of rooms terminated in an open gallery with balustrades, running at right angles along another side of the garden. The whole apartment, so delicate and elegant in its decorations, so choice and sequestered in its situation along this retired little garden, and so different in architecture from the neighboring halls, awakened an interest in its history. I found on inquiry that it was an apartment fitted up by Italian artists in the early part of the last century, at the time when Philip V. and his second wife, the beautiful Elizabeth of Farnese, were expected at the Alhambra. It was destined for the queen and the ladies of her train. One of the loftiest chambers had been her sleeping-room. A narrow staircase, now walled up, led up to a delightful belvedere, which was fitted up as a boudoir for the fair Elizabeth, and still retains the name of the Queen's Toilet.

One window of the royal sleeping-room commanded a prospect of the Generalife and its embowered terraces; another looked out into the little secluded garden I have mentioned, which was decidedly Moorish in its character, and also had its history. It was in fact the garden of Lindaraxa, so often mentioned in descriptions of the Alhambra, but who this Lindaraxa was I had never heard explained. A little research gave me the few particulars known about her. She was a Moorish beauty who flourished in the court of Mohamed the Left-Handed, and was the daughter of his loyal adherent, the governor of Malaga, who sheltered him in his city when driven from the throne. On regaining his crown, the governor was rewarded for his fidelity. His daughter had her apartment in the Alhambra, and was given by the king in marriage to Nasar, a young prince descended from Aben Hud the Just.

Four centuries had elapsed since the fair Lindaraxa passed away, yet how much of the fragile beauty of the scenes she inhabited remained! The garden still bloomed in which she delighted; the fountain still presented the crystal mirror in which her charms may once have been reflected; the alabaster, it is true, had lost its whiteness; the basin beneath, overrun with weeds, had become the lurking-place of the lizard, but there was something in the very decay that enhanced the interest of the scene, speaking as it did of that mutability, the irrevocable lot of man and all his works.

The desolation too of these chambers, once the abode of the proud and elegant Elizabeth, had a more touching charm for me than if I had beheld them in their pristine splendor, glittering with the pageantry of a court.

When I returned to my quarters, in the governor's apartment, everything seemed tame and commonplace after the poetic region I had left. The thought suggested itself: Why could I not change my quarters to these vacant chambers? that would indeed be living in the Alhambra, surrounded by its gardens and fountains, as in the time of the Moorish sovereigns. I proposed the change to Dame Antonia and her family, and it occasioned vast surprise. They could not conceive any rational inducement for the choice of an apartment so forlorn, remote, and solitary. Dolores exclaimed at its frightful loneliness; nothing but bats and owls flitting about,—and then a fox and wildcat were kept in the vaults of the neighboring baths, and roamed about at night. The good Tia had more reasonable objections. The neighborhood was infested by vagrants; gipsies swarmed in the caverns of the adjacent hills; the palace was ruinous and easy to be entered in many places; the rumor of a stranger quartered alone in one of the remote and ruined apartments, out of the hearing of the rest of the inhabitants, might tempt unwelcome visitors in the night, especially as foreigners were always supposed to be well stocked with money. I was not to be diverted from my humor, however, and my will was law with these good people. So, calling in the assistance of a carpenter, and the ever officious Mateo Ximenes, the doors and windows were soon placed in a state of tolerable security, and the sleeping-room of the stately Elizabeth prepared for my reception. Mateo kindly volunteered as a body-guard to sleep in my antechamber; but I did not think it worth while to put his valor to the proof.

With all the hardihood I had assumed and all the precautions I had taken, I must confess the first night passed in these quarters was inexpressibly dreary. I do not think it was so much the apprehension of dangers from without that affected me, as the character of the place itself, with all its strange associations: the deeds of violence committed there; the tragical ends of many of those who had once reigned there in splendor.

The whole family escorted me to my chamber, and took leave of me as of one engaged on a perilous enterprise; and when I heard their retreating steps die away along the waste antechambers and echoing galleries, and turned the key of my door, I was reminded of those stories, where the hero is left to accomplish the adventure of an enchanted house.

Even the thoughts of the fair Elizabeth, and the beauties of her court, who had once graced these chambers, now, by a perversion of fancy, added to the gloom. Here was the scene of their transient gayety and loveliness; here were the very traces of their elegance and enjoyment; but what and where were they? Dust and ashes! tenants of the tomb! phantoms of the memory!

A vague and indescribable awe was creeping over me. I would fain have ascribed it to the thoughts of robbers awakened by the evening's conversation, but I felt it was something more unreal and absurd. The long-buried superstitions of the nursery were reviving, and asserting their power over my imagination. Everything began to be affected by the working of my mind. I cast my eyes into the garden of Lindaraxa; the groves presented a gulf of shadows; the thickets, indistinct and ghastly shapes. I was glad to close the window, but my chamber itself became infected. There was a slight rustling noise overhead; a bat suddenly emerged from a broken panel of the ceiling, flitting about the room and athwart my solitary lamp; and as the fateful bird almost flouted my face with his noiseless wing, the grotesque faces carved in high relief in the cedar ceiling, whence he had emerged, seemed to mope and mow at me.

Rousing myself, and half smiling at this temporary weakness, I resolved to brave it out in the true spirit of the hero of the enchanted house; so, taking lamp in hand; I sallied forth to make a tour of the palace. Notwithstanding every mental exertion the task was a severe one. I had to traverse waste halls and mysterious galleries, where the rays of the lamp extended but a short distance around me. I walked, as it were, in a mere halo of light, walled in by impenetrable darkness. The vaulted corridors were as caverns; the ceilings of the halls were lost in gloom. I recalled all that had been said of the danger from interlopers in these remote and ruined apartments. Might not some vagrant foe be lurking before or behind me, in the outer darkness? My own shadow, cast upon the wall, began to disturb me. The echoes of my own footsteps along the corridors made me pause and look round. I was traversing scenes fraught with dismal recollections. One dark passage led down to the mosque where Yusef, the Moorish monarch, the finisher of the Alhambra, had been basely murdered. In another place I trod the gallery where another monarch had been struck down by the poniard of a relative whom he had thwarted in his love.

A low murmuring sound, as of stifled voices and clanking chains, now reached me. I knew it to be the rush of water through subterranean channels, but it sounded strangely in the night, and reminded me of the dismal stories to which it had given rise.

I had no desire for further perambulation; but returned to my chamber with infinitely more alacrity than I had sallied forth, and drew my breath more freely when once more within its walls and the door bolted behind me. When I awoke in the morning, with the sun shining in at my window and lighting up every part of the building with his cheerful and truth-telling beams, I could scarcely recall the shadows and fancies conjured up by the gloom of the preceding night; or believe that the scenes around me, so naked and apparent, could have been clothed with such imaginary horrors.

In the course of a few evenings a thorough change took place in the scene and its associations. The moon, which when I took possession of my new apartments was invisible, gradually gained each evening upon the darkness of the night, and at length rolled in full splendor above the towers, pouring a flood of tempered light into every court and hall. The garden beneath my window, before wrapped in gloom, was gently lighted up; the orange and citron trees were tipped with silver; the fountain sparkled in the moonbeams, and even the blush of the rose was faintly visible.

I now felt the poetic merit of the Arabic inscription on the walls,—"How beauteous is this garden; where the flowers of the earth vie with the stars of heaven. What can compare with the vase of yon alabaster fountain filled with crystal water? nothing but the moon in her fulness, shining in the midst of an unclouded sky!"

On such heavenly nights I would sit for hours at my window inhaling the sweetness of the garden, and musing on the checkered fortunes of those whose history was dimly shadowed out in the elegant memorials around. Sometimes, when all was quiet, and the clock from the distant cathedral of Granada struck the midnight hour, I have sallied out on another tour and wandered over the whole building; but how different from my first tour! No longer dark and mysterious; no longer peopled with shadowy foes; no longer recalling scenes of violence and murder; all was open, spacious, beautiful; everything called up pleasing and romantic fancies; Lindaraxa once more walked in her garden; the gay chivalry of Moslem Granada once more glittered about the Court of Lions! Who can do justice to a moonlight night in such a climate and such a place? The temperature of a summer midnight in Andalusia is perfectly ethereal. We seem lifted up into a purer atmosphere; we feel a serenity of soul, a buoyancy of spirits, an elasticity of frame, which render mere existence happiness. But when moonlight is added to all this, the effect is like enchantment. Under its plastic sway the Alhambra seems to regain its pristine glories. Every rent and chasm of time; every mouldering tint and weather-stain is gone; the marble resumes its original whiteness; the long colonnades brighten in the moonbeams; the halls are illuminated with a softened radiance,—we tread the enchanted palace of an Arabian tale!

What a delight, at such a time, to ascend to the little airy pavilion of the Queen's Toilet, which, like a bird-cage, overhangs the valley of the Darro, and gaze from its light arcades upon the moonlight prospect! To the right, the swelling mountains of the Sierra Nevada, robbed of their ruggedness and softened into a fairy land, with their snowy summits gleaming like silver clouds against the deep blue sky. And then to lean over the parapet and gaze down upon Granada spread out like a map below; all buried in deep repose; the white palaces and convents sleeping in the moonshine, and beyond all these the vapory Vega fading away like a dreamland in the distance.

Sometimes the faint click of castanets rises from the public walk, where some gay Andalusians are dancing away the summer night. Sometimes the dubious tones of a guitar and the notes of an amorous voice, tell perchance the whereabout of some moonstruck lover serenading his lady's window.

Such is a faint picture of the moonlight nights I have passed loitering about the courts and halls and balconies of this most suggestive pile; "feeding my fancy with sugared suppositions," and enjoying that mixture of reverie and sensation which steal away existence in a southern climate; so that it has been almost morning before I have retired to bed, and been lulled to sleep by the falling waters of the fountain of Lindaraxa.

Panorama from the Tower of Comares

It is a serene and beautiful morning: the sun has not gained sufficient power to destroy the freshness of the night. What a morning to mount to the summit of the Tower of Comares, and take a bird's-eye view of Granada and its environs!

Come then, worthy reader and comrade, follow my steps into this vestibule, ornamented with rich tracery, which opens into the Hall of Ambassadors. We will not enter the hall, however, but turn to this small door opening into the wall. Have a care! here are steep winding steps and but scanty light; yet up this narrow, obscure, and spiral staircase, the proud monarchs of Granada and their queens have often ascended to the battlements to watch the approach of invading armies, or gaze with anxious hearts on the battles in the Vega.

At length we have reached the roof, and may take breath for a moment, while we cast a general eye over the splendid panorama of city and country; of rocky mountain, verdant valley, and fertile plain; of castle, cathedral, Moorish towers, and Gothic domes, crumbling ruins, and blooming groves. Let us approach the battlements, and cast our eyes immediately below. See, on this side we have the whole plain of the Alhambra laid open to us, and can look down into its courts and gardens. At the foot of the tower is the Court of the Alberca, with its great tank or fish-pool, bordered with flowers; and yonder is the Court of Lions, with its famous fountain, and its light Moorish arcades; and in the centre of the pile is the little garden of Lindaraxa, buried in the heart of the building, with its roses and citrons and shrubbery of emerald green.

That belt of battlements, studded with square towers, straggling round the whole brow of the hill, is the outer boundary of the fortress. Some of the towers, you may perceive, are in ruins, and their massive fragments buried among vines, fig-trees, and aloes. Let us look on this northern side of the tower. It is a giddy height; the very foundations of the tower rise above the groves of the steep hillside. And see! a long fissure in the massive walls shows that the tower has been rent by some of the earthquakes which from time to time have thrown Granada into consternation; and which, sooner or later, must reduce this crumbling pile to a mere mass of ruin. The deep narrow glen below us, which gradually widens as it opens from the mountains, is the valley of the Darro; you see the little river winding its way under embowered terraces, and among orchards and flower-gardens. It is a stream famous in old times for yielding gold, and its sands are still sifted occasionally, in search of the precious ore. Some of those white pavilions, which here and there gleam from among groves and vine-yards, were rustic retreats of the Moors, to enjoy the refreshment of their gardens. Well have they been compared by one of their poets to so many pearls set in a bed of emeralds.

The airy palace, with its tall white towers and long arcades, which breasts yon mountain, among pompous groves and hanging gardens, is the Generalife, a summer palace of the Moorish kings, to which they resorted during the sultry months to enjoy a still more breezy region than that of the Alhambra. The naked summit of the height above it, where you behold some shapeless ruins, is the Seat of the Moor, so called from having been a retreat of the unfortunate Boabdil during the time of an insurrection, where he seated himself, and looked down mournfully upon his rebellious city.

A murmuring sound of water now and then rises from the valley. It is from the aqueduct of yon Moorish mill, nearly at the foot of the hill. The avenue of trees beyond is the Alameda, along the bank of the Darro; a favorite resort in evenings, and a rendezvous of lovers in the summer nights, when the guitar may be heard at a late hour from the benches along its walks. At present you see none but a few loitering monks there, and a group of water-carriers. The latter are burdened with water-jars of ancient Oriental construction, such as were used by the Moors. They have been filled at the cold and limpid spring called the fountain of Avellanos. Yon mountain path leads to the fountain, a favorite resort of Moslems as well as Christians; for this is said to be the "Fountain of Tears," celebrated in the histories and romances of the Moors.

You start! 'tis nothing but a hawk that we have frightened from his nest. This old tower is a complete breeding-place for vagrant birds; the swallow and martlet abound in every chink and cranny, and circle about it the whole day long; while at night, when all other birds have gone to rest, the moping owl comes out of its lurking-place, and utters its boding cry from the battlements. See how the hawk we have dislodged sweeps away below us, skimming over the tops of the trees, and sailing up to the ruins above the Generalife!

I see you raise your eyes to the snowy summit of yon pile of mountains, shining like a white summer cloud in the blue sky. It is the Sierra Nevada, the pride and delight of Granada; the source of her cooling breezes and perpetual verdure; of her gushing fountains and perennial streams. It is this glorious pile of mountains which gives to Granada that combination of delights so rare in a southern city,—the fresh vegetation and temperate airs of a northern climate, with the vivifying ardor of a tropical sun, and the cloudless azure of a southern sky. It is this aerial treasury of snow, which, melting in proportion to the increase of the summer heat, sends down rivulets and streams through every glen and gorge of the Alpuxarras, diffusing emerald verdure and fertility throughout a chain of happy and sequestered valleys.

Those mountains may be well called the glory of Granada. They dominate the whole extent of Andalusia, and may be seen from its most distant parts. The muleteer hails them, as he views their frosty peaks from the sultry level of the plain; and the Spanish mariner on the deck of his bark, far, far off on the bosom of the blue Mediterranean, watches them with a pensive eye, thinks of delightful Granada, and chants, in low voice, some old romance about the Moors.

See to the south at the foot of those mountains a line of arid hills, down which a long train of mules is slowly moving. Here was the closing scene of Moslem domination. From the summit of one of those hills the unfortunate Boabdil cast back his last look upon Granada, and gave vent to the agony of his soul. It is the spot famous in song and story, "The last sigh of the Moor."

Further this way these arid hills slope down into the luxurious Vega, from which he had just emerged: a blooming wilderness of grove and garden, and teeming orchard, with the Xenil winding through it in silver links, and feeding innumerable rills; which, conducted through ancient Moorish channels, maintain the landscape in perpetual verdure. Here were the beloved bowers and gardens, and rural pavilions, for which the unfortunate Moors fought with such desperate valor. The very hovels and rude granges, now inhabited by boors, show, by the remains of arabesques and other tasteful decorations, that they were elegant residences in the days of the Moslems. Behold, in the very centre of this eventful plain, a place which in a manner links the history of the Old World with that of the New. Yon line of walls and towers gleaming in the morning sun, is the city of Santa Fe, built by the Catholic sovereigns during the siege of Granada, after a conflagration had destroyed their camp. It was to these walls Columbus was called back by the heroic queen, and within them the treaty was concluded which led to the discovery of the Western World. Behind yon promontory to the west is the bridge of Pinos, renowned for many a bloody fight between Moors and Christians. At this bridge the messenger overtook Columbus when, despairing of success with the Spanish sovereigns, he was departing to carry his project of discovery to the court of France.

Above the bridge a range of mountains bounds the Vega to the west,—the ancient barrier between Granada and the Christian territories. Among their heights you may still discern warrior towns; their gray walls and battlements seeming of a piece with the rocks on which they are built. Here and there a solitary watchtower, perched on a mountain peak, looks down as it were from the sky into the valley on either side. How often have these towers given notice, by fire at night or smoke by day, of an approaching foe! It was down a cragged defile of these mountains, called the Pass of Lope, that the Christian armies descended into the Vega. Round the base of yon gray and naked mountain (the mountain of Elvira), stretching its bold rocky promontory into the bosom of the plain, the invading squadrons would come bursting into view, with flaunting banners and clangor of drum and trumpet.

Five hundred years have elapsed since Ismael ben Ferrag, a Moorish king of Granada, beheld from this very tower an invasion of the kind, and an insulting ravage of the Vega; on which occasion he displayed an instance of chivalrous magnanimity, often witnessed in the Moslem princes; "whose history," says an Arabian writer, "abounds in generous actions and noble deeds that will last through all succeeding ages, and live forever in the memory of man."—But let us sit down on this parapet, and I will relate the anecdote.

It was in the year 1319, that Ismael ben Ferrag beheld from this tower a Christian camp whitening the skirts of yon mountain of Elvira. The royal princes, Don Juan and Don Pedro, regents of Castile during the minority of Alphonso XI., had already laid waste the country from Alcaudete to Alcalá la Real, capturing the castle of Illora, and setting fire to its suburbs, and they now carried their insulting ravages to the very gates of Granada, defying the king to sally forth and give them battle.

Ismael, though a young and intrepid prince, hesitated to accept the challenge. He had not sufficient force at hand, and awaited the arrival of troops summoned from the neighboring towns. The Christian princes, mistaking his motives, gave up all hope of drawing him forth, and having glutted themselves with ravage, struck their tents and began their homeward march. Don Pedro led the van, and Don Juan brought up the rear, but their march was confused and irregular, the army, being greatly encumbered by the spoils and captives they had taken.

By this time King Ismael had received his expected resources, and putting them under the command of Osmyn, one of the bravest of his generals, sent them forth in hot pursuit of the enemy. The Christians were overtaken in the defiles of the mountains. A panic seized them; they were completely routed, and driven with great slaughter across the borders. Both of the princes lost their lives. The body of Don Pedro was carried off by his soldiers, but that of Don Juan was lost in the darkness of the night. His son wrote to the Moorish king, entreating that the body of his father might be sought and honorably treated. Ismael forgot in a moment that Don Juan was an enemy, who had carried ravage and insult to the very gate of his capital; he only thought of him as a gallant cavalier and a royal prince. By his command diligent search was made for the body. It was found in a ravine and brought to Granada. There Ismael caused it to be laid out in state on a lofty bier, surrounded by torches and tapers, in one of these halls of the Alhambra. Osmyn and other of the noblest cavaliers were appointed as a guard of honor, and the Christian captives were assembled to pray around it.

In the meantime, Ismael wrote to the son of Prince Juan to send a convoy for the body, assuring him it should be faithfully delivered up. In due time, a band of Christian cavaliers arrived for the purpose. They were honorably received and entertained by Ismael, and, on their departure with the body, the guard of honor of Moslem cavaliers escorted the funeral train to the frontier.

The Balcony

I have spoken of a balcony of the central window of the Hall of Ambassadors. It served as a kind of observatory, where I used often to take my seat, and consider not merely the heaven above but the earth beneath. Besides the magnificent prospect which it commanded of mountain, valley, and plain, there was a little busy scene of human life laid open to inspection immediately below. At the foot of the hill was a public walk, which, though not so fashionable as the more modern and splendid promenade of the Xenil, still boasted a varied and picturesque concourse. Hither resorted the small gentry of the suburbs, together with the beaux and belles of the lower classes, in their Andalusian dresses; swaggering smugglers, and sometimes half-muffled and mysterious loungers of the higher ranks.

It was a moving picture of Spanish life and character, which I delighted to study; and as the astronomer has his grand telescope with which to sweep the skies, and, as it were, bring the stars nearer for his inspection, so I had a smaller one, of pocket size, for the use of my observatory, with which I could sweep the regions below, and bring the countenances of the motley groups so close as almost, at times, to make me think I could divine their conversation by the play and expression of their features. I was thus, in a manner, an invisible observer, and, without quitting my solitude, could throw myself in an instant into the midst of society,—a rare advantage to one of somewhat shy and quiet habits, and fond, like myself, of observing the drama of life without becoming an actor in the scene.

There was a considerable suburb lying below the Alhambra, filling the narrow gorge of the valley, and extending up the opposite hill of the Albaycin. Many of the houses were built in the Moorish style, round courts, cooled by fountains and open to the sky; and as the inhabitants passed much of their time in these courts, and on the terraced roofs during the summer season, it follows that many a glance at their domestic life might be obtained by an aerial spectator like myself, who could look down on them from the clouds.

I occasionally amused myself with noting from this balcony the gradual changes of the scenes below, according to the different stages of the day.

Scarce has the gray dawn streaked the sky, and the earliest cock crowed from the cottages of the hillside, when the suburbs give sign of reviving animation;

for the fresh hours of dawning are precious in the summer season in a sultry climate. All are anxious to get the start of the sun, in the business of the day. The muleteer drives forth his loaded train for the journey; the traveller slings his carbine behind his saddle, and mounts his steed at the gate of the hostel; the brown peasant from the country urges forward his loitering beasts, laden with panniers of sunny fruit and fresh dewy vegetables, for already the thrifty housewives are hastening to the market.

The sun is up and sparkles along the valley, tipping the transparent foliage of the groves. The matin bells resound melodiously through the pure, bright air, announcing the hour of devotion. The muleteer halts his burdened animals before the chapel, thrusts his staff through his belt behind, and enters with hat in hand, smoothing his coal-black hair, to put up a prayer for a prosperous wayfaring across the sierra.

As the morning advances, the din of labor augments on every side; the streets are thronged with man, and steed, and beast of burden, and there is a hum and murmur, like the surges of the ocean. As the sun ascends to his meridian, the hum and bustle gradually decline; at the height of noon there is a pause. The panting city sinks into lassitude, and for several hours there is a general repose. The windows are closed, the curtains drawn, the inhabitants retired into the coolest recesses of their mansions; the brawny porter lies stretched on the pavement beside his burden; the peasant and the laborer sleep beneath the trees of the promenade, lulled by the sultry chirping of the locust. The streets are deserted, except by the water-carrier, who refreshes the ear by proclaiming the merits of his sparkling beverage, colder than the mountain snow."

As the sun declines, there is again a gradual reviving, and when the vesper bell rings out his sinking knell, all nature seems to rejoice that the tyrant of the day has fallen. Now begins the bustle of enjoyment, when the citizens pour forth to breathe the evening air, and revel away the brief twilight in the walks and gardens of the Darro and Xenil.

As night closes, the capricious scene assumes new features. Light after light gradually twinkles forth; here a taper from a balconied window; there a votive lamp before the image of a Saint. Thus, by degrees, the city emerges from the, pervading gloom, and sparkles with scattered lights, like the starry firmament. Now break forth from court and garden, and street and lane, the tinkling of innumerable guitars, and the clicking of castanets; blending, at this lofty height, in a faint but general concert.

I was one evening seated in the balcony, enjoying the light breeze that came rustling along the side of the hill, among the tree-tops, when my humble historiographer Mateo, who was at my elbow, pointed out a spacious house, in an obscure street of the Albaycin, about which he related, as nearly as I can recollect, the following anecdote.

The Adventure of the Mason

"There was once upon a time a poor mason, or brick-layer, in Granada, who kept all the saints' days and holidays, and yet, with all his devotion, he grew poorer and poorer, and could scarcely earn bread for his numerous family. One night he was roused from his first sleep by a knocking at his door. He opened it, and beheld before him a tall, meagre, cadaverous-looking person.

"'Hark ye, honest friend!' said the stranger; 'I have observed that you are a good Christian, and one to be trusted; will you undertake a job this very night?'

"'With all my heart, Señor, on condition that I am paid accordingly.'

"'That you shall be; but you must suffer yourself to be blindfolded.'

"To this the mason made no objection. So, being hood-winked, he was led by the stranger through various rough lanes and winding passages, until they stopped before the portal of a house. The stranger then applied a key, turned a creaking lock, and opened what sounded like a ponderous door. They entered, the door was closed and bolted, and the mason was conducted through an echoing corridor and a spacious hall to an interior part of the building. Here the bandage was removed from his eyes, and he found himself in a court, dimly lighted by a single lamp. In the centre was the dry basin of an old Moorish fountain, under which the stranger requested him to form a small vault, bricks and mortar being at hand for the purpose. He accordingly worked all night, but without finishing the job. Just before daybreak the stranger put a piece of gold into his hand, and having again blindfolded him, conducted him back to his dwelling.

"'Are you willing,' said he, 'to return and complete your work?'

"'Gladly, Señor, provided I am so well paid.'

"'Well, then, to-morrow at midnight I will call again.'" He did so, and the vault was completed.

"'Now,' said the stranger, 'you must help me to bring forth the bodies that are to be buried in this vault.'

"The poor mason's hair rose on his head at these words: he followed the stranger, with trembling steps, into a retired chamber of the mansion, expecting to behold some ghastly spectacle of death, but was relieved on perceiving three or four portly jars standing in one corner. They were evidently full of money, and it was with great labor that he and the stranger carried them forth and consigned them to their tomb. The vault was then closed, the pavement replaced, and all traces of the work were obliterated. The mason was again hoodwinked and led forth by a route different from that by which he had come. After they had wandered for a long time through a perplexed maze of lanes and alleys, they halted, The stranger then put two pieces of gold into his hand: 'Wait here,' said he, 'until you hear the cathedral bell toll for matins. If you presume to uncover your eyes before that time, evil will befall you': so saying, he departed. The mason waited faithfully, amusing himself by weighing the gold pieces in his hand, and clinking them against each other. The moment the cathedral bell rang its matin peal, he uncovered his eyes, and found himself on the banks of the Xenil; whence he made the best of his way home, and revelled with his family for a whole fortnight on the profits of his two nights' work; after which he was as poor as ever.

"He continued to work a little, and keep saints' days and holidays, from year to year, while his family grew up as gaunt and ragged as a crew of gipsies. As he was seated one evening at the door of his hovel, he was accosted by a rich old curmudgeon, who was noted for owning many houses, and being a griping landlord. The man of money eyed him for a moment from beneath a pair of anxious shagged eyebrows.

"'I am told, friend, that you are very poor.'

"'There is no denying the fact, Señor,—it speaks for itself.'

'I presume, then, that you will be glad of a job, and will work cheap.'

"'As cheap, my master, as any mason in Granada.'

"'That's what I want. I have an old house fallen into decay, which costs me more money than it is worth to keep it in repair, for nobody will live in it; so I must contrive to patch it up and keep it together at as small expense as possible.'

"The mason was accordingly conducted to a large deserted house that seemed going to ruin. Passing through several empty halls and chambers, he entered an inner court, where his eye was caught by an old Moorish fountain. He paused for a moment, for a dreaming recollection of the place came over him.

"'Pray,' said he, 'who occupied this house formerly?'

"'A pest upon him!' cried the landlord; 'it was an old miser, who cared for nobody but himself. He was said to be immensely rich, and, having no relations, it was thought he would leave all his treasures to the Church. He died suddenly, but nothing could be found but a few ducats in a leathern purse. The worst luck has fallen on me, for, since his death, the old fellow continues to occupy my house without paying rent, and there is no taking the law of a dead man. The people pretend to hear the clinking of gold all night in the chamber where the old miser slept, as if he were counting over his money, and sometimes a groaning and moaning about the court. Whether true or false, these stories have brought a bad name on my house, and not a tenant will remain in it.'

'Enough,' said the mason sturdily: 'let me live in your house rent-free until some better tenant present, and I will engage to put it in repair, and to quiet the troubled spirit that disturbs it. I am a good Christian and a poor man, and am not to be daunted by the Devil himself, even though he should come in the shape of a big bag of money!'

"The offer of the honest mason was gladly accepted; he moved with his family into the house, and fulfilled all his engagements. By little and little he restored it to its former state; the clinking of gold was no more heard at night in the chamber of the defunct miser, but began to be heard by day in the pocket of the living mason. In a word, he increased rapidly in wealth, to the admiration of all his neighbors, became one of the richest men in Granada, and never revealed the secret of the vault until on his death-bed to his son and heir."

The Court of Lions

The peculiar charm of this old dreamy palace is its power of calling up vague reveries and picturings of the past, and thus clothing naked realities with the illusions of the memory and the imagination. As I delight to walk in these "vain shadows," I am prone to seek those parts of the Alhambra which are most favorable to this phantasmagoria of the mind; and none are more so than the Court of Lions, and its surrounding halls. Here the hand of time has fallen the lightest, and the traces of Moorish elegance and splendor exist in almost their original brilliancy. Earthquakes have shaken the foundations of this pile, and rent its rudest towers; yet see! not one of those slender columns has been displaced, not an arch of that light and fragile colonnade given way, and all the fairy fretwork of these domes, apparently as unsubstantial as the crystal fabrics of a morning's frost, exist after the lapse of centuries, almost as fresh as if from the hand of the Moslem artist. I write in the midst of these mementos of the past, in the fresh hour of early morning. Everything here appears calculated to inspire kind and happy feelings, for everything is delicate and beautiful. Through the ample and fretted arch of the portal I behold the Court of Lions, with brilliant sunshine gleaming along its colonnades and sparkling in its fountains. The lively swallow dives into the court, and, rising with a surge, darts away twittering over the roofs; the busy bee toils humming among the flower-beds; and painted butterflies hover from plant to plant, and flutter up and sport with each other in the sunny air.

He, however, who would behold this scene under an aspect more in unison with its fortunes, let him come when the shadows of evening temper the brightness of the court, and throw a gloom into the surrounding halls. Then nothing can be more serenely melancholy, or more in harmony with the tale of departed grandeur.

At such times I am apt to seek the Hall of Justice, whose deep shadowy arcades extend across the upper end of the court. Here was performed, in presence of Ferdinand and Isabella and their triumphant court, the pompous ceremonial of high mass, on taking possession of the Alhambra. The very cross is still to be seen upon the wall, where the altar was erected, and where officiated the Grand Cardinal of Spain, and others of the highest religious dignitaries of the land. I picture to myself the scene when this place was filled with the conquering host, that mixture of mitred prelate and shaven monk, and steel-clad knight and silken courtier; when religious standards were mingled with proud armorial ensigns and the banners of the haughty chiefs of Spain, and flaunted in triumph through these Moslem halls. I picture to myself Columbus, the future discoverer of a world, taking his modest stand in a remote corner, the humble and neglected spectator of the pageant. I see in imagination the Catholic sovereigns, prostrating themselves before the altar, and pouring forth thanks for their victory; while the vaults resound with sacred minstrelsy, and the deep-toned Te Deum.

The transient illusion is over,—the pageant melts from the fancy,—monarch, priest, and warrior return into oblivion with the poor Moslems over whom they exulted. The hall of their triumph is waste and desolate. The bat flits about its twilight vault; and the owl hoots from the neighboring tower of Comares.

Entering the Court of the Lions a few evenings since, I was almost startled at beholding a turbaned Moor quietly seated near the fountain. For a moment one of the fictions of the place seemed realized an enchanted Moor had broken the spell of centuries, and become visible. He proved, however, to be a mere ordinary mortal: a native of Barbary, who had a shop in Granada, where he sold rhubarb, trinkets, and perfumes. As he spoke Spanish fluently, I was enabled to hold conversation with him, and found him shrewd and intelligent. He told me that he came up the hill occasionally in the summer, to pass a part of the day in the Alhambra, which reminded him of the old palaces in Barbary, being built and adorned in similar style, though with more magnificence.

As we walked about the palace, he pointed out several of the Arabic inscriptions, as possessing much poetic beauty.

"Ah, señor," said he, "when the Moors held Granada, they were a gayer people than they are nowadays. They thought only of love, music, and poetry. They made stanzas upon every occasion, and set them all to music. He who could make the best verses, and she who had the most tuneful voice, might be sure of favor and preferment. In those days if any one asked for bread, the reply was, make me a couplet; and the poorest beggar, if he begged in rhyme, would often be rewarded with a piece of gold."

"And is the popular feeling for poetry," said I, "entirely lost among you?"

"By no means, señor; the people of Barbary, even those of the lower classes, still make couplets, and good ones too, as in old times; but talent is not rewarded as it was then: the rich prefer the jingle of their gold to the sound of poetry or music."

As he was talking, his eye caught one of the inscriptions which foretold perpetuity to the power and glory of the Moslem monarchs, the masters of this pile. He shook his head, and shrugged his shoulders, as he interpreted it. "Such might have been the case," said he; "the Moslems might still have been reigning in the Alhambra, had not Boabdil been a traitor, and given up his capital to the Christians. The Spanish monarchs would never have been able to conquer it by open force."

I endeavored to vindicate the memory of the unlucky Boabdil from this aspersion, and to show that the dissensions which led to the downfall of the Moorish throne originated in the cruelty of his tiger-hearted father; but the Moor would admit of no palliation.

"Muley Abul Hassan," said he, "might have been cruel; but he was brave, vigilant, and patriotic. Had he been properly seconded, Granada would still have been ours; but his son Boabdil thwarted his plans, crippled his power, sowed treason in his palace and dissension in his camp. May the curse of God light upon him for his treachery!" With these words the Moor left the Alhambra.

The indignation of my turbaned companion agrees with an anecdote related by a friend who, in the course of a tour in Barbary, had an interview with the Pacha of Tetuan. The Moorish governor was particular in his inquiries about Spain, and especially concerning the favored region of Andalusia, the delights of Granada, and the remains of its royal palace. The replies awakened all those fond recollections, so deeply cherished by the Moors, of the power and splendor of their ancient empire in Spain. Turning to his Moslem attendants, the Pacha stroked his beard, and broke forth in passionate lamentations, that such a sceptre should have fallen from the sway of true believers. He consoled himself, however, with the persuasion that the power and prosperity of the Spanish nation were on the decline; that a time would come when the Moors would conquer their rightful domains; and that the day was perhaps not far distant when Mohammedan worship would again be offered up in the Mosque of Cordova, and a Mohammedan prince sit on his throne in the Alhambra.

Such is the general aspiration and belief among the Moors of Barbary; who consider Spain, or Andaluz, as it was anciently called, their rightful heritage, of which they have been despoiled by treachery and violence. These ideas are fostered and perpetuated by the descendants of the exiled Moors of Granada, scattered among the cities of Barbary. Several of these reside in Tetuan, preserving their ancient names, and refraining from intermarriage with any families who cannot claim the same high origin. Their vaunted lineage is regarded with a degree of popular deference rarely shown in Mohammedan communities to any hereditary distinction, excepting in the royal line.

These families, it is said, continue to sigh after the terrestrial paradise of their ancestors, and to put up prayers in their mosques on Fridays, imploring Allah to hasten the time when Granada shall be restored to the faithful: an event to which they look forward as fondly and confidently as did the Christian crusaders to the recovery of the Holy Sepulchre. Nay, it is added, that some of them retain the ancient maps and deeds of the estates and gardens of their ancestors of Granada, and even the keys of the houses; holding them as evidences of their hereditary claims, to be produced at the anticipated day of restoration.

Local Traditions

The common people of Spain have an Oriental passion for story-telling, and are fond of the marvellous. They will gather round the doors of their cottages in summer evenings, or in the great cavernous chimney-corners in the winter, and listen with insatiable delight to miraculous legends of saints, perilous adventures of travellers, and daring exploits of robbers and smugglers. The wild and solitary character of the country, the imperfect diffusion of knowledge, the scarceness of general topics of conversation, and the romantic adventurous life that every one leads in a land where travelling is yet in its primitive state, all contribute to cherish this love of oral narration, and to produce a strong infusion of the extravagant and incredible. There is no theme, however, more prevalent and popular than that of treasures buried by the Moors; it pervades the whole country. In traversing the wild sierras, the scenes of ancient foray and exploit, you cannot see a Moorish watch-tower perched among the cliffs, or beetling above its rock-built village, but your muleteer, on being closely questioned, will suspend the smoking of his cigarette to tell some tale of Moslem gold buried beneath its foundations; nor is there a ruined fortress in a city but has its golden tradition, handed down from generation to generation among the poor people of the neighborhood.

These, like most popular fictions, have sprung from some scanty groundwork of fact. During the wars between Moor and Christian, which distracted this country for centuries, towns and castles were liable frequently and suddenly to change owners, and the inhabitants, during sieges and assaults, were fain to bury their money and jewels in the earth, or hide them in vaults and wells, as is often done at the present day in the despotic and belligerent countries of the East. At the time of the expulsion of the Moors also, many of them concealed their most precious effects, hoping that their exile would be but temporary, and that they would be enabled to return and retrieve their treasures at some future day. It is certain that from time to time hoards of gold and silver coin have been accidentally digged up, after a lapse of centuries, from among the ruins of Moorish fortresses and habitations; and it requires but a few facts of the kind to give birth to a thousand fictions.

The hidden wealth is always laid under magic spell, and secured by a charm. Sometimes it is guarded by uncouth monsters or fiery dragons, sometimes by enchanted Moors, who sit by it in armor, with drawn swords, but motionless as statues, maintaining a sleepless watch for ages.

The Alhambra of course, from the peculiar circumstances of its history, is a stronghold for popular fictions of the kind; and various relics, digged up from time to time, have contributed to strengthen them. At one time an earthen vessel was found containing Moorish coins and the skeleton of a cock, which, according to the opinion of certain shrewd inspectors, must have been buried alive. At another time a vessel was dug up containing a great beetle of baked clay, covered with Arabic inscriptions, which was pronounced a prodigious amulet of occult virtues. In this way the wits of the ragged brood who inhabit the Alhambra have been set wool-gathering, until there is not a hall, nor tower, nor vault, of the old fortress, that has not been made the scene of some marvellous tradition. Having, I trust, in the preceding papers made the reader in some degree familiar with the localities of the Alhambra, I shall now launch out more largely into the wonderful legends connected with it, and which I have diligently wrought into shape and form, from various legendary scraps and hints picked up in the course of my walks—in the same manner that an antiquary works out a regular historical document from a few scattered letters of an almost defaced inscription.

If anything in these legends should shock the faith of the over-scrupulous reader, he must remember the nature of the place, and make due allowances. He must not expect here the same laws of probability that govern commonplace scenes and everyday life; he must remember that he treads the halls of an enchanted palace, and that all is "haunted ground."

The House of the Weathercock

On the brow of the lofty hill of the Albaycin, the highest part of Granada, and which rises from the narrow valley of the Darro, directly opposite to the Alhambra, stands all that is left of what was once a royal palace of the Moors. It has, in fact, fallen into such obscurity, that it cost me much trouble to find it, though aided in my researches by the sagacious and all-knowing Mateo Ximenes. This edifice has borne for centuries the name of "The House of the Weathercock," from a bronze figure on one of its turrets, in ancient times, of a warrior on horseback, and turning with every breeze. This weathercock was considered by the Moslems of Granada a portentous talisman. According to some traditions, it bore an Arabic inscription, which has been rendered into English:—

In this way, says Aben Habuz the Wise, Andaluz guards against surprise.

This Aben Habuz, according to some of the old Moorish chronicles, was a captain in the invading army of Taric, one of the conquerors of Spain, who left him as Governor of Granada. He is supposed to have intended this effigy as a perpetual warning to the Moslems of Andaluz, that, surrounded by foes, their safety depended upon their being always on their guard and ready for the field.

Another version of this portentous inscription is given by a Moslem historian, on the authority of Sidi Hasan, a faquir who flourished about the time of Ferdinand and Isabella, and who was present at the taking down of the weathercock, when the old palace was undergoing repairs.

"I saw it," says the venerable faquir, "with my own eyes: it had the following inscription in verse:

"'The palace at fair Granada presents a talisman.'

"'The horseman, though a solid body, turns with every wind.'

"'This to a wise man reveals a mystery. In a little while comes a calamity to ruin both the palace and its owner.'"

In effect it was not long after this meddling with the portentous weathercock that the following event occurred. As old Muley Abul Hasan, the king of Granada, was seated under a sumptuous pavilion, reviewing his troops, who paraded before him in armor of polished steel and gorgeous silken robes, mounted on fleet steeds, and equipped with swords, spears, and shields embossed with gold and silver,—suddenly a tempest was seen hurrying from the southwest. In a little while black clouds over-shadowed the heavens and burst forth with a deluge of rain. Torrents came roaring down from the mountains, bringing with them rocks and trees; the Darro overflowed its banks; mills were swept away, bridges destroyed, gardens laid waste; the inundation rushed into the city, undermining houses, drowning their inhabitants, and overflowing even the square of the Great Mosque. The people rushed in affright to the mosques to implore the mercy of Allah, regarding this uproar of the elements as the harbinger of dreadful calamities; and, indeed, according to an Arabian historian, it was but a type and prelude of the direful war which ended in the downfall of the Moslem kingdom of Granada.

I have thus given historic authorities sufficient to show the portentous mysteries connected with the House of the Weathercock, and its talismanic horseman.

I now proceed to relate still more surprising things about Aben Habuz and his palace; for the truth of which, should any doubt be entertained, I refer the dubious reader to Mateo Ximenes and his fellow-historiographers of the Alhambra.

Legend of the Arabian Astrologer

In old times, many hundred years ago, there was a Moorish king named Aben Habuz, who reigned over the kingdom of Granada. He was a retired conqueror, that is to say, one who, having in his more youthful days led a life of constant foray and depredation, now that he was grown feeble and superannuated, "languished for repose," and desired nothing more than to live at peace with all the world, to husband his laurels, and to enjoy in quiet the possessions he had wrested from his neighbors.

It so happened, however, that this most reasonable and pacific old monarch had young rivals to deal with; princes full of his early passion for fame and fighting, and who were disposed to call him to account for the scores he had run up with their fathers. Certain distant districts of his own territories, also, which during the days of his vigor he had treated with a high hand, were prone, now that he languished for repose, to rise in rebellion and threaten to invest him in his capital. Thus he had foes on every side; and as Granada is surrounded by wild and craggy mountains, which hide the approach of an enemy, the unfortunate Aben Habuz was kept in a constant state of vigilance and alarm, not knowing in what quarter hostilities might break out.

It was in vain that he built watch-towers on the mountains, and stationed guards at every pass with orders to make fires by night and smoke by day, on the approach of an enemy. His alert foes, baffling every precaution, would break out of some unthought-of defile, ravage his lands beneath his very nose, and then make off with prisoners and booty to the mountains. Was ever peaceable and retired conqueror in a more uncomfortable predicament?

While Aben Habuz was harassed by these perplexities and molestations, an ancient Arabian physician arrived at his court. His gray beard descended to his girdle, and he had every mark of extreme age, yet he had travelled almost the whole way from Egypt on foot, with no other aid than a staff, marked with hieroglyphics. His fame had preceded him. His name was Ibrahim; he was said to have lived ever since the days of Mahomet, and to be son of Abu Ayub, the last of the companions of the Prophet. He had, when a child, followed the conquering army of Amru into Egypt, where he had remained many years studying the dark sciences, and particularly magic, among the Egyptian priests.

It was, moreover, said that he had found out the secret of prolonging life, by means of which he had arrived to the great age of upwards of two centuries, though, as he did not discover the secret until well stricken in years, he could only perpetuate his gray hairs and wrinkles.

This wonderful old man was honorably entertained by the king; who, like most superannuated monarchs, began to take physicians into great favor. He would have assigned him an apartment in his palace, but the astrologer preferred a cave in the side of the hill which rises above the city of Granada, being the same on which the Alhambra has since been built. He caused the cave to be enlarged so as to form a spacious and lofty hall, with a circular hole at the top, through which, as through a well, he could see the heavens and behold the stars even at mid-day. The walls of this hall were covered with Egyptian hieroglyphics with cabalistic symbols, and with the figures of the stars in their signs. This hall he furnished with many implements, fabricated under his directions by cunning artificers of Granada, but the occult properties of which were known only to himself.

In a little while the sage Ibrahim became the bosom counsellor of the king, who applied to him for advice in every emergency. Aben Habuz was once inveighing against the injustice of his neighbors, and bewailing the restless vigilance he had to observe to guard himself against their invasions; when he had finished, the astrologer remained silent for a moment, and then replied, "Know, O king, that, when I was in Egypt, I beheld a great marvel devised by a pagan priestess of old. On a mountain, above the city of Borsa, and overlooking the great valley of the Nile, was a figure of a ram, and above it a figure of a cock, both of molten brass, and turning upon a pivot. Whenever the country was threatened with invasion, the ram would turn in the direction of the enemy, and the cock would crow upon this the inhabitants of the city knew of the danger, and of the quarter from which it was approaching, and could take timely means to guard against it."

"Allah is great!" exclaimed the pacific Aben Habuz, "what a treasure would be such a ram to keep an eye upon these mountains around me; and then such a cock, to crow in time of danger! Allah is great! how securely I might sleep in my palace with such sentinels on the top!"

The astrologer waited until the ecstasies of the king had subsided, and then proceeded:

"After the victorious Armu (may he rest in peace!) had finished his conquest of Egypt, I remained among the priests of the land, studying the rites and ceremonies of their idolatrous faith, and seeking to make myself master of the hidden knowledge for which they are renowned. I was one day seated on the banks of the Nile, conversing with an ancient priest, when he pointed to the mighty pyramids which rose like mountains out of the neighboring desert. 'All that we can teach thee,' said he, 'is nothing to the knowledge locked up in those mighty piles. In the centre of the central pyramid is a sepulchral chamber, in which is enclosed the mummy of the high-priest who aided in rearing that stupendous pile; and with him is buried a wondrous book of knowledge, containing all the secrets of magic and art. This book was given to Adam after his fall, and was handed down from generation to generation to King Solomon the Wise, and by its aid he built the Temple of Jerusalem. How it came into the possession of the builder of the pyramids is known to Him alone who knows all things.'

"When I heard these words of the Egyptian priest, my heart burned to get possession of that book. I could command the services, of many of the soldiers of our conquering army, and of a number of the native Egyptians: with these I set to work, and pierced the solid mass of the pyramid, until, after great toil, I came upon one of its interior and hidden passages. Following this up, and threading a fearful labyrinth, I penetrated into the very heart of the pyramids, even to the sepulchral chamber, where the mummy of the high-priest had lain for ages. I broke through the outer cases of the mummy, unfolded its many wrappers and bandages, and at length found the precious volume on its bosom. I seized it with a trembling hand, and groped my way out of the pyramid, leaving the mummy in its dark and silent sepulchre, there to await the final day of resurrection and judgment."

"Son of Abu Ayub," exclaimed Aben Habuz, "thou hast been a great traveller, and seen marvellous things; but of what avail to me is the secret of the pyramid, and the volume of knowledge of the wise Solomon?"

"This it is, O king! By the study of that book I am instructed in all magic arts, and can command the assistance of genii to accomplish my plans. The mystery of the Talisman of Borsa is therefore familiar to me, and such a talisman can I make, nay, one of greater virtues."

"O wise son of Abu Ayub," cried Aben Habuz, "better were such a talisman than all the watch-towers on the hills, and sentinels upon the borders. Give me such a safeguard, and the riches of my treasury are at thy command."

The astrologer immediately set to work to gratify the wishes of the monarch. He caused a great tower to be erected upon the top of the royal palace, which stood on the brow of the hill of the Albaycin. The tower was built of stones brought from Egypt, and taken, it is said, from one of the pyramids. In the upper part of the tower was a circular hall, with windows looking towards every point of the compass, and before each window was a table, on which was arranged, as on a chess-board, a mimic army of horse and foot, with the effigy of the potentate that ruled in that direction, all carved of wood. To each of these tables there was a small lance, on which were engraved certain characters. This hall was kept constantly closed, by a gate of brass, with a great lock of steel, the key of which was in possession of the king.

On the top of the tower was a bronze figure of a Moorish horseman, fixed on a pivot, with a shield on one arm, and his lance elevated perpendicularly. The face of this horseman was towards the city, as if keeping guard over it; but if any foe were at hand, the figure would turn in that direction, and would level the lance as if for action.

When this talisman was finished, Aben Habuz was all impatient to try its, virtues, and longed as ardently for an invasion as he had ever sighed after repose. His desire was soon gratified. Tidings were brought, early one morning, by the sentinel appointed to watch the tower, that the face of the bronze horseman was turned towards the mountains of Elvira, and that his lance pointed directly against the Pass of Lope.

"Let the drums and trumpets sound to arms, and all Granada be put on the alert," said Aben Habuz.

"O king," said the astrologer, "let not your city be disquieted, nor your warriors called to arms; we need no aid of force to deliver you from your enemies. Dismiss your attendants, and let us proceed alone to the secret hall of the tower."

The ancient Aben Habuz mounted the staircase of the tower, leaning on the arm of the still more ancient Ibrahim. They unlocked the brazen door and entered. The window that looked towards the Pass of Lope was open. "In this direction," said the astrologer, "lies the danger; approach, O king, and behold the mystery of the table."

King Aben Habuz approached the seeming chess-board, on which were arranged the small wooden effigies, when, to his surprise, he perceived that they were all in motion. The horses pranced and curveted, the warriors brandished their weapons, and there was a faint sound of drums and trumpets, and the clang of arms, and neighing of steeds; but all no louder, nor more distinct, than the hum of the bee, or the summer-fly, in the drowsy ear of him who lies at noontide in the shade.

"Behold, O king," said the astrologer, "a proof that thy enemies are even now in the field. They must be advancing through yonder mountains, by the Pass of Lope. Would you produce a panic and confusion amongst them, and cause them to retreat without loss of life, strike these effigies with the butt-end of this magic lance; would you cause bloody feud and carnage, strike with the point."

A livid streak passed across the countenance of Aben Habuz; he seized the lance with trembling eagerness; his gray beard wagged with exultation as he tottered toward the table: "Son of Abu Ayub," exclaimed he, in chuckling tone, "I think we will have a little blood!"

So saying, he thrust the magic lance into some of the pigmy effigies, and belabored others with the butt-end, upon which the former fell as dead upon the board, and the rest turning upon each other, began, pell-mell, a chance-medley fight.

It was with difficulty the astrologer could stay the hand of the most pacific of monarchs, and prevent him from absolutely exterminating his foes; at length he prevailed upon him to leave the tower, and to send out scouts to the mountains by the Pass of Lope.

They returned with the intelligence that a Christian army had advanced through the heart of the Sierra, almost within sight of Granada, where a dissension had broken out among them; they had turned their weapons against each other, and after much slaughter had retreated over the border.

Aben Habuz was transported with joy on thus proving the efficacy of the talisman. "At length," said he, "I shall lead a life of tranquillity, and have all my enemies in my power. O wise son of Abu Ayub, what can I bestow on thee in reward for such a blessing?"

"The wants of an old man and a philosopher, O king, are few and simple; grant me but the means of fitting up my cave as a suitable hermitage, and I am content"

"How noble is the moderation of the truly wise!" exclaimed Aben Habuz, secretly pleased at the cheapness of the recompense. He summoned his treasurer, and bade him dispense whatever sums might be required by Ibrahim to complete and furnish his hermitage.

The astrologer now gave orders to have various chambers hewn out of the solid rock, so as to form ranges of apartments connected with his astrological hall; these he caused to be furnished with luxurious ottomans and divans, and the walls to be hung with the richest silks of Damascus. "I am an old man," said he, "and can no longer rest my bones on stone couches, and these damp walls require covering."

He had baths too constructed, and provided with all kinds of perfumes and aromatic oils. "For a bath," said he, "is necessary to counteract the rigidity of age, and to restore freshness and suppleness to the frame withered by study."

He caused the apartments to be hung with innumerable silver and crystal lamps, which he filled with a fragrant oil prepared according to a receipt discovered by him in the tombs of Egypt. This oil was perpetual in its nature, and diffused a soft radiance like the tempered light of day. "The light of the sun," said he, "is too garish and violent for the eyes of an old man, and the light of the lamp is more congenial to the studies of a philosopher."

The treasurer of King Aben Habuz groaned at the sums daily demanded to fit up this hermitage, and he carried his complaints to the king. The royal word, however, had been given; Aben Habuz shrugged his shoulders: "We must have patience," said he; "this old man has taken his idea of a philosophic retreat from the interior of the pyramids, and of the vast ruins of Egypt; but all things have an end, and so will the furnishing of his cavern."

The king was in the right; the hermitage was at length complete, and formed a sumptuous subterranean palace.

While the philosophic Ibrahim passed his time in his hermitage, the pacific Aben Habuz carried on furious campaigns in effigy in his tower. It was a glorious thing for an old man, like himself, of quiet habits, to have war made easy, and to be enabled to amuse himself in his chamber by brushing away whole armies like so many swarms of flies.

For a time he rioted in the indulgence of his humors, and even taunted and insulted his neighbors, to induce them to make incursions; but by degrees they grew wary from repeated disasters, until no one ventured to invade his territories. For many months the bronze horseman remained on the peace establishment, with his lance elevated in the air; and the worthy old monarch began to repine at the want of his accustomed sport, and to grow peevish at his monotonous tranquillity.

At length, one day, the talismanic horseman veered suddenly round, and lowering his lance, made a dead point towards the mountains of Guadix. Aben Habuz hastened to his tower, but the magic table in that direction remained quiet: not a single warrior was in motion. Perplexed at the circumstance, he set forth a troop of horse to scour the mountains and reconnoitre. They returned after three days' absence.

"We have searched every mountain pass," said they, "but not a helm nor spear was stirring. All that we have found in the course of our foray, was a Christian damsel of surpassing beauty, sleeping at noontide beside a fountain, whom we have brought away captive."

"A damsel of surpassing beauty!" exclaimed Aben Habuz, his eyes gleaming with animation; "let her be conducted into my presence."

The beautiful damsel was accordingly conducted into his presence. She was arrayed with all the luxury of ornament that had prevailed among the Gothic Spaniards at the time of the Arabian conquest. Pearls of dazzling whiteness were entwined with her raven tresses; and jewels sparkled on her forehead, rivaling the lustre of her eyes. Around her neck was a golden chain, to which was suspended a silver lyre, which hung by her side.

The flashes of her dark eye were like sparks of fire on the withered yet combustible heart of Aben Habuz. "Fairest of women," cried he, "who and what art thou?"

"The daughter of one of the Gothic princes, who but lately ruled over this land. The armies of my father have been destroyed, as if by magic, among these mountains; he has been driven into exile, and his daughter is a captive."

"Beware, O king!" whispered Ibrahim, "this may be one of those northern sorceresses of whom we have heard, who assume the most seductive forms to beguile the unwary. Methinks I read witchcraft in her eye, and sorcery in every movement. Doubtless this is the enemy pointed out by the talisman."

Son of Abu Ayub," replied the king, "thou art a wise man, I grant, a conjurer for aught I know; but thou art little versed in the ways of woman. As to this damsel, I see no harm in her; she is fair to look upon, and finds favor in my eyes."

Further remonstrances of the astrologer only provoked a more peremptory reply from the monarch, and they parted in high displeasure. The sage shut himself up in his hermitage; ere he departed, however, he gave the king one more warning to beware of his dangerous captive. But where is the old man in love that will listen to counsel? His only study was how to render himself amiable in the eyes of the Gothic beauty. He had not youth to recommend him, it is true, but then he had riches; and when a lover is old, he is generally generous. The shops of Granada were ransacked for the most precious merchandise of the East; silks, jewels, precious gems, exquisite perfumes, all that Asia and Africa yielded that was rich and rare, were lavished upon the princess. All kinds of spectacles and festivities were devised for her entertainment; minstrelsy, dancing, tournaments, bull-fights;—Granada for a time was a scene of perpetual pageant. The Gothic princess regarded all this splendor with the air of one accustomed to magnificence. She received everything as a homage due to her rank, or rather to her beauty; for beauty is more lofty in its exactions even than rank. Nay, she seemed to take a secret pleasure in exciting the monarch to expenses that made his treasury shrink, and then treating his extravagant generosity as a mere matter of course. With all his assiduity and munificence, also, the venerable lover could not flatter himself that he had made any impression on her heart. She never frowned on him, it is true, but then she never smiled. Whenever he began to plead his love, she struck her silver lyre. There was a mystic charm in the sound. In an instant the monarch began to nod; a drowsiness stole over him, and he gradually sank into a sleep.

At length a danger burst on the head of Aben Habuz, against which his talisman yielded him no warning. An insurrection broke out in his very capital; his palace was surrounded by an armed rabble, who menaced his life and the life of the Christian damsel. A spark of his ancient warlike spirit was awakened in the breast of the monarch. At the head of a handful of his guards he sallied forth, put the rebels to flight, and crushed the insurrection in the bud.

When quiet was again restored, he sought the astrologer, who still remained shut up in his hermitage.

Aben Habuz approached him with a conciliatory tone. "O wise son of Abu Ayub," said he, "well didst thou predict dangers to me from this captive beauty: tell me then, thou who art so quick at foreseeing peril, what I should do to avert it."

"Put from thee the infidel damsel who is the cause." "Sooner would I part with my kingdom," cried Aben Habuz.

"Thou art in danger of losing both," replied the astrologer.

"Be not harsh and angry, O most profound of philosophers; consider the double distress of a monarch and a lover, and devise some means of protecting me from the evils by which I am menaced. I care not for grandeur, I care not for power, I languish only for repose; would that I had some quiet retreat where I might take refuge from the world, and all its cares, and pomps, and troubles, and devote the remainder of my days to tranquillity and love."

The astrologer regarded him for a moment from under his bushy eyebrows.

"And what wouldst thou give, if I could provide thee such a retreat?"

"Thou shouldst name thy own reward; and whatever it might be, if within the scope of my power, as my soul liveth, it should be thine."

"Thou hast heard, O king, of the garden of Irem, one of the prodigies of Arabia the happy."

"I have heard of that garden; it is recorded in the Koran, even in the chapter entitled 'The Dawn of Day.' I have, moreover, heard marvellous things related of it by pilgrims who had been to Mecca; but I considered them wild fables, such as travellers are wont to tell who have visited remote countries."

"Discredit not, O king, the tales of travellers," rejoined the astrologer, gravely, "for they contain precious rarities of knowledge brought from the ends of the earth. As to the palace and garden of Irem, what is generally told of them is true; I have seen them with mine own eyes;—listen to my adventure, for it has a bearing upon the object of your request.

"In my younger days, when a mere Arab of the desert, I tended my father's camels. In traversing the desert of Aden, one of them strayed from the rest and was lost. I searched after it for several days, but in vain, until, wearied and faint, I laid myself down at noontide, and slept under a palm-tree by the side of a scanty well. When I awoke I found myself at the gate of a city. I entered, and beheld noble streets, and squares, and market-places; but all were silent and without an inhabitant. I wandered on until I came to a sumptuous palace, with a garden adorned with fountains and fish-ponds, and groves and flowers, and orchards laden with delicious fruit; but still no one was to be seen. Upon which, appalled at this loneliness, I hastened to depart; and, after issuing forth at the gate of the city, I turned to look upon the place, but it was no longer to be seen; nothing but the silent desert extended before my eyes.

"In the neighborhood I met with an aged dervise, learned in the traditions and secrets of the land, and related to him what had befallen me. 'This,' said he, 'is the far-famed garden of Irem, one of the wonders of the desert. It only appears at times to some wanderer like thyself, gladdening him with the sight of towers and palaces and garden-walls overhung with richly-laden fruit-trees, and then vanishes, leaving nothing but a lonely desert. And this is the story of it. In old times, when this country was inhabited by the Addites, King Sheddad, the son of Ad, the great-grandson of Noah, founded here a splendid city. When it was finished, and he saw its grandeur, his heart was puffed up with pride and arrogance, and he determined to build a royal palace, with gardens which should rival all related in the Koran of the celestial paradise. But the curse of heaven fell upon him for his presumption. He and his subjects were swept from the earth, and his splendid city and palace, and gardens, were laid under a perpetual spell, which hides them from human sight, excepting that they are seen at intervals, by way of keeping his sin in perpetual remembrance.'

"This story, O king, and the wonders I had seen, ever dwelt in my mind; and in after-years, when I had been in Egypt, and was possessed of the book of knowledge of Solomon the Wise, I determined to return and revisit the garden of Irem. I did so, and found it revealed to my instructed sight. I took possession of the palace of Sheddad, and passed several days in his mock paradise. The, genii who watch over the place were obedient to my magic power, and revealed to me the spells by which the whole garden had been, as it were, conjured into existence, and by which it was rendered invisible. Such a palace and garden, O king, can I make for thee, even here, on the mountain above thy city. Do I not know all the secret spells? And am I not in possession of the book of knowledge of Solomon the Wise?"

"O wise son of Abu Ayub!" exclaimed Aben Habuz, trembling with eagerness, "thou art a traveller indeed, and hast seen and learned marvellous things! Contrive me such a paradise, and ask any reward, even to the half of my kingdom."

"Alas!" replied the other, "thou knowest I am an old man, and a philosopher, and easily satisfied; all the reward I ask is the first beast of burden, with its load, which shall enter the magic portal of the palace."

The monarch gladly agreed to so moderate a stipulation, and the astrologer began his work. On the summit of the hill, immediately above his subterranean hermitage, he caused a great gateway or barbican to be erected, opening through the centre of a strong tower.

There was an outer vestibule or porch, with a lofty arch, and within it a portal secured by massive gates. On the keystone of the portal the astrologer, with his own hand, wrought the figure of a huge key; and on the keystone of the outer arch of the vestibule, which was loftier than that of the portal, he carved a gigantic hand. These were potent talismans, over which he repeated many sentences in an unknown tongue.

When this gateway was finished, he shut himself up for two days in his astrological hall, engaged in secret incantations; on the third he ascended the hill, and passed the whole day on its summit. At a late hour of the night he came down, and presented himself before Aben Habuz. "At length, O king," said he, "my labor is accomplished. On the summit of the hill stands one of the most delectable palaces that ever the head of man devised, or the heart of man desired. It contains sumptuous halls and galleries, delicious gardens, cool fountains, and fragrant baths; in a word, the whole mountain is converted into a paradise. Like the garden of Irem, it is protected by a mighty charm, which hides it from the view and search of mortals, excepting such as possess the secret of its talismans."

"Enough!" cried Aben Habuz, joyfully, "to-morrow morning with the first light we will ascend and take possession." The happy monarch slept but little that night. Scarcely had the rays of the sun begun to play about the snowy summit of the Sierra Nevada, when he mounted his steed, and, accompanied only by a few chosen attendants, ascended a steep and narrow road leading up the hill. Beside him, on a white palfrey, rode the Gothic princess, her whole dress sparkling with jewels, while round her neck was suspended her silver lyre. The astrologer walked on the other side of the king, assisting his steps with his hieroglyphic staff, for he never mounted steed of any kind.

Aben Habuz looked to see the towers of the palace brightening above him, and the embowered terraces of its gardens stretching along the heights; but as yet nothing of the kind was to be descried. "That is the mystery and safeguard of the place," said the astrologer, "nothing can be discerned until you have passed the spell-bound gateway, and been put in possession of the place."

As they approached the gateway, the astrologer paused, and pointed out to the king the mystic hand and key carved upon the portal of the arch. "These," said he, "are the talismans which guard the entrance to this paradise. Until yonder hand shall reach down and seize that key, neither mortal power nor magic artifice can prevail against the lord of this mountain."

While Aben Habuz was gazing, with open mouth and silent wonder, at these mystic talismans, the palfrey of the princess proceeded, and bore her in at the portal, to the very centre of the barbican.

"Behold," cried the astrologer, "my promised reward; the first animal with its burden which should enter the magic gateway."

Aben Habuz smiled at what he considered a pleasantry of the ancient man; but when he found him to be in earnest, his gray beard trembled with indignation.

"Son of Abu Ayub," said he, sternly, "what equivocation is this? Thou knowest the meaning of my promise: the first beast of burden with its load, that should enter this portal. Take the strongest mule in my stables, load it with the most precious things of my treasury, and it is thine; but dare not raise thy thoughts to her who is the delight of my heart."

"What need I of wealth?" cried the astrologer, scornfully; "have I not the book of knowledge of Solomon the Wise, and through it the command of the secret treasures of the earth? The princess is mine by right; thy royal word is pledged; I claim her as my own."

The princess looked down haughtily from her palfrey, and a light smile of scorn curled her rosy lip at this dispute between two gray-beards for the possession of youth and beauty. The wrath of the monarch got the better of his discretion. "Base son of the desert," cried he, thou mayst be master of many arts, but know me for thy master, and presume not to juggle with thy king."

"My master my king!" echoed the astrologer,—"the monarch of a mole-hill to claim sway over him who possesses the talismans of Solomon! Farewell, Aben Habuz; reign over thy petty kingdom, and revel in thy paradise of fools; for me, I will laugh at thee in my philosophic retirement."

So saying, he seized the bridle of the palfrey, smote the earth with his staff, and sank with the Gothic princess through the centre of the barbican. The earth closed over them, and no trace remained of the opening by which they had descended.

Aben Habuz was struck dumb for a time with astonishment. Recovering himself, he ordered a thousand workmen to dig, with pickaxe and spade, into the ground where the astrologer had disappeared. They digged and digged, but in vain; the flinty bosom of the hill resisted their implements; or if they did penetrate a little way, the earth filled in again as fast as they threw it out. Aben Habuz sought the mouth of the cavern at the foot of the hill, leading to the subterranean palace of the astrologer; but it was nowhere to be found. Where once had been an entrance, was a solid surface of primeval rock. With the disappearance of Ibrahim ceased the benefit of his talismans. The bronze horseman remained fixed, with his face turned toward the hill, and his spear pointed to the spot where the astrologer had descended, as if there still lurked the deadliest foe of Aben Habuz.

From time to time the sound of music, and the tones of a female voice, could be faintly heard from the bosom of the hill; and a peasant one day brought word to the king, that in the preceding night he had found a fissure in the rock, by which he had crept in, until he looked down into a subterranean hall, in which sat the astrologer, on a magnificent divan, slumbering and nodding to the silver lyre of the princess, which seemed to hold a magic sway over his senses.

Aben Habuz sought the fissure in the rock, but it was again closed. He renewed the attempt to unearth his rival, but all in vain. The spell of the hand and key was too potent to be counteracted by human power. As to the summit of the mountain, the site of the promised palace and garden, it remained a naked waste; either the boasted elysium was hidden from sight by enchantment, or was a mere fable of the astrologer. The world charitably supposed the latter, and some used to call the place "The King's Folly "; while others named it "The Fool's Paradise."

To add to the chagrin of Aben Habuz, the neighbors whom he had defied and taunted, and cut up at his leisure while master of the talismanic horseman, finding him no longer protected by magic spell, made inroads into his territories from all sides, and the remainder of the life of the most pacific of monarchs was a series of turmoils.

At length Aben Habuz died, and was buried. Ages have since rolled away. The Alhambra has been built on the eventful mountain, and in some measure realizes the fabled delights of the garden of Irem. The spell-bound gateway still exists entire, protected no doubt by the mystic hand and key, and now forms the Gate of Justice, the grand entrance to the fortress. Under that gateway, it is said, the old astrologer remains in his subterranean hall, nodding on his divan, lulled by the silver lyre of the princess.

The old invalid sentinels, who mount guard at the gate hear the strains occasionally in the summer nights; and, yielding to their soporific power, doze quietly at their posts. Nay, so drowsy an influence pervades the place, that even those who watch by day may generally be seen nodding on the stone benches of the barbican, or sleeping under the neighboring trees; so that in fact it is the drowsiest military post in all Christendom. All this, say the ancient legends, will endure from age to age. The princess will remain captive to the astrologer; and the astrologer bound up in magic slumber by the princess, until the last day, unless the mystic hand shall grasp the fated key, and dispel the whole charm of this enchanted mountain.

Legend of Prince Ahmed Al Kamel.

There was once a Moorish king of Granada, who had but one son, whom he named Ahmed, to which his courtiers added the surname of the Perfect, from the indubitable signs of super excellence which they perceived in him in his very infancy. The astrologers countenanced them in their foresight, predicting everything in his favor that could make a perfect prince and a prosperous sovereign. One cloud only rested upon his destiny, and even that was of a roseate hue: he would be of an amorous temperament, and run great perils from the tender passion of love. If, however, he could be kept from its allurements until of mature age, these dangers would be averted, and his life thereafter be one uninterrupted course of felicity.

To prevent all danger of this kind, the king wisely determined to rear the prince in a seclusion where he should never see a female face, nor hear even the name of love. For this purpose he built a beautiful palace on the brow of the hill above the Alhambra, in the midst of delightful gardens, but surrounded by lofty walls, being, in fact, the same palace known at the present day by the name of the Generalife. In this palace the youthful prince was shut up, and intrusted to the guardianship and instruction of Eben Bonabben, one of the wisest and dryest of Arabian sages, who had passed the greatest part of his life in Egypt, studying hieroglyphics, and making researches among the tombs and pyramids, and who saw more charms in an Egyptian mummy than in the most tempting of living beauties. The sage was ordered to instruct the prince in all kinds of knowledge but one,—he was to be kept utterly ignorant of love. "Use every precaution for the purpose you may think proper," said the king, "but remember, O Eben Bonabben, if my son learns aught of that forbidden knowledge while under your care, your head shall answer for it." A withered smile came over the dry visage of the wise Bonabben, at the menace. "Let your majesty's heart be as easy about your son, as mine is about my head: am I a man likely to give lessons in the idle passion?"

Under the vigilant care of the philosopher, the prince grew up in the seclusion of the palace and its gardens. His mental endowments were the peculiar care of Eben Bonabben, who sought to initiate him into the abstruse lore of Egypt; but in this the prince made little progress, and it was soon evident that he had no turn for philosophy.

He was, however, amazingly ductile for a youthful prince, ready to follow any advice, and always guided by the last counsellor. He suppressed his yawns, and listened patiently to the long and learned discourses of Eben Bonabben, from which he imbibed a smattering of various kinds of knowledge, and thus happily attained his twentieth year, a miracle of princely wisdom—but totally ignorant of love.

About this time, however, a change came over the conduct of the prince. He completely abandoned his studies, and took to strolling about the gardens, and musing by the side of the fountains. He had been taught a little music among his various accomplishments; it now engrossed a great part of his time, and a turn for poetry became apparent. The sage Eben Bonabben took the alarm, and endeavored to work these idle humors out of him by a severe course of algebra; but the prince turned from it with distaste. "I cannot endure algebra," said he; "it is an abomination to me. I want something that speaks more to the heart."

The sage Eben Bonabben shook his dry head at the words. "Here is an end to philosophy," thought he. "The prince has discovered he has a heart!" He now kept anxious watch upon his pupil, and saw that the latent tenderness of his nature was in activity, and only wanted an object. He wandered about the gardens of the Generalife in an intoxication of feelings of which he knew not the cause. Sometimes he would sit plunged in a delicious reverie; then he would seize his lute and draw from it the most touching notes, and then throw it aside, and break forth into sighs and ejaculations.

By degrees this loving disposition began to extend to inanimate objects; he had his favorite flowers, which he cherished with tender assiduity; then he became attached to various trees, and there was one in particular, of a graceful form and drooping foliage, on which he lavished his devotion, carving his name on its bark, hanging garlands on its branches, and singing couplets in its praise, to the accompaniment of his lute.

Eben Bonabben was alarmed at this excited state of his pupil. He saw him on the very brink of forbidden knowledge—the least hint might reveal to him the fatal secret. Trembling for the safety of the prince and the security of his own head, he hastened to draw him from the seductions of the garden, and shut him up in the highest tower of the Generalife. It contained beautiful apartments, and commanded an almost boundless prospect, but was elevated far above that atmosphere of sweets and those witching bowers so dangerous to the feelings of the too susceptible Ahmed.

What was to be done, however, to reconcile him to this restraint and to beguile the tedious hours? He had exhausted almost all kinds of agreeable knowledge; and algebra was not to be mentioned. Fortunately Eben Bonabben had been instructed, when in Egypt, in the language of birds by a Jewish Rabbi, who had received it in lineal transmission from Solomon the Wise, who had been taught it by the queen of Sheba. At the very mention of such a study, the eyes of the prince sparkled with animation, and he applied himself to it with such avidity, that he soon became as great an adept as his master.

The Tower of the Generalife was no longer a solitude; he had companions at hand with whom he could converse. The first acquaintance he formed was with a hawk, who built his nest in a crevice of the lofty battlements, whence he soared far and wide in quest of prey. The prince, however, found little to like or esteem in him. He was a mere pirate of the air, swaggering and boastful, whose talk was all about rapine and carnage, and desperate exploits.

His next acquaintance was an owl, a mighty wise-looking bird, with a huge head and staring eyes, who sat blinking and goggling all day in a hole in the wall, but roamed forth at night. He had great pretensions to wisdom, talked of astrology and the moon, and the prince found his prosings even more ponderous than those of the sage Eben Bonabben.

Then there was a bat, that hung all day by his heels in the dark corner of a vault, but sallied out in slipshod style at twilight. He, however, had but twilight ideas on all subjects, derided things of which he had taken but an imperfect view, and seemed to take delight in nothing.

Besides these there was a swallow, with whom the prince was at first much taken. He was a smart talker, but restless, bustling, and forever on the wing; seldom remaining long enough for any continued conversation. He turned out in the end to be a mere smatterer, who did but skim over the surface of things, pretending to know everything, but knowing nothing thoroughly:

These were the only feathered associates with whom the prince had any opportunity of exercising his newly acquired language: the tower was too high for any other birds to frequent it. He soon grew weary of his new acquaintances, whose conversation spoke so little to the head and nothing to the heart, and gradually relapsed into his loneliness. A winter passed away, spring opened with all its bloom and verdure and breathing sweetness, and the happy time arrived for birds to pair and build their nests. Suddenly, as it were, a universal burst of song and melody broke forth from the groves and gardens of the Generalife, and reached the prince in the solitude of his tower. From every side he heard the same universal theme—love—love—love—chanted forth, and responded to in every variety of note and tone. The prince listened in silence and perplexity. "What can be this love," thought he, "of which the world seems so full, and of which I know nothing?" He applied for information to his friend the hawk. The ruffian bird answered in a tone of scorn: "You must apply," said he, "to the vulgar peaceable birds of earth, who are made for the prey of us princes of the air. My trade is war, and fighting my delight. I am a warrior, and know nothing of this thing called love."

The prince turned from him with disgust, and sought the owl in his retreat. "This is a bird," said he, "of peaceful habits, and may be able to solve my question." So he asked the owl to tell him what was this love about which all the birds in the groves below were singing.

Upon this the owl put on a look of offended dignity. "My nights," said he, "are taken up in study and research, and my days in ruminating in my cell upon all that I have learnt. As to these singing birds of whom you talk, I never listen to them—I despise them and their themes. Allah be praised, I cannot sing; I am a philosopher, and know nothing of this thing called love."

The prince now repaired to the vault, where his friend the bat was hanging by the heels, and propounded the same question. The bat wrinkled up his nose into a most snappish expression. "Why do you disturb me in my morning's nap with such an idle question?" said he, peevishly. "I only fly by twilight, when all birds are asleep, and never trouble myself with their concerns. I am neither bird nor beast, and I thank heaven for it. I have found out the villany of the whole of them, and hate them one and all. I know nothing of this thing called love."

As a last resort, the prince now sought the swallow, and stopped him just as he was circling about the summit of the tower. The swallow, as usual, was in a prodigious hurry, and had scarce time to make a reply. "Upon my word," said he, I have so much public business to attend to, and so many pursuits to follow, that I have had no time to think on the subject. I have every day a thousand visits to pay; a thousand affairs of importance to examine into, that leave me not a moment of leisure for these little sing-song matters. In a word, I am a citizen of the world—I know nothing of this thing called love." So saying, the swallow dived into the valley, and was out of sight in a moment.

The prince remained disappointed and perplexed, but with his curiosity still more piqued by the difficulty of gratifying it. While in this mood, his ancient guardian entered the tower. The prince advanced eagerly to meet him. "O Eben Bonabben," cried he, "thou hast revealed to me much of the wisdom of the earth; but there is one thing of which I remain in utter ignorance, and would fain be informed."

"My prince has but to make the inquiry, and everything within the limited range of his servant's intellect is at his command."

"Tell me then, O most profound of sages, what is the nature of this thing called love?"

Eben Bonabben was struck as with a thunderbolt. He trembled and turned pale, and felt as if his head sat but loosely on his shoulders.

"What could suggest such a question to my prince,—where could he have learned so idle a word?"

The prince led him to the window of the tower. "Listen, Eben Bonabben," said he. The sage listened. The nightingale sat in a thicket below the tower, singing to the rose; from every blossomed spray and tufted grove rose a strain of melody; and love—love—love—was still the unvarying strain.

"Allah is great!" exclaimed the wise Bonabben. "Who shall pretend to keep this secret from the heart of man, when even the birds of the air conspire to betray it?"

Then turning to Ahmed "O my prince," cried he, "shut thine ears to these seductive strains. Close thy mind against this dangerous knowledge. Know that this love is the cause of half the ills of wretched mortality. It is this which produces bitterness and strife between brethren and friends; which causes treacherous murder and desolating war. Care and sorrow, weary days and sleepless nights, are its attendants. It withers the bloom and blights the joy of youth, and brings on the ills and griefs of premature old age. Allah preserve thee, my prince, in total ignorance of this thing called love!"

The sage Eben Bonabben hastily retired, leaving the prince plunged in still deeper perplexity. It was in vain he attempted to dismiss the subject from his mind; it still continued uppermost in his thoughts, and teased and exhausted him with vain conjectures. Surely, said he to himself, as he listened to the tuneful strains of the birds, there is no sorrow in those notes; everything seems tenderness and joy. If love be a cause of such wretchedness and strife, why are not these birds drooping in solitude, or tearing each other in pieces, instead of fluttering cheerfully about the groves, or sporting with each other among the flowers?

He lay one morning on his couch, meditating on this inexplicable matter. The window of his chamber was open to admit the soft morning breeze, which came laden with the perfume of orange-blossoms from the valley of the Darro. The voice of the nightingale was faintly heard, still chanting the wonted theme. As the prince was listening and sighing, there was a sudden rushing noise in the air; a beautiful dove, pursued by a hawk, darted in at the window, and fell panting on the floor, while the pursuer, balked of his prey, soared off to the mountains.

The prince took up the gasping bird, smoothed its feathers, and nestled it in his bosom. When he had soothed it by his caresses, he put it in a golden cage, and offered it, with his own hands, the whitest and finest of wheat and the purest of water. The bird, however, refused food, and sat drooping and pining, and uttering piteous moans.

"What aileth thee?" said Ahmed. "Hast thou not everything thy heart can wish?"

"Alas, no!" replied the dove; "am I not separated from the partner of my heart, and that too in the happy spring-time, the very season of love!"

"Of love!" echoed Ahmed. "I pray thee, my pretty bird, canst thou then tell me what is love?"

"Too well can I, my prince. It is the torment of one, the felicity of two, the strife and enmity of three. It is a charm which draws two beings together, and unites them by delicious sympathies, making it happiness to be with each other, but misery to be apart. Is there no being to whom you are drawn by these ties of tender affection?"

"I like my old teacher Eben Bonabben better than any other being; but he is often tedious, and I occasionally feel myself happier without his society."

"That is not the sympathy I mean. I speak of love, the great mystery and principle of life: the intoxicating revel of youth; the sober delight of age. Look forth, my prince, and behold how at this blest season all nature is full of love. The most insignificant bird sings to its mate; the very beetle woos its lady-beetle, and yon butterflies which you see fluttering high above the tower and toying in the air, are happy in each other's loves. Alas, my prince! hast thou spent so many of the precious days of youth without knowing anything of love? Is there no gentle being of another sex—no beautiful princess nor lovely damsel who has ensnared your heart, and filled your bosom with a soft tumult of pleasing pains and tender wishes?"

"I begin to understand," said the prince, sighing; "but where should I seek for an object such as you describe in this dismal solitude?"

A little further conversation ensued, and the first lesson of the prince was complete.

"Alas!" said he, "if love be indeed such a delight, and its interruption such a misery, Allah forbid that I should mar the joy of any of its votaries." He opened the cage, took out the dove, and having fondly kissed it, carried it to the window. "Go, happy bird," said he, "rejoice with the partner of thy heart in the days of youth and spring-time. Why should I make thee a fellow-prisoner in this dreary tower where love can never enter?"

The dove flapped its wings in rapture, gave one vault into the air, and then swooped downward on whistling wings to the blooming bowers of the Darro.

The prince followed him with his eyes, and then gave way to bitter repining. The singing of the birds, which once delighted him, now added to his bitterness. Love! love! love! Alas, poor youth! he now understood the strain.

His eyes flashed fire when next he beheld the sage Bonabben. "Why hast thou kept me in this abject ignorance?" cried he. Why has the great mystery and principle of life been withheld from me, in which I find the meanest insect is so learned? Behold all nature is in a revel of delight. Every created being rejoices with its mate. This—this is the love about which I have sought instruction. Why am I alone debarred its enjoyment? Why has so much of my youth been wasted without a knowledge of it?"

The sage Bonabben saw that all further reserve was useless; for the prince had acquired the dangerous and forbidden knowledge. He revealed to him, therefore, the predictions of the astrologers and the precautions that had been taken in his education to avert the threatened evils. "And now, my prince," added he, "my life is in your hands. Let the king your father discover that you have learned the passion of love while under my guardianship, and my head must answer for it."

The prince was as reasonable as most young men of his age, and easily listened to the remonstrances of his tutor, since nothing pleaded against them. Besides, he really was attached to Eben Bonabben, and being as yet but theoretically acquainted with the passion of love, he consented to confine the knowledge of it to his own bosom, rather than endanger the head of the philosopher.

His discretion was doomed, however, to be put to still further proofs. A few mornings afterwards, as he was ruminating on the battlements of the tower, the dove which had been released by him came hovering in the air, and alighted fearlessly upon his shoulder.

The prince fondled it to his heart. "Happy bird," said he, "who can fly, as it were, with the wings of the morning to the uttermost parts of the earth. Where hast thou been since we parted?"

"In a far country, my prince, whence I bring you tidings in reward for my liberty. In the wild compass of my flight, which extends over plain and mountain, as I was soaring in the air, I beheld below me a delightful garden with all kinds of fruits and flowers. It was in a green meadow, on the banks of a wandering stream: and in the centre of the garden was a stately palace. I alighted in one of the bowers to repose after my weary flight. On the green bank below me was a youthful princess, in the very sweetness and bloom of her years. She was surrounded by female attendants, young like herself, who decked her with garlands and coronets of flowers; but no flower of field or garden could compare with her for loveliness. Here, however, she bloomed in secret, for the garden was surrounded by high walls, and no mortal man was permitted to enter. When I beheld this beauteous maid, thus young and innocent and unspotted by the world, I thought, here is the being formed by heaven to inspire my prince with love."

The description was a spark of fire to the combustible heart of Ahmed, and he conceived an immeasurable passion for the princess. He wrote a letter, couched in the most impassioned language, breathing his fervent devotion, but bewailing the unhappy thraldom of his person, which prevented him from seeking her out and throwing himself at her feet. He added couplets of the most tender and moving eloquence, for he was a poet by nature, and inspired by love. He addressed his letter—"To the Unknown Beauty, from the captive Prince Ahmed"; then perfuming it with musk and roses, he gave it to the dove.

"Away, trustiest of messengers!" said he. "Fly over mountain, and valley, and river, and plain; rest not in bower, nor set foot on earth, until thou hast given this letter to the mistress of my heart."

The dove soared high in air, and taking his course darted away in one undeviating direction. The prince followed him with his eye until he was a mere speck on a cloud, and gradually disappeared behind a mountain.

Day after day he watched for the return of the messenger of love, but he watched in vain. He began to accuse him of forgetfulness, when towards sunset one evening the faithful bird fluttered into his apartment, and, falling at his feet, expired. The arrow of some wanton archer had pierced his breast, yet he had struggled with the lingerings of life to execute his mission. As the prince bent with grief over this gentle martyr to fidelity, he beheld a chain of pearls round his neck, attached to which, beneath his wing, was a small enameled picture. It represented a lovely princess in the very flower of her years. It was doubtless the unknown beauty of the garden; but who and where was she?—how had she received his letter? and was this picture sent as a token of her approval of his love? Unfortunately the death of the faithful dove left everything in mystery and doubt.

The prince gazed on the picture till his eyes swam with tears. He pressed it to his lips and to his heart; he sat for hours contemplating it almost in an agony of tenderness. "Beautiful image!" said he, "alas, thou art but an image! Yet thy dewy eyes beam tenderly upon me; those rosy lips look as though they would speak encouragement: vain fancies! Have they not looked the same on some more happy rival? But where in this wide world shall I hope to find the original? Who knows what mountains, what realms, may separate us; what adverse chances may intervene? Perhaps now, even now, lovers may be crowding around her, while I sit here a prisoner in a tower, wasting my time in adoration of a painted shadow."

The resolution of Prince Ahmed was taken. "I will fly from this palace," said he, "which has become an odious prison; and, a pilgrim of love, will seek this unknown princess throughout the world." To escape from the tower in the day, when every one was awake, might be a difficult matter; but at night the palace was slightly guarded; for no one apprehended any attempt of the kind from the prince, who had always been so passive in his captivity. How was he to guide himself, however, in his darkling flight, being ignorant of the country? He bethought him of the owl, who was accustomed to roam at night, and must know every by-lane and secret pass. Seeking him in his hermitage, he questioned him touching his knowledge of the land. Upon this the owl put on a mighty self-important look. "You must know, O prince," said he, "that we owls are of a very ancient and extensive family, though rather fallen to decay, and possess ruinous castles and palaces in all parts of Spain. There is scarcely a tower of the mountains, or a fortress of the plains, or an old citadel of a city, but has some brother, or uncle, or cousin quartered in it; and in going the rounds to visit this my numerous kindred, I have pried into every nook and corner, and made myself acquainted with every secret of the land."

The prince was overjoyed to find the owl so deeply versed in topography, and now informed him, in confidence, of his tender passion and his intended elopement, urging him to be his companion and counsellor.

"Go to!" said the owl, with a look of displeasure; "am I a bird to engage in a love-affair?—I, whose whole time is devoted to meditation and the moon?"

"Be not offended, most solemn owl," replied the prince; "abstract thyself for a time from meditation and the moon, and aid me in my flight, and thou shalt have whatever heart can wish."

"I have that already," said the owl: "a few mice are sufficient for my frugal table, and this hole in the wall is spacious enough for my studies; and what more does a philosopher like myself desire?"

Bethink thee, most wise owl, that while moping in thy cell and gazing at the moon, all thy talents are lost to the world. I shall one day be a sovereign prince, and may advance thee to some post of honor and dignity."

The owl, though a philosopher and above the ordinary wants of life, was not above ambition, so he was finally prevailed on to elope with the prince, and be his guide and mentor in his pilgrimage.

The plans of a lover are promptly executed. The prince collected all his jewels, and concealed them about his person as travelling funds. That very night he lowered himself by his scarf from a balcony of the tower, clamored over the outer walls of the Generalife, and, guided by the owl, made good his escape before morning to the mountains.

He now held a council with his mentor as to his future course.

"Might I advise," said the owl, "I would recommend you to repair to Seville. You must know that many years since I was on a visit to an uncle, an owl of great dignity and power, who lived in a ruined wing of the castle of that place. In my hoverings at night over the city I frequently remarked a light burning in a lonely tower. At length I alighted on the battlements, and found it to proceed from the lamp of an Arabian magician: he was surrounded by his magic books, and on his shoulder was perched an ancient raven who had come with him from Egypt. I am acquainted with that raven, and owe to him a great part of the knowledge I possess. The magician is since dead, but the raven still inhabits the tower, for these birds are of wonderful long life. I would advise you, O prince, to seek that raven, for he is a soothsayer and a conjurer, and deals in the black art, for which all ravens, and especially those of Egypt, are renowned.

The prince was struck with the wisdom of this advice, and accordingly bent his course towards Seville. He travelled only in the night to accommodate his companion, and lay by during the day in some dark cavern or mouldering watch-tower, for the owl knew every hiding-hole of the kind, and had a most antiquarian taste for ruins.

At length one morning at daybreak they reached the city of Seville, where the owl, who hated the glare and bustle of crowded streets, halted without the gate, and took up his quarters in a hollow tree.

The prince entered the gate, and readily found the magic tower, which rose above the houses of the city, as a palm-tree rises above the shrubs of the desert; it was in fact the same tower standing at the present day, and known as the Giralda, the famous Moorish tower of Seville.

The prince ascended by a great winding staircase to the summit of the tower, where he found the cabalistic raven,—an old, mysterious, gray-headed bird, ragged in feather, with a film over one eye that gave him the glare of a specter.

He was perched on one leg, with his head turned on one side, poring with his remaining eye on a diagram described on the pavement.

The prince approached him with the awe and reverence naturally inspired by his venerable appearance and super-natural wisdom. "Pardon me, most ancient and darkly wise raven," exclaimed he, "if for a moment I interrupt those studies which are the wonder of the world. You behold before you a votary of love, who would fain seek your counsel how to obtain the object of his passion."

"In other words," said the raven, with a significant look, you seek to try my skill in palmistry. Come, show me your hand, and let me decipher the mysterious lines of fortune."

"Excuse me," said the prince, "I come not to pry into the decrees of fate, which are hidden by Allah from the eyes of mortals; I am a pilgrim of love, and seek but to find a clue to the object of my pilgrimage. I seek one unknown beauty, the original of this picture; and I beseech thee, most potent raven, if it be within the scope of thy knowledge or the reach of thy art, inform me where she may be found?"

"What know I," replied the gray-headed raven, dryly, "of youth and beauty? my visits are to the old and withered, not the fresh and fair; the harbinger of fate am I; who croak bodings of death from the chimney-top, and flap my wings at the sick man's window. You must seek else-where for tidings of your unknown beauty."

"And where can I seek if not among the sons of wisdom, versed in the book of destiny? Know that I am a royal prince, fated by the stars, and sent on a mysterious enterprise on which may hang the destiny of empires."

When the raven heard that it was a matter of vast moment, in which the stars took interest, he changed his tone and manner, and listened with profound attention to the story of the prince. When it was concluded, he replied, "Touching this princess, I can give thee no information of myself, for my flight is not among gardens, or around ladies' bowers; but hie thee to Cordova, seek the palm-tree of the great Abderahman, which stands in the court of the principal mosque: at the foot of it thou wilt find a great traveller who has visited all countries and courts, and been a favorite with queens and princesses. He will give thee tidings of the object of thy search."

"Many thanks for this precious information," said the prince. "Farewell, most venerable conjurer."

"Farewell, pilgrim of love," said the raven, dryly, and again fell to pondering, on the diagram.

The prince sallied forth from Seville, sought his fellow-traveller the owl, who was still dozing in the hollow tree, and set off for Cordova.

He approached it along hanging gardens, and orange and citron groves, overlooking the fair valley of the Guadalquivir. When arrived at its gates the owl flew up to a dark hole in the wall, and the prince proceeded in quest of the palm-tree planted in days of yore by the great Abderahman. It stood in the midst of the great court of the mosque, towering from amidst orange and cypress trees. Dervises and faquirs were seated in groups under the cloisters of the court, and many of the faithful were performing their ablutions at the fountains before entering the mosque.

At the foot of the palm-tree was a crowd listening to the words of one who appeared to be talking with great volubility. "This," said the prince to himself, "must be the great traveller who is to give me tidings of the unknown princess." He mingled in the crowd, but was astonished to perceive that they were all listening to a parrot, who with his bright-green coat, and consequential top-knot, had the air of a bird on excellent terms with himself.

"How is this," said the prince to one of the by-standers, "that so many grave persons can be delighted with a chattering bird?"

"You know not whom you speak of," said the other; "this parrot is a descendant of the famous parrot of Persia, renowned for his story-telling talent. He has all the learning of the East at the tip of his tongue, and can quote poetry as fast as he can talk. He has visited various foreign courts, where he has been considered an oracle of erudition. He has been a universal favorite also with the fair sex, who have a vast admiration for erudite parrots that can quote poetry."

"Enough," said the prince, "I will have some private talk with this distinguished traveller."

He sought a private interview, and expounded the nature of his errand. He had scarcely mentioned it when the parrot burst into a fit of dry laughter, that absolutely brought tears into his eyes. "Excuse my merriment," said he "but the mere mention of love always sets me laughing."

The prince was shocked at this ill-timed mirth. "Is not love," said he, "the great mystery of nature, the secret principle of life, the universal bond of sympathy?"

"A fig's end!" cried the parrot, interrupting him; "prithee where hast thou learned this sentimental jargon? trust me, love is quite out of vogue; one never hears of it in company of wits and people of refinement."

The prince sighed as he recalled the different language of his friend the dove. But this parrot, thought he, has lived about the court, he affects the wit and the fine gentleman, he knows nothing of the thing called love. Unwilling to provoke any more ridicule of the sentiment which filled his heart, he now directed his inquiries to the immediate purport of his visit.

"Tell me," said he, "most accomplished parrot, thou who hast everywhere been admitted to the most secret bowers of beauty, hast thou in the course of thy travels met with the original of this portrait?"

The parrot took the picture in his claw, turned his head from side to side, and examined it curiously with either eye. "Upon my honor," said he, "a very pretty face, very pretty; but then one sees so many pretty women in one's travels that one can hardly—but hold—bless me! now I look at it again—sure enough, this is the Princess Aldegonda: how could I forget one that is so prodigious a favorite with me!"

"The Princess Aldegonda!" echoed the prince; "and where is she to be found?"

"Softly, softly," said the parrot; "easier to be found than gained. She is the only daughter of the Christian king who reigns at Toledo, and is shut up from the world until her seventeenth birthday, on account of some prediction of those meddlesome fellows the astrologers. You'll not get a sight of her; no mortal man can see her. I was admitted to her presence to entertain her, and I assure you, on the word of a parrot who has seen the world, I have conversed with much sillier princesses in my time."

"A word in confidence, my dear parrot," said the prince. "I am heir to a kingdom, and shall one day sit upon a throne. I see that you are a bird of parts, and understand the world. Help me to gain possession of this princess, and I will advance you to some distinguished place about court."

"With all my heart," said the parrot; "but let it be a sinecure if possible, for we wits have a great dislike to labor."

Arrangements were promptly made: the prince sallied forth from Cordova through the same gate by which he had entered; called the owl down from the hole in the wall, introduced him to his new travelling companion as a brother savant, and away they set off on their journey.

They travelled much more slowly than accorded with the impatience of the prince; but the parrot was accustomed to high life, and did not like to be disturbed early in the morning. The owl, on the other hand, was for sleeping at mid-day, and lost a great deal of time by his long siestas. His antiquarian taste also was in the way; for he insisted on pausing and inspecting every ruin, and had long legendary tales to tell about every old tower and castle in the country. The prince had supposed that he and the parrot, being both birds of learning, would delight in each other's society, but never had he been more mistaken. They were eternally bickering. The one was a wit, the other a philosopher. The parrot quoted poetry, was critical on new readings and eloquent on small points of erudition; the owl treated all such knowledge as trifling, and relished-nothing but metaphysics. Then the parrot would sing songs and repeat bon-mots and crack jokes upon his solemn neighbor, and laugh outrageously at his own wit; all which proceedings the owl considered as a grievous invasion of his dignity, and would scowl and sulk and swell, and be silent for a whole day together.

The prince heeded not the wranglings of his companions, being wrapped up in the dreams of his own fancy and the contemplation of the portrait of the beautiful princess. In this way they journeyed through the stern passes of the Sierra Morena, across the sunburnt plains of La Mancha and Castile, and along the banks of the "Golden Tagus," which winds its wizard mazes over one half of Spain and Portugal. At length they came in sight of a strong city with walls and towers built on a rocky promontory, round the foot of which the Tagus circled with brawling violence.

"Behold," exclaimed the owl, "the ancient and renowned city of Toledo; a city famous for its antiquities. Behold those venerable domes and towers, hoary with time and clothed with legendary grandeur, in which so many of my ancestors have meditated."

"Pish!" cried the parrot, interrupting his solemn antiquarian rapture, "what have we to do with antiquities, and legends, and your ancestry? Behold what is more to the purpose—behold the abode of youth and beauty—behold at length, O prince, the abode of your long-sought princess."

The prince looked in the direction indicated by the parrot, and beheld, in a delightful green meadow on the banks of the Tagus, a stately palace rising from amidst the bowers of a delicious garden. It was just such a place as had been described by the dove as the residence of the original of the picture. He gazed at it with a throbbing heart; "perhaps at this moment," thought he, "the beautiful princess is sporting beneath those shady bowers, or pacing with delicate step those stately terraces, or reposing beneath those lofty roofs!" As he looked more narrowly, he perceived that the walls of the garden were of great height, so as to defy access, while numbers of armed guards patrolled around them.

The prince turned to the parrot. "O most accomplished of birds," said he, "thou hast the gift of human speech. Hie thee to yon garden; seek the idol of my soul, and tell her that Prince Ahmed, a pilgrim of love, and guided by the stars, has arrived in quest of her on the flowery banks of the Tagus."

The parrot, proud of his embassy, flew away to the garden, mounted above its lofty walls, and after soaring for a time over the lawns and groves, alighted on the balcony of a pavilion that overhung the river. Here, looking in at the casement, he beheld the princess reclining on a couch, with her eyes fixed on a paper, while tears gently stole after each other down her pallid cheek.

Pluming his wings for a moment, adjusting his bright green coat, and elevating his top-knot, the parrot perched himself beside her with a gallant air; then assuming a tenderness of tone, "Dry thy tears, most beautiful of princesses," said he; "I come to bring solace to thy heart."

The princess was startled on hearing a voice, but turning and seeing nothing but a little green-coated bird bobbing and bowing before her, "Alas! what solace canst thou yield," said she, "seeing thou art but a parrot?"

The parrot was nettled at the question. "I have consoled many beautiful ladies in my time," said he; "but let that pass. At present I come ambassador from a royal prince. Know that Ahmed, the prince of Granada, has arrived in quest of thee, and is encamped even now on the flowery banks of the Tagus."

The eyes of the beautiful princess sparkled at these words even brighter than the diamonds in her coronet. "O sweetest of parrots," cried she, "joyful indeed are thy tidings, for I was faint and weary, and sick almost unto death with doubt of the constancy of Ahmed. Hie thee back, and tell him that the words of his letter are engravers in my heart, and his poetry has been the food of my soul. Tell him, however, that he must prepare to prove his love by force of arms; to-morrow is my seventeenth birthday, when the king my father holds a great tournament; several princes are to enter the lists, and my hand is to be the prize of the victor."

The parrot again took wing, and rustling through the groves, flew back to where the prince awaited his return. The rapture of Ahmed on finding the original of his adored portrait, and finding her kind and true, can only be conceived by those favored mortals who have had the good fortune to realize day-dreams and turn a shadow into substance: still there was one thing that alloyed his transport this impending tournament. In fact, the banks of the Tagus were already glittering with arms, and resounding with trumpets of the various knights, who, with proud retinues, were prancing on towards Toledo to attend the ceremonial. The same star that had controlled the destiny of the prince had governed that of the princess, and until her seventeenth birthday she had been shut up from the world, to guard her from the tender passion. The fame of her charms, however, had been enhanced rather than obscured by this seclusion. Several powerful princes had contended for her hand; and her father, who was a king of wondrous shrewdness, to avoid making enemies by showing partiality, had referred them to the arbitrament of arms. Among the rival candidates were several renowned for strength and prowess. What a predicament for the unfortunate Ahmed, unprovided as he was with weapons, and unskilled in the exercise of chivalry! "Luckless prince that I am!" said he, "to have been brought up in seclusion under the eye of a philosopher! Of what avail are algebra and philosophy in affairs of love? Alas, Eben Bonabben! why hast thou neglected to instruct me in the management of arms?" Upon this the owl broke silence, preluding his harangue with a pious ejaculation, for he was a devout Mussulman.

"Allah is great!" exclaimed he; "in his hands are all secret things—he alone governs the destiny of princes! Know, O prince, that this land is full of mysteries, hidden from all but those who, like myself, can grope after knowledge in the dark. Know that in the neighboring mountains there is a cave, and in that cave there is an iron table, and on that table there lies a suit of magic armor, and beside that table there stands a spell-bound steed, which have been shut up there for many generations."

The prince stared with wonder, while the owl, blinking his huge round eyes, and erecting his horns, proceeded.

"Many years since I accompanied my father to these parts on a tour of his estates, and we sojourned in that cave; and thus became I acquainted with the mystery. It is a tradition in our family which I have heard from my grandfather, when I was yet but a very little owlet, that this armor belonged to a Moorish magician, who took refuge in this cavern when Toledo was captured by the Christians, and died here, leaving his steed and weapons under a mystic spell, never to be used but by a Moslem, and by him only from sunrise to mid-day. In that interval, whoever uses them will overthrow every opponent."

"Enough: let us seek this cave!" exclaimed Ahmed.

Guided by his legendary mentor, the prince found the cavern, which was in one of the wildest recesses of those rocky cliffs which rise around Toledo; none but the mousing eye of an owl or an antiquary could have discovered the entrance to it. A sepulchral lamp of everlasting oil shed a solemn light through the place. On an iron table in the centre of the cavern lay the magic armor, against it leaned the lance, and beside it stood an Arabian steed, caparisoned for the field, but motionless as a statue. The armor was bright and unsullied as it had gleamed in days of old; the steed in as good condition as if just from the pasture; and when Ahmed laid his hand upon his neck, he pawed the ground and gave a loud neigh of joy that shook the walls of the cavern. Thus amply provided with "horse and rider and weapon to wear," the prince determined to defy the field in the impending tourney.

The eventful morning arrived. The lists for the combat were prepared in the Vega, or plain, just below the cliff-built walls of Toledo, where stages and galleries were erected for the spectators, covered with rich tapestry, and sheltered from the sun by silken awnings. All the beauties of the land were assembled in those galleries, while below pranced plumed knights with their pages and esquires, among whom figured conspicuously the princes who were to contend in the tourney. All the beauties of the land, however, were eclipsed when the Princess Aldegonda appeared in the royal pavilion, and for the first time broke forth upon the gaze of an admiring world. A murmur of wonder ran through the crowd at her transcendent loveliness; and the princes who were candidates for her hand, merely on the faith of her reported charms, now felt ten-fold ardor for the conflict.

The princess, however, had a troubled look. The color came and went from her cheek, and her eye wandered with a restless and unsatisfied expression over the plumed throng of knights. The trumpets were about sounding for the encounter, when the herald announced the arrival of a strange knight; and Ahmed rode into the field. A steel helmet studded with gems rose above his turban; his cuirass was embossed with gold; his cimeter and dagger were of the workmanship of Fez, and flamed with precious stones. A round shield was at his shoulder, and in his hand he bore the lance of charmed virtue. The caparison of his Arabian steed was richly embroidered and swept the ground, and the proud animal pranced and snuffed the air, and neighed with joy at once more beholding the array of arms. The lofty and graceful demeanor of the prince struck every eye, and when his appellation was announced, "The Pilgrim of Love," a universal flutter and agitation prevailed among the fair dames in the galleries.

When Ahmed presented himself at the lists, however, they were closed against him: none but princes, he was told, were admitted to the contest. He declared his name and rank. Still worse!—he was a Moslem, and could not engage in a tourney where the hand of a Christian princess was a prize.

The rival princes surrounded him with haughty and menacing aspects; and one of insolent demeanor and herculean frame sneered at his light and youthful form, and scoffed at his amorous appellation. The ire of the prince was roused. He defied his rival to the encounter. They took distance, wheeled, and charged; and at the first touch, of the magic lance, the brawny scoffer was tilted from his saddle. Here the prince would have paused, but, alas! he had to deal with a demoniac horse and armor; once in action, nothing could control them. The Arabian steed charged into the thickest of the throng; the lance overturned everything that presented; the gentle prince was carried pell-mell about the field, strewing it with high and low, gentle and simple, and grieving at his own involuntary exploits. The king stormed and raged at this outrage on his subjects and his guests. He ordered out all his guards—they were unhorsed as fast as they came up. The king threw off his robes, grasped buckler and lance, and rode forth to awe the stranger with the presence of majesty itself. Alas! majesty fared no better than the vulgar; the steel and lance were no respecters of persons; to the dismay of Ahmed, he was borne full tilt against the king, and in a moment the royal heels were in the air, and the crown was rolling in the dust.

At this moment the sun reached the meridian; the magic spell resumed its power; the Arabian steed scoured across the plain, leaped the barrier, plunged into the Tagus, swam its raging current, bore the prince breathless and amazed to the statue, beside the iron table. The prince dismounted right gladly, and replaced the armor, to abide the further decrees of fate. Then seating himself in the cavern, he ruminated on the desperate state to which this demoniac steed and armor had reduced him. Never should he dare to show his face at Toledo after inflicting such disgrace upon its chivalry, and such an outrage on its king. What too would the princess think of so rude and riotous an achievement? Full of anxiety, he sent forth his winged messengers to gather tidings. The parrot resorted to all the public places and crowded resorts of the city, and soon returned with a world of gossip. All Toledo was in consternation. The princess had been borne off senseless to the palace; the tournament had ended in confusion; every one was talking of the sudden apparition, prodigious exploits, and strange disappearance of the Moslem knight. Some pronounced him a Moorish magician; others thought him a demon who had assumed a human shape, while others related traditions of enchanted warriors hidden in the caves of the mountains, and thought it might be one of these, who had made a sudden irruption from his den. All agreed that no mere ordinary mortal could have wrought such wonders, or unhorsed such accomplished and stalwart Christian warriors.

The owl flew forth at night and hovered about the dusky city, perching on the roofs and chimneys. He then wheeled his flight up to the royal palace, which stood on a rocky summit of Toledo, and went prowling about its terraces and battlements, eavesdropping at every cranny, and glaring in with his big goggling eyes at every window where there was a light, so as to throw two or three maids of honor into fits. It was not until the gray dawn began to peer above the mountains that he returned from his mousing expedition, and related to the prince what he had seen.

As I was prying about one of the loftiest towers of the palace," said he, "I beheld through a casement a beautiful princess. She was reclining on a couch with attendants and physicians around her, but she would none of their ministry and relief. When they retired, I beheld her draw forth a letter from her bosom, and read and kiss it, and give way to loud lamentations; at which, philosopher as I am, I could but be greatly moved."

The tender heart of Ahmed was distressed at these tidings. "Too true were thy words, O sage Eben Bonabben," cried he; "care and sorrow and sleepless nights are the lot of lovers. Allah preserve the princess from the blighting influence of this thug called love!"

Further intelligence from Toledo corroborated the report of the owl. The city was a prey to uneasiness and alarm. The princess was conveyed to the highest tower of the palace, every avenue to which was strongly guarded. In the meantime a devouring melancholy had seized upon her, of which no one could divine the cause—she refused food and turned a deaf ear to every consolation. The most skillful physicians had essayed their art in vain; it was thought some magic spell had been practised upon tier, and the king made proclamation, declaring that whoever should effect her cure should receive the richest jewel in the royal treasury.

When the owl, who was dozing in a corner, heard of this proclamation, he rolled his large eyes and looked more mysterious than ever.

"Allah is great!" exclaimed he, "happy the man that shall effect that cure, should he but know what to choose from the royal treasury."

"What mean you, most reverend owl?" said Ahmed.

"Hearken, O prince, to what I shall relate. We owls, you must know, are a learned body, and much given to dark and dusty research. During my late prowling at night about the domes and turrets of Toledo, I discovered a college of antiquarian owls, who hold their meetings in a great vaulted tower where the royal treasury is deposited. Here they were discussing the forms and inscriptions and designs of ancient gems and jewels, and of golden and silver vessels, heaped up in the treasury, the fashion of every country and age; but mostly they were interested about certain relics and talismans that have remained in the treasury since the time of Roderick the Goth. Among these was a box of sandal-wood secured by bands of steel of Oriental workmanship, and inscribed with mystic characters known only to the learned few. This box and its inscription had occupied the college for several sessions, and had caused much long and grave dispute. At the time of my visit a very ancient owl, who had recently arrived from Egypt, was seated on the lid of the box, lecturing upon the inscription, and he proved from it that the coffer contained the silken carpet of the throne of Solomon the Wise; which doubtless had been brought to Toledo by the Jews who took refuge there after the downfall of Jerusalem."

When the owl had concluded his antiquarian harangue, the prince remained for a time absorbed in thought. "I have heard," said he, "from the sage Eben Bonabben, of the wonderful properties of that talisman, which disappeared at the fall of Jerusalem, and was supposed to be lost to mankind. Doubtless it remains a sealed mystery to the Christians of Toledo. If I can get possession of that carpet, my fortune is secure."

The next day the prince laid aside his rich attire, and arrayed himself in the simple garb of an Arab of the desert. He dyed his complexion to a tawny hue, and no one could have recognized in him the splendid warrior who had caused such admiration and dismay at the tournament. With staff in hand, and scrip by his side, and a small pastoral reed, he repaired to Toledo, and presenting himself at the gate of the royal palace, announced himself as a candidate for the reward offered for the cure of the princess. The guards would have driven him away with blows. "What can a vagrant Arab like thyself pretend to do," said they, "in a case where the most learned of the land have failed?" The king, however, overheard the tumult, and ordered the Arab to be brought into his presence.

"Most potent king," said Ahmed, "you behold before you a Bedouin Arab, the greater part of whose life has been passed in the solitudes of the desert. These solitudes, it is well known, are the haunts of demons and evil spirits, who beset us poor shepherds in our lonely watchings, enter into and possess our flocks and herds, and sometimes render even the patient camel furious; against these, our counter-charm is music; and we have legendary airs handed down from generation to generation, that we chant and pipe, to cast forth these evil spirits. I am of a gifted line, and possess this power in its fullest force. If it be any evil influence of the kind that holds a spell over thy daughter, I pledge my head to free her from its sway."

The king, who was a man of understanding, and knew the wonderful secrets possessed by the Arabs, was inspired with hope by the confident language of the prince. He conducted him immediately to the lofty tower, secured by several doors, in the summit of which was the chamber of the princess. The windows opened upon a terrace with balustrades, commanding a view over Toledo and all the surrounding country. The windows were darkened, for the princess lay within, a prey to a devouring grief that refused all alleviation.

The prince seated himself on the terrace, and performed several wild Arabian airs on his pastoral pipe, which he had learnt from his attendants in the Generalife at Granada. The princess continued insensible, and the doctors who were present shook their heads, and smiled with incredulity and contempt: at length the prince laid aside the reed, and, to a simple melody, chanted the love verses of the letter which had declared his passion.

The princess recognized the strain—a fluttering joy stole to her heart; she raised her head and listened; tears rushed to her eyes and streamed down her cheeks; her bosom rose and fell with a tumult of emotions. She would have asked for the minstrel to be brought into her presence, but maiden coyness held her silent. The king read her wishes, and at his command Ahmed was conducted into the chamber. The lovers were discreet: they but exchanged glances, yet those glances spoke volumes. Never was triumph of music more complete. The rose had returned to the soft cheek of the princess, the freshness to her lip, and the dewy light to her languishing eyes.

All the physicians present stared at each other with astonishment. The king regarded the Arab minstrel with admiration mixed with awe. "Wonderful youth!" exclaimed he, "thou shalt henceforth be the first physician of my court, and no other prescription will I take but thy melody. For the present receive thy reward, the most precious jewel in my treasury."

"O king," replied Ahmed, "I care not for silver or gold or precious stones. One relic halt thou in the treasury, handed down from the Moslems who once owned Toledo—a box of sandal-wood containing a silken carpet: give me that box, and I am content."

All present were surprised at the moderation of the Arab, and still more when the box of sandal-wood was brought and the carpet drawn forth. It was of fine green silk, covered witty Hebrew and Chaldaic characters. The court physicians looked at each other, shrugged their shoulders, and smiled at the simplicity of this new practitioner, who could be content with so paltry a fee.

"This carpet," said the prince, once covered the throne of Solomon the wise; it is worthy of being placed beneath the feet of beauty."

So saying, he spread it on the terrace beneath an ottoman that had been brought forth for the princess; then seating himself at her feet—

"Who," said he, "shall counteract what is written in the book of fate? Behold the prediction of the astrologers verified. Know, O king, that your daughter and I have long loved each other in secret. Behold in me the Pilgrim of Love!"

These words were scarcely from his lips when the carpet rose in the air, bearing off the prince and princess. The king and the physicians gazed after it with open mouths and straining eyes until it became a little speck on the white bosom of a cloud, and then disappeared in the blue vault of heaven.

The king in a rage summoned his treasurer. "How is this," said he, "that thou has suffered an infidel to get possession of such a talisman?"

"Alas, sir, we knew not its nature, nor could we decipher the inscription of the box. If it be indeed the carpet of the throne of the wise Solomon, it is possessed of magic power, and can transport its owner from place to place through the air."

The king assembled a mighty army, and set off for Granada in pursuit of the fugitives. His march was long and toilsome. Encamping in the Vega, he sent a herald to demand restitution of his daughter. The king himself came forth with all his court to meet him. In the king he beheld the real minstrel, for Ahmed had succeeded to the throne on the death of his father, and the beautiful Aldegonda was his sultana.

The Christian king was easily pacified when he found that his daughter was suffered to continue in her faith; not that he was particularly pious, but religion is always a point of pride and etiquette with princes. Instead of bloody battles, there was a succession of feasts and rejoicings, after which the king returned well pleased to Toledo, and the youthful couple continued to reign as happily as wisely, in the Alhambra.

It is proper to add, that the owl and the parrot had severally followed the prince by easy stages to Granada; the former travelling by night, and stopping at, the various hereditary possessions of his family; the latter figuring in gay circles of every town and city on his route.

Ahmed gratefully requited the services which they had rendered on his pilgrimage. He appointed the owl his prime minister, the parrot his master of ceremonies. It is needless to say that never was a realm more sagely administered, nor a court conducted with more exact punctilio.

Legend of the Moor's Legacy

Just within the fortress of the Alhambra, in front of the royal palace, is a broad open esplanade, called the Square of the Cisterns, so called from being undermined by reservoirs of water, hidden from sight, and which have existed from the time of the Moors. At one corner of this esplanade is a Moorish well, cut through the living rock to a great depth, the water of which is cold as ice and clear as crystal. The wells made by the Moors are always in repute, for it is well known what pains they took to penetrate to the purest and sweetest springs and fountains. The one of which we now speak is famous throughout Granada, insomuch that water-carriers, some baring great water-jars on their shoulders, others driving asses before them laden with earthen vessels, are ascending and descending the steep woody avenues of the Alhambra, from early dawn until a late hour of the night.

Fountains and wells, ever since the scriptural days, have been noted gossiping-places in hot climates; and at the well in question there is a kind of perpetual club kept up during the livelong day, by the invalids, old women, and other curious do-nothing folk of the fortress, who sit here on the stone benches, under an awning spread over the well to shelter the toll-gatherer from the sun, and dawdle over the gossip of the fortress, and question every water-carrier that arrives about the news of the city, and make long comments on everything they hear and see. Not an hour of the day but loitering housewives and idle maid-servants may be seen, lingering, with pitcher on head or in hand, to hear the last of the endless tattle of these worthies.

Among the water-carriers who once resorted to this well, there was a sturdy, strong-backed, bandy-legged little fellow, named Pedro Gil, but called Peregil for shortness, who had begun business with merely a great earthen jar which he carried upon his shoulder. By degrees he rose in the world, and was enabled to purchase a stout shaggy-haired donkey. On each side of this his long-eared aid-de-camp, in a kind of pannier, were slung his water-jars, covered with fig-leaves to protect them from the sun. There was not a more industrious water-carrier in all Granada, nor one more merry withal. The streets rang with his cheerful voice as he trudged after his donkey, singing forth the usual summer note that resounds through the Spanish towns:. "Who wants water—water colder than snow? Who wants water from the well of the Alhambra, cold as ice and clear as crystal?" When he served a customer with a sparkling glass, it was always with a pleasant word that caused a smile; and if, perchance, it was a comely dame or dimpling damsel, it was always with a compliment to her beauty that was irresistible. Thus Peregil was noted throughout all Granada for being one of the civilest, pleasantest, and happiest of mortals. Yet it is not he who sings loudest and jokes most that has the lightest heart. Under all this air of merriment, honest Peregil had his cares and troubles. He had a large family of ragged children to support, who were hungry and clamorous as a nest of young swallows, and beset him with their outcries for food whenever he came home of an evening. He had a helpmate, too, who was anything but a help to him. She had been a village beauty before marriage, noted for her skill at dancing the bolero and rattling the castanets; and she still retained her early propensities, spending the hard earnings of honest Peregil in frippery, and laying the very donkey under requisition for junketing parties into the country on Sundays and those innumerable holidays, which are rather more numerous in Spain than the days of the week. With all this she was a slattern and a gossip of the first water; neglecting house, household, and everything else, to loiter slipshod in the houses of her gossip neighbors.

Peregil bore all the heavy dispensations of wife and children with as meek a spirit as his donkey bore the water-jars; and, however he might shake his ears in private, never ventured to question the household virtues of his slattern spouse.

He loved his children, too, even as an owl loves its owlets, seeing in them his own image multiplied and perpetuated; for they were a sturdy, long-backed, bandy-legged little brood. The great pleasure of honest Peregil was, whenever he could afford himself a scanty holiday, and had a handful of pennies to spare, to take the whole family forth with him, some in his arms, some tugging at his skirts, and some trudging at his heels, and to treat them to a gambol among the orchards of the Vega, while his wife was dancing with her holiday friends.

It was a late hour one summer night, and most of the water-carriers had desisted from their toils. The day had been uncommonly sultry; the night was one of those delicious moonlights which tempt the inhabitants of southern climes to indemnify themselves for the heat and inaction of the day, by lingering in the open air, and enjoying its tempered sweetness until after midnight. Customers for water were therefore still abroad. Peregil, like a considerate, painstaking father, thought of his hungry children. "One more journey to the well," said he to himself, "to earn a Sunday's dinner for the little ones." So saying, he trudged manfully up the steep avenue of the Alhambra, singing as he went, and now and then bestowing a hearty thwack with a cudgel on the flanks of his donkey, either by way of cadence to the song, or refreshment to the animal; for dry blows serve instead of provender in Spain for all beasts of burden.

When arrived at the well, he found it deserted by every one except a solitary stranger in Moorish garb, seated on a stone bench in the moonlight. Peregil paused at first and regarded him with surprise, not unmixed with awe, but the Moor feebly beckoned him to approach. "I am faint and ill," said he; "aid me to return to the city, and I will pay thee double what thou couldst gain by thy jars of water."

The honest heart of the little water-carrier was touched with compassion at the appeal of the stranger. "God forbid," said he, "that I should ask fee or reward for doing a common act of humanity." He accordingly helped the Moor on his donkey, and set off slowly for Granada, the poor Moslem being so weak that it was necessary to hold him on the animal to keep him from falling to the earth.

When they entered the city, the water-carrier demanded whither he should conduct him. "Alas!" said the Moor, faintly, "I have neither home nor habitation; I am a stranger in the land. Suffer me to lay my head this night beneath thy, roof and thou shalt be amply repaid."

Honest Peregil thus saw himself unexpectedly saddled with an infidel guest, but he was too humane to refuse a night's shelter to a fellow-being in so forlorn a plight; so he conducted the Moor to his dwelling. The children, who had sallied forth open-mouthed as usual on hearing the tramp of the donkey, ran back with affright when they beheld the turbaned stranger, and hid themselves behind their mother. The latter stepped forth intrepidly, like a ruffling hen before her brood when a vagrant dog approaches.

"What infidel companion," cried she, "is this you have brought home at this late hour?"

"Be quiet, wife," replied Peregil; "here is a poor sick stranger, without friend or home; wouldst thou turn him forth to perish in the streets?"

The wife would still have remonstrated, for although she lived in a hovel, she was a furious stickler for the credit of her house; the little water-carrier, however, for once was stiff-necked, and refused to bend beneath the yoke. He assisted the poor Moslem to alight, and spread a mat and a sheep-skin for him, on the ground, in the coolest part of the house; being the only kind of bed that his poverty afforded.

In a little while the Moor was seized with violent convulsions, which defied all the ministering skill of the simple water-carrier. The eye of the poor patient acknowledged his kindness. During an interval of his fits he called him to his side, and addressing him in a low voice, "My end," said he, "I fear is at hand. If I die, I bequeath you this box as a reward for your charity:" so saying, he opened his cloak, and showed a small box of sandal-wood, strapped round his body. "God grant, my friend," replied the worthy little water-carrier, that you may live many years to enjoy your treasure, whatever it may be." The Moor shook his head; he laid his hand upon the box, and would have said something more concerning it, but his convulsions returned with increasing violence, and in a little while he expired.

The water-carrier's wife was now as one distracted. "This comes," said she, "of your foolish good-nature, always running into scrapes to oblige others. What will become of us when this corpse is found in our house? We shall be sent to prison as murderers; and if we escape with our lives, shall be ruined by notaries and constables."

Poor Peregil was in equal tribulation, and almost repented himself of having done a good deed. At length a thought struck him. "It is not yet day," said he; "I can convey the dead body out of the city, and bury it in the sands on the banks of the Xenil. No one saw the Moor enter our dwelling, and no one will know anything of his death."

So said, so done. The wife aided him; they rolled the body of the unfortunate Moslem in the mat on which he had expired, laid it across the ass, and Peregil set out with it for the banks of the river.

As ill luck would have it, there lived opposite to the water-carrier a barber named Pedrillo Pedrugo, one of the most prying, tattling, and mischief-making of his gossip tribe. He was a weasel-faced, spider-legged varlet, supple and insinuating; he had a, universal knowledge of the affairs of others, and he had no more power of retention than a sieve. It was said that he slept but with one eye at a time, and kept one ear uncovered, so that even in his sleep he might see and hear all that was going on. Certain it is, he was a sort of scandalous chronicle for the quidnuncs of Granada, and had more customers than all the rest of his fraternity.

This meddlesome barber heard Peregil arrive at an unusual hour at night, and the exclamations of his wife and children. His head was instantly popped out of a little window which served him as a lookout, and he saw his neighbor assist a man in Moorish garb into his dwelling. This was so strange an occurrence, that Pedrillo Pedrugo slept not a wink that night. Every five minutes he was at his loophole, watching the lights that gleamed through the chinks of his neighbor's door, and before daylight he beheld Peregil sally forth with his donkey unusually laden.

The inquisitive barber was in a fidget; he slipped on his clothes, and, stealing forth silently, followed the water-carrier at a distance, until he saw him dig a hole in the sandy bank of the Xenil, and bury something that had the appearance of a dead body.

The barber hied him home, and fidgeted about his shop, setting everything upside down, until sunrise. He then took a basin under his arm, and sallied forth to the house of his daily customer the judge.

The judge was just risen. Pedrillo Pedrugo seated him in a chair, threw a napkin round his neck, put a basin of hot water under his chin, and began to mollify his beard with his fingers.

"Strange doings!" said Pedrugo, who played barber and newsmonger at the same time,—"strange doings! Robbery, and murder, and burial all in one night!"

"Hey!—how!—what is that you say?" cried the judge.

"I say," replied the barber, rubbing a piece of soap over the nose and mouth of the dignitary, for a Spanish barber disdains to employ a brush,—"I say that Peregil the water-carrier has robbed and murdered a Moorish Mussulman, and buried him, this blessed night. Accursed be the night for the same!"

"But how do you know all this?" demanded the judge.

"Be patient, Señor, and you shall hear all about it," replied Pedrillo, taking him by the nose and sliding a razor over his cheek. He then recounted all that he had seen, going through both operations at the same time, shaving his beard, washing his chin, and wiping him dry with a dirty napkin, while he was robbing, murdering, and burying the Moslem.

Now it so happened that this judge was one of the most overbearing, and at the same time most griping and corrupt curmudgeons in all Granada. It could not be denied, however, that he set a high value upon justice, for he sold it at its weight in gold. He presumed the case in point to be one of murder and robbery; doubtless there must be a rich spoil; how was it to be secured into the legitimate hands of the law; for as to merely entrapping the delinquent—that would be feeding the gallows; but entrapping the booty—that would be enriching the judge, and such, according to his creed, was the great end of justice. So thinking, he summoned to his presence his trustiest constable—a gaunt, hungry-looking varlet, clad, according to the custom of his order, in the ancient Spanish garb, a broad black beaver turned up at its sides; a quaint ruff; a small black cloak dangling from his shoulders; rusty black underclothes that set off his spare, wiry frame, while in his hand he bore a slender white wand, the dreaded insignia of his office. Such was the legal bloodhound of the ancient Spanish breed, that he put upon the traces of the unlucky water-carrier, and such was his speed and certainty, that he was upon the haunches of poor Peregil before he had returned to his dwelling, and brought both him and his donkey before the dispenser of justice.

The judge bent upon him one of the most terrific frowns. "Hark ye, culprit!" roared he, in a voice that made the knees of the little water-carrier smite together,—"hark ye, culprit! there is no need of denying thy guilt, everything is known to me. A gallows is the proper reward for the crime thou hast committed, but I am merciful, and readily listen to reason. The man that has been murdered in thy house was a Moor, an infidel, the enemy of our faith. It was doubtless in a fit of religious zeal that thou hast slain him. I will be indulgent, therefore; render up the property of which thou hast robbed him, and we will hush the matter up."

The water-carrier related the whole story of the dying Moor with the straightforward simplicity of truth, but it was all in vain. "Wilt thou persist in saying," demanded the judge, "that this Moslem had neither gold nor jewels, which were the object of thy cupidity?"

"As I hope to be saved, your worship," replied the water-carrier, he had nothing but a small box of sandal-wood, which he bequeathed to me in reward for my services."

"A box of sandal-wood; a box of sandal-wood?" exclaimed the judge, his eyes sparkling at the idea of precious jewels.

"And where is this box? where have you concealed it?"

"An' it please your grace," replied the water-carrier, "it is in one of the panniers of my mule, and heartily at the service of your worship."

He had hardly spoken the words, when the keen constable darted off, and reappeared in an instant with the mysterious box of sandal-wood. The judge opened it with an eager and trembling hand; all pressed forward to gaze upon the treasure it was expected to contain; when, to their disappointment, nothing appeared within, but a parchment scroll, covered with Arabic characters, and an end of a waxen taper.

When there is nothing to be gained by the conviction of a prisoner, justice, even in Spain, is apt to be impartial. The judge, having recovered from his disappointment, and found that there was really no booty in the case, now listened dispassionately to the explanation of the water carrier, which was corroborated by the testimony of his wife. Being convinced, therefore, of his innocence, he discharged him from arrest; nay, more, he permitted him to carry off the Moor's legacy, the box of sandal-wood and its contents, as the well-merited reward of his humanity; but he retained his donkey in payment of costs and charges.

Behold the unfortunate little Peregil reduced once more to the necessity of being his own water-carrier, and trudging up to the well of the Alhambra with a great earthen jar upon his shoulder.

As he toiled up the hill in the heat of a summer noon, his usual good-humor forsook him. "Dog of a judge!" would he cry, "to rob a poor man of the means of his subsistence, of the best friend he had in the world!" And then at the remembrance of the beloved companion of his labors, all the kindness of his nature would break forth. "Ah, donkey of my heart!" would he exclaim; resting his burden on a stone, and wiping the sweat from his brow,—"ah, donkey of my heart! I warrant me thou thinkest of thy old master! I warrant me thou missest the water-jars—poor beast."

To add to his afflictions, his wife received him, on his return home, with whimperings and repinings; she had clearly the vantage-ground of him, having warned him not to commit the egregious act of hospitality which had brought on him all these misfortunes; and, like a knowing woman, she took every occasion to throw her superior sagacity in his teeth. If her children lacked food, or needed a new garment, she could answer with a sneer, "Go to your father—he is heir to king Chico of the Alhambra: ask him to help you out of the Moor's strong box."

Was ever poor mortal so soundly punished for having done a good action? The unlucky Peregil was grieved in flesh and spirit, but still he bore meekly with the railings of his spouse. At length, one evening, when, after a hot day's toil, she taunted him in the usual manner, he lost all patience. He did not venture to retort upon her, but his eye rested upon the box of sandal-wood, which lay on a shelf with lid half open, as if laughing in mockery at his vexation. Seizing it up, he dashed it with indignation to the floor. "Unlucky was the day that I ever set eyes on thee," he cried, "or sheltered thy master beneath my roof!"

As the box struck the floor, the lid flew wide open, and the parchment scroll rolled forth.

Peregil sat regarding the scroll for some time in moody silence. At length rallying his ideas, "Who knows," thought he, "but this writing may be of some importance, as the Moor seems to have guarded it with such care?" Picking it up therefore, he put it in his bosom, and the next morning, as he was crying water through the streets, he stopped at the shop of a Moor, a native of Tangiers, who sold trinkets and perfumery, and asked him to explain the contents.

The Moor read the scroll attentively, then stroked his beard and smiled. "This manuscript," said he, "is a form of incantation for the recovery of hidden treasure that is under the power of enchantment. It is said to have such virtue that the strongest bolts and bars, nay the hardest rock itself, will yield before it!"

"Bah!" cried Peregil, "what is all that to me? I am no enchanter, and know nothing of buried treasure." So saying, he shouldered his water-jar, left the scroll in the hands of the Moor, and trudged forward on his daily rounds.

That evening, however, as he rested himself about twilight at the well of the Alhambra, he found a number of gossips assembled at the place, and their conversation, as is not unusual at that shadowy hour, turned upon old tales and traditions of a supernatural nature. Being all poor as rats, they dwelt with peculiar fondness upon the popular theme of enchanted riches left by the Moors in various parts of the Alhambra. Above all they concurred in the belief that there were great treasures buried deep in the earth under the tower of the seven floors.

These stories made an unusual impression on the mind of the honest Peregil, and they sank deeper and deeper into his thoughts as he returned alone down the dark avenues. "If, after all, there should be treasure hid beneath that tower: and if the scroll I left with the Moor should enable me to get at it!" In the sudden ecstasy of the thought he had well-nigh let fall his water-jar.

That night he tumbled and tossed, and could scarcely get a wink of sleep for the thoughts that were bewildering his brain. Bright and early he repaired to the shop of the Moor, and told him all that was passing in his mind. "You can read Arabic," said he; "suppose we go together to the tower, and try the effect of the charm; if it fails, we are no worse off than before; but if it succeeds, we will share equally all the treasure, we may discover."

"Hold," replied the Moslem; "this writing is not sufficient of itself; it must be read at midnight, by the light of a taper singularly compounded and prepared, the ingredients of which are not within my reach. Without such a taper the scroll is of no avail."

"Say no more!" cried little Peregil; "I have such a taper at hand, and will bring it here in a moment." So saying, he hastened home, and soon returned with the end of yellow wax taper that he had found in the box of sandal-wood.

The Moor felt it and smelt of it. "Here are rare and costly perfumes," said he, "combined with this yellow wax. This is the kind of taper specified in the scroll. While this burns, the strongest walls and most secret caverns will remain open. Woe to him, however, who lingers within until it be extinguished. He will remain enchanted with the treasure."

It was now agreed between them to try the charm that very night. At a late hour, therefore, when nothing was stirring but bats and owls, they ascended the woody hill of the Alhambra, and approached that awful tower, shrouded by trees and rendered formidable by so many traditionary tales. By the light of a lantern they groped their way through bushes, and over fallen stones, to the door of a vault beneath the tower. With fear and trembling they descended a flight of steps cut into the rock. It led to an empty chamber, damp and drear, from which another flight of steps led to a deeper vault. In this way they descended four several flights, leading into as many vaults, one below the other, but the floor of the fourth was solid; and though, according to tradition, there remained three vaults still below, it was said to be impossible to penetrate further, the residue being shut up by strong enchantment. The air of this vault was damp and chilly, and had an earthy smell, and the light scarce cast forth any rays. They. paused here for a time, in breathless suspense, until they faintly heard the clock of the watch-tower strike midnight; upon this they lit the waxen taper, which diffused an odor of myrrh and frankincense and storax.

The Moor began to read in a hurried voice. He had scarce finished when there was a noise as of subterraneous thunder. The earth shook, and the floor, yawning open, disclosed a flight of steps. Trembling with awe, they descended, and by the light of the lantern found themselves in another vault covered with Arabic inscriptions. In the centre stood a great chest, secured with seven bands of steel, at each end of which sat an enchanted Moor in armor, but motionless as a statue, being controlled by the power of the incantation. Before the chest were several jars filled with gold and silver and precious stones. In the largest of these they thrust their arms up to the elbow, and at every dip hauled forth handfuls of broad yellow pieces of Moorish gold, or bracelets and ornaments of the same precious metal, while occasionally a necklace of Oriental pearl would stick to their fingers. Still they trembled and breathed short while cramming their pockets with the spoils; and cast many a fearful glance at the two enchanted Moors, who sat grim and motionless, glaring upon them with unwinking eyes. At length, struck with a sudden panic at some fancied noise, they both rushed up the staircase, tumbled over one mother into the upper apartment, overturned and extinguished the waxen taper, and the pavement again closed with a thundering sound.

Filled with dismay, they did not pause until they had groped their way out of the tower, and beheld the stars shining through the trees. Then seating themselves upon the grass, they divided the spoil, determining to content themselves for the present with this mere skimming of the jars, but to return on some future night and drain them to the bottom. To make sure of each other's good faith, also, they divided the talismans between them, one retaining the scroll and the other the taper; this done, they set off with light hearts and well-lined pockets for Granada.

As they wended their way down the hill, the shrewd Moor whispered a word of council in the ear of the simple little water-carrier.

"Friend Peregil," said he, "all this affair must be kept a profound secret until we have secured the treasure, and conveyed it out of harm's way. If a whisper of it gets to the ear of the judge, we are undone!"

"Certainly," replied Peregil, "nothing can be more true."

"Friend Peregil," said the Moor, "you are a discreet man, and I make no doubt can keep a secret; but you have a wife."

"She shall not know a word of it," replied the little water-carrier, sturdily.

Enough," said the Moor, "I depend upon thy discretion and thy promise."

Never was promise more positive and sincere; but, alas! what man can keep a secret from his wife? Certainly not such a one as Peregil the water-carrier, who was one of the most loving and tractable of husbands. On his return home, he found his wife moping in a corner. "Mighty well," cried she as he entered, "you've come at last, after rambling about until this hour of the night. I wonder you have not brought home another Moor as a house-mate." Then bursting into tears, she began to wring her hands and smite her breast. "Unhappy woman that I am!" exclaimed she, "what will become of me? My house stripped and plundered by lawyers and constables; my husband a do-no-good, that no longer brings home bread to his family, but goes rambling about day and night, with infidel Moors! O my children! my children! what will become of us? We shall all have to beg in the streets!"

Honest Peregil was so moved by the distress of his spouse, that he could not help whimpering also. His heart was as full as his pocket, and not to be restrained. Thrusting his hand into the latter he hauled forth three or four broad gold pieces, and slipped them into her hand. The poor woman stared with astonishment, and could not understand the meaning of this golden shower. Before she could recover her surprise, her husband drew forth a chain of gold and dangled it before her, capering with exultation, his mouth distended from ear to ear.

"What hast thou been doing, Peregil?" exclaimed the wife; "surely thou hast not been committing murder and robbery!"

The idea scarce entered the brain of the poor woman, than it became a certainty with her. She saw a prison and a gallows in the distance, and a little bandy-legged water-carrier hanging pendent from it; and, overcome by the horrors conjured up by imagination, fell into violent hysterics.

What could the poor man do? He had no other means of pacifying his wife, and dispelling the phantoms of her fancy, than by relating the whole story of his good fortune. This, however, he did not do until he had exacted from her the most solemn promise to keep it a profound secret from every living being.

To describe her joy would be impossible. She flung her arms round the neck of her husband, and almost strangled him with her caresses. "Now, wife," exclaimed the little man with honest exultation, "what say you now to the Moor's legacy? Henceforth never abuse me for helping a fellow-creature in distress."

The honest Peregil retired to his sheep-skin mat, and slept as soundly as if on a bed of down. Not so his wife; she emptied the whole contents of his pockets upon the mat, and sat counting gold pieces of Arabic coin, trying on necklaces and earrings, and fancying the figure she should one day make when permitted to enjoy her riches.

On the following morning the honest water-carrier took a broad golden coin, and repaired with it to a jeweler's shop to offer it for sale, pretending to have found it among the ruins of the Alhambra. The jeweler saw that it had an Arabic inscription, and was of the purest gold; he offered, however, but a third of its value, with which the water-carrier was perfectly content. Peregil now bought new clothes for his little flock, and all kinds of toys, together with ample provisions for a hearty meal, and returning to his dwelling, set all his children dancing around him, while he capered in the midst, the happiest of fathers.

The wife of the water-carrier kept her promise of secrecy with surprising strictness. For a whole day and a half she went about with a look of mystery and a heart swelling almost to bursting, yet she held her peace, though surrounded by her gossips. It is true, she could not help giving herself a few airs, apologized for her ragged dress, and talked of ordering a new basquina all trimmed with gold lace and bugles, and a new lace mantilla. She threw out hints of her husband's intention of leaving off his trade of water-carrying, as it did not altogether agree with his health. In fact she thought they should all retire to the country for the summer, that the children might have the benefit of the mountain air, for there was no living in the city this sultry season.

The neighbors stared at each other, and thought the poor woman had lost her wits; and her airs and graces and elegant pretensions were the theme of universal scoffing and merriment among her friends, the moment her back was turned.

If she restrained herself abroad, however, she indemnified herself at home, and putting a string of rich Oriental pearls round her neck, Moorish bracelets on her arms, and an aigrette of diamonds on her head, sailed backwards and forwards in her slattern rags about the room, now and then stopping to admire herself in a broken mirror. Nay, in the impulse of her simple vanity, she could not resist, on one occasion, showing herself at the window to enjoy the effect of her finery on the passers-by.

As the fates would have it, Pedrillo Pedrugo, the meddlesome barber, was at this moment sitting idly in his shop on the opposite side of the street, when his ever-watchful eye caught the sparkle of a diamond. In an instant he was at his loophole reconnoitring the slattern spouse of the water-carrier, decorated with the splendor of an eastern bride. No sooner had he taken an accurate inventory of her ornaments, than he posted off with all speed to the judge. In a little while the hungry constable was again on the scent, and before the day was over the unfortunate Peregil was once more dragged into the presence of the judge.

"How is this, villain!" cried the judge, in a furious voice. "You told me that the infidel who died in your house left nothing behind but an empty coffer, and now I hear of your wife flaunting in her rags decked out with pearls and diamonds. Wretch that thou art! prepare to render up the spoils of thy miserable victim, and to swing on the gallows that is already tired of waiting for thee."

The terrified water-carrier fell on his knees, and made a full relation of the marvellous manner in which he had gained his wealth. The judge, the constable, and the inquisitive barber listened with greedy ears to this Arabian tale of enchanted treasure. The constable was dispatched to bring the Moor who had assisted in the incantation. The Moslem entered half frightened out of his wits at finding himself in the clutches of the law. When he beheld the water-carrier standing with sheepish looks and down-cast countenance, he comprehended the whole matter. "Miserable animal," said he, as he passed near him, "did I not warn thee against babbling to thy wife?"

The story of the Moor coincided exactly with that of his colleague; but the judge affected to be slow of belief, and threw out menaces of imprisonment and rigorous investigation.

"Softly, good Sir judge," said the Mussulman, who by this time had recovered his usual shrewdness and self-possession. "Let us not mar fortune's favors in the scramble for them. Nobody knows anything of this matter but ourselves; let us keep the secret. There is wealth enough in the cave to enrich us all. Promise a fair division, and all shall be produced; refuse, and the cave shall remain forever closed."

The judge consulted apart with the constable. The latter was an old fox in his profession. Promise anything," said he, "until you get possession of the treasure. You may then seize upon the whole, and if he and his accomplice dare to murmur, threaten them with the fagot and the stake as infidels and sorcerers."

The judge relished the advice. Smoothing his brow and turning to the Moor, "This is a strange story," said he, "and may be true, but I must have ocular proof of it. This very night you must repeat the incantation in my presence. If there be really such treasure, we will share it amicably between us, and say nothing further of the matter; if ye have deceived me, expect no mercy at my hands. In the meantime you must remain in custody."

The Moor and the water-carrier cheerfully agreed to these conditions, satisfied that the event would prove the truth of their words.

Towards midnight the judge sallied forth secretly, attended by the constable and the meddlesome barber, all strongly armed. They conducted the Moor and the water-carrier as prisoners, and were provided with the stout donkey of the latter to bear off the expected treasure. They arrived at the tower without being observed, and tying the donkey to a fig-tree, descended into the fourth vault of the tower.

The scroll was produced, the yellow waxen taper lighted, and the Moor read the form of incantation. The earth trembled as before, and the pavement opened with a thundering sound, disclosing the narrow flight of steps. The judge, the constable, and the barber were struck aghast, and could not summon courage to descend. The Moor and the water-carrier entered the lower vault, and found the two Moors seated as before, silent and motionless. They removed two of the great jars, filled with golden coin and precious stones. The water-carrier bore them up one by one upon his shoulders, but though a strong-backed little man, and accustomed to carry burdens, he staggered beneath their weight, and found, when slung on each side of his donkey, they were as much as the animal could bear.

"Let us be content for the present," said the Moor; "here is as much treasure as we can carry off without being perceived, and enough to make us all wealthy to our heart's desire."

"Is there more treasure remaining behind?" demanded the judge.

"The greatest prize of all," said the Moor, "a huge coffer bound with bands of steel, and filled with pearls and precious stones."

"Let us have up the coffer by all means," cried the grasping judge.

"I will descend for no more," said the Moor, doggedly; "enough is enough for a reasonable man—more is superfluous."

"And I," said the water-carrier, will bring up no further burden to break the back of my poor donkey."

Finding commands, threats, and entreaties equally vain, the judge turned to his two adherents. "Aid me," said he, "to bring up the coffer, and its contents shall be divided between us." So saying, he descended the steps, followed with trembling reluctance by the constable and the barber.

No sooner did the Moor behold them fairly earthed than he extinguished the yellow taper; the pavement closed with its usual crash, and the three worthies remained buried beneath it.

He then hastened up the different flight of steps, nor stopped until in the open air. The little water-carrier followed him as fast as his short legs would permit.

"What hast thou done?" cried Peregil, as soon as he could recover breath. "The judge and the other two are shut up in the vault."

"It is the will of Allah!" said the Moor, devoutly.

"And will you not release them?" demanded the water-carrier.

"Allah forbid!" replied the Moor, smoothing his beard. "It is written in the book of fate that they shall remain enchanted until some future adventurer arrive to break the charm. The will of Allah be done!" so saying, he hurled the end of the waxen taper far among the gloomy thickets of the glen.

There was now no remedy; so the Moor and the water-carrier proceeded with the richly laden donkey toward the city, nor could honest Peregil refrain from hugging and kissing his long-eared fellow-laborer, thus restored to him from the clutches of the law; and, in fact, it is doubtful which gave the simple-hearted little man most joy at the moment, the gaining of the treasure, or the recovery of the donkey.

The two partners in good luck divided their spoil amicably and fairly, except that the Moor, who had a little taste for trinketry, made out to get into his heap the most of the pearls and precious stones, but then he always gave the water-carrier instead magnificent jewels of massy gold, of five times the size, with which the latter was heartily content. They took care not to linger within reach of accidents, but made off to enjoy their wealth undisturbed in other countries. The Moor returned to Africa, to his native city of Tangiers, and the water-carrier, with his wife, his children, and his donkey, made the best of his way to Portugal. Here, under the admonition and tuition of his wife, he became a personage of some consequence, for she made the worthy little man array his long body and short legs in doublet and hose, with a feather in his hat and a sword by his side, and laying aside his familiar appellation of Peregil, assumed the more sonorous title of Don Pedro Gil: his progeny grew up a thriving and merry-hearted, though short and bandy-legged generation, while Señor a Gil, befringed, belaced, and betasselled from her head to her heels, with glittering rings on every finger, became a model of slattern fashion and finery.

As to the judge and his associates, they remained shut up under the great tower of the seven floors, and there they remain spellbound at the present day. Whenever there shall be a lack in Spain of meddling barbers, sharking constables, and corrupt judges, they may be sought after; but if they have to wait until such time for their deliverance, there is danger of their enchantment enduring until doomsday

Legend of the Three Beautiful Princesses

In old times there reigned a Moorish king in Granada, whose name was Mohamed, to which his subjects added the appellation of "The Left-handed." Some say he was so called on account of his being really more expert with his sinister than his dexter hand; others, because he was prone to take everything by the wrong end, or, in other words, to mar wherever he meddled. Certain it is, either through misfortune or mismanagement, he was continually in trouble: thrice was he driven from his throne, and on one occasion barely escaped to Africa with his life, in the disguise of a fisherman. Still he was as brave as he was blundering; and though left-handed, wielded his cimeter to such purpose, that he each time reëstablished himself upon his throne by dint of hard fighting. Instead, however, of learning wisdom from adversity, he hardened his neck, and stiffened his left arm in willfulness. The evils of a public nature which he thus brought upon himself and his kingdom may be learned by those who will delve into the Arabian annals of Granada; the present legend deals but with his domestic policy.

As this Mohamed was one day riding forth with a train of his courtiers, by the foot of the mountain of Elvira, he met a band of horsemen returning from a foray into the land of the Christians. They were conducting a long string of mules laden with spoil, and many captives of both sexes, among whom the monarch was struck with the appearance of a beautiful damsel, richly attired, who sat weeping on a low palfrey, and heeded not the consoling words of a duenna who rode beside her.

The monarch was struck with her beauty, and, on inquiring of the captain of the troop, found that she was the daughter of the governor of a frontier fortress, that had been surprised and sacked in the course of the foray. Mohamed claimed her as his royal share of the booty, and had her conveyed to the Alhambra. There everything was devised to soothe her melancholy; and the monarch sought to make her his queen. The Spanish maid at first repulsed his addresses: he was an infidel; he was the open foe of her country; what was worse, he was stricken in years!

The monarch, finding his assiduities of no avail, determined to enlist in his favor the duenna, who had been captured with the lady. She was an Andalusian by birth, whose Christian name is forgotten, being mentioned in Moorish legends by no other appellation than that of the discreet Kadiga; and discreet in truth she was, as her whole history makes evident. No sooner had the Moorish king held a little private conversation with her, than she saw at once the cogency of his reasoning, and undertook his cause with her young mistress.

"Go to, now!" cried she; "what is there in all this to weep and wail about?, Is it not better to be mistress of this beautiful palace, with all its gardens and fountains, than to be shut up within your father's old frontier tower? As to this Mohamed being an infidel, what is that to the purpose? You marry him, not his religion; and if he is waxing a little old, the sooner will you be a widow, and mistress of yourself; at any rate, you are in his power, and must either be a queen or a slave."

The arguments of the discreet Kadiga prevailed: The Spanish lady dried her tears, and became the spouse of Mohamed the Left-handed; she even conformed, in appearance, to the faith of her royal husband; and her discreet duenna immediately became a zealous convert to the Moslem doctrines: it was then the latter received the Arabian name of Kadiga, and was permitted to remain in the confidential employ of her mistress.

In time the Moorish king was made the proud and happy father of three lovely daughters, all born at the same time.

As usual with all Moslem monarchs, he summoned his astrologers on this happy event. They cast the nativities of the three princesses, and shook their heads. "Daughters, O king!" said they, "are always precarious property; but these will most need your watchfulness when they arrive at a marriageable age; at that time gather them under your wings, and trust them to no other guardianship."

Mohamed the Left-handed was acknowledged to be a wise king by his courtiers, and was certainly so considered by himself. The prediction of the astrologers caused him but little disquiet, trusting to his ingenuity to guard his daughters and outwit the Fates.

The queen died within a few years, bequeathing her infant daughters to his love, and to the fidelity of the discreet Kadiga.

Many years had yet to elapse before the princesses would arrive at that period of danger—the marriageable age. "It is good, however, to be cautious in time," said the shrewd monarch; so he determined to have them reared in the royal castle of Salobreña. This was a sumptuous palace, incrusted, as it were, in a powerful Moorish fortress on the summit of a hill overlooking the Mediterranean sea. It was a royal retreat, in which the Moslem monarchs shut up such of their relatives as might endanger their safety; allowing them all kinds of luxuries and amusements, in the midst of which they passed their lives in voluptuous indolence.

Here the princesses remained, immured from the world, but surrounded by enjoyment, and attended by female slaves who anticipated their wishes. They had delightful gardens for their recreation, filled with the rarest fruits and flowers, with aromatic groves and perfumed baths. On three sides the castle looked down upon a rich valley, enriched with all kinds of culture, and bounded by the lofty Alpuxarra mountains; on the other side it overlooked the broad sunny sea.

In this delicious abode, in a propitious climate, and under a cloudless sky, the three princesses grew up into wondrous beauty; but, though all reared alike, they gave early tokens of diversity of character. Their names were Zayda, Zorayda, and Zorahayda.

Zayda, the eldest, was of an intrepid spirit, and took the lead of her sisters in everything. She was curious and inquisitive, and fond of getting at the bottom of things.

Zorayda had a great feeling for beauty, which was the reason, no doubt, of her delighting to regard her own image in a mirror or a fountain, and of her fondness for flowers, and jewels, and other tasteful ornaments.

As to Zorahayda, the youngest, she was soft and timid, and extremely sensitive, with a vast deal of disposable tenderness, as was evident from her number of pet flowers, and pet birds, and pet animals, all of which she cherished with the fondest care. Her amusements, too, were of a gentle nature, and mixed up with musing and reverie. She would sit for hours in a balcony, gazing on the sparkling stars of a summer's night, or on the sea when lit up by the moon; and at such times, the song of a fisherman, faintly heard from the beach, or the notes of a Moorish flute from some gliding bark, sufficed to elevate her feelings into ecstasy. The least uproar of the elements, however, filled her with dismay; and a clap of thunder was enough to throw her into a swoon.

Years rolled on smoothly and serenely; the discreet Kadiga, to whom the princesses were confided, was faithful to her trust, and attended them with unremitting care.

The castle of Salobreña, as has been said, was built upon a hill on the sea-coast. One of the exterior walls straggled down the profile of the hill; until it reached a jutting rock overhanging the sea, with a narrow sandy beach at its foot, laved by the rippling billows. A small watch-tower on this rock had been fitted up as a pavilion, with latticed windows to admit the sea-breeze. Here the princesses used to pass the sultry hours of mid-day.

The curious Zayda was one day seated at a window of the pavilion, as her sisters, reclining on ottomans, were taking the siesta or noontide slumber. Her attention was attracted to a galley which came coasting along, with measured strokes of the oar. As it drew near she observed that it was filled with armed men. The galley anchored at the foot of the tower: a number of Moorish soldiers landed on the narrow beach, conducting several Christian prisoners. The curious Zayda awakened her sisters, and all three peeped cautiously through the close jalousies of the lattice which screened them from sight. Among the prisoners were three Spanish cavaliers, richly dressed. They were in the flower of youth, and of noble presence; and the lofty manner in which they carried themselves, though loaded with chains and surrounded with enemies, bespoke the grandeur of their souls. The princesses gazed with intense and breathless interest. Cooped up as they had been in this castle among female attendants, seeing nothing of the male sex but black slaves, or the rude fishermen of the sea-coast, it is not to be wondered at that the appearance of three gallant cavaliers, in the pride of youth and manly beauty, should produce some commotion in their bosoms.

"Did ever nobler being tread the earth than that cavalier in crimson?" cried Zayda, the eldest of the sisters.

"See how proudly he bears himself, as though all around him were his slaves!"

"But notice that one in green!" exclaimed Zorayda. "What grace! what elegance! what spirit!"

The gentle Zorahayda said nothing, but she secretly gave preference to the cavalier in blue.

The princesses remained gazing until the prisoners were out of sight; then heaving long-drawn sighs, they turned round, looked at each other for a moment, and sat down, musing and pensive, on their ottomans.

The discreet Kadiga found them in this situation; they related what they had seen, and even the withered heart of the duenna was warmed. "Poor youths!" exclaimed she, "I'll warrant their captivity makes many a fair and high-born lady's heart ache in their native land! Ah! my children, you have little idea of the life these cavaliers lead in their own country. Such sporting at tournaments! such devotion to the ladies! such courting and serenading!"

The curiosity of Zayda was fully aroused; she was insatiable in her inquiries, and drew from the duenna the most animated pictures of the scenes of her youthful days and native land. The beautiful Zorayda bridled up, and slyly regarded herself in a mirror, when the theme turned upon the charms of the Spanish ladies; while Zorahayda suppressed a struggling sigh at the mention of moonlight serenades.

Every day the curious Zayda renewed her inquiries, and every day the sage duenna repeated her stories, which were listened to with profound interest, though with frequent sighs by her gentle auditors. The discreet old woman awoke at length to the mischief she might be doing. She had been accustomed to think of the princesses only as children; but they had imperceptibly ripened beneath her eye, and now bloomed before her three lovely damsels of the marriageable age. It is time, thought the duenna, to give notice to the king.

Mohamed the Left-handed was seated one morning on a divan in a cool hall of the Alhambra, when a slave arrived from the fortress of Salobreña, with a message from the sage Kadiga, congratulating him on the anniversary of his daughters' birthday. The slave at the same time presented a delicate little basket decorated with flowers, within which, on a couch of vine and fig-leaves, lay a peach, an apricot, and a nectarine, with their bloom and down and dewy sweetness upon them, and all in the early stage of tempting ripeness. The monarch was versed in the Oriental language of fruits and flowers, and rapidly divined the meaning of this emblematical offering.

"So," said he, "the critical period pointed out by the astrologers is arrived: my daughters are at a marriageable age. What is to be done? They are shut up from the eyes of men; they are under the eyes of the discreet Kadiga,—all very good,—but still they are not under my own eye, as was prescribed by the astrologers: I must gather them under my wing, and trust to no other guardianship."

So saying, he ordered that a tower of the Alhambra should be prepared for their reception, and departed at the head of his guards for the fortress of Salobreña, to conduct them home in person.

About three years had elapsed since Mohamed had beheld his daughters, and he could scarcely credit his eyes at the wonderful change which that small space of time had made in their appearance. During the interval, they had passed that wondrous boundary line in female life which separates the crude, unformed, and thoughtless girl from the blooming, blushing, meditative woman. It is like passing from the flat, bleak, uninteresting plains of La Mancha to the voluptuous valleys and swelling hills of Andalusia.

Zayda was tall and finely formed, with a lofty demeanor and a penetrating eye. She entered with a stately and decided step, and made a profound reverence to Mohamed, treating him more as her sovereign than her father. Zorayda was of the middle height, with an alluring look and swimming gait, and a sparkling beauty, heightened by the assistance of the toilet. She approached her father with a smile, kissed his hand, and saluted him with several stanzas from a popular Arabian poet, with which the monarch was delighted. Zorahayda was shy and timid, smaller than her sisters, and with a beauty of that tender beseeching kind which looks for fondness and protection. She drew near to her father, with a timid and almost faltering step, and would have taken his hand to kiss, but on looking up into his face, and seeing it beaming with a paternal smile, the tenderness of her nature broke forth, and she threw herself upon his neck.

Mohamed the Left-handed surveyed his blooming daughters with mingled pride and perplexity, for while he exulted in their charms, he bethought himself of the prediction of the astrologers.

He prepared for his return to Granada, by sending heralds before him, commanding every one to keep out of the road by which he was to pass, and that all doors and windows should be closed at the approach of the princesses. This done, he set forth, escorted by a troop of black horsemen of hideous aspect, and clad in shining armor.

The princesses rode beside the king, closely veiled, on beautiful white palfreys, with velvet caparisons, embroidered with gold, and sweeping the ground; the bits and stirrups were of gold, and the silken bridles adorned with pearls and precious stones. The palfreys were covered with little silver bells, which made the most musical tinkling as they ambled gently along. Woe to the unlucky wight, however, who lingered in the way when he heard the tinkling of these bells!—the guards were ordered to cut him down without mercy.

The cavalcade was drawing near to Granada, when it overtook, on the banks of the river Xenil, a small body of Moorish soldiers with a convoy of prisoners. It was too late for the soldiers to get out of the way, so they threw themselves on their faces on the earth, ordering their captives to do the like. Among the prisoners were the three identical cavaliers whom the princesses had seen from the pavilion. They either did not understand, or were too haughty to obey the order, and remained standing and gazing upon the cavalcade as it approached.

The ire of the monarch was kindled at this flagrant defiance of his orders. Drawing his cimeter, and pressing forward, he was about to deal a left-handed blow that might have been fatal to at least one of the gazers, when the princesses crowded round him, and implored mercy for the prisoners; even the timid Zorahayda forgot her shyness, and became eloquent in their behalf.

Mohamed paused, with uplifted cimeter, when the, captain of the guard threw himself at his feet. "Let not your highness," said he, "do a deed that may cause great scandal throughout the kingdom. These are three brave and noble Spanish knights, who have been taken in battle, fighting like lions; they are of high birth, and may bring great ransoms." "—Enough!" said the king. "I will spare their lives, but punish their audacity—let them be taken to the Vermilion Towers, and put to hard labor."

Mohamed was making one of his usual left-handed blunders. In the tumult and agitation of this blustering scene, the veils of the three princesses had been thrown back, and the radiance of their beauty revealed; and in prolonging the parley, the king had given that beauty time to have its full effect. In those days people fell in love much more suddenly than at present, as all ancient stories make manifest: it is not a matter of wonder, therefore, that the hearts of the three cavaliers were completely captured; especially as gratitude was added to their admiration; it is a little singular, however, though no less certain, that each of them was enraptured with a different beauty. As to the princesses, they were more than ever struck with the noble demeanor of the captives, and cherished in their breasts all that they had heard of their valor and noble lineage.

The cavalcade resumed its march; the three princesses rode pensively along on their tinkling palfreys, now and then stealing a glance behind in search of the Christian captives, and the latter were conducted to their allotted prison in the Vermilion Towers.

The residence provided for the princesses was one of the most dainty that fancy could devise. It was in a tower somewhat apart from the main palace of the Alhambra, though connected with it by the wall which encircled the whole summit of the hill. On one side it looked into the interior of the fortress, and had, at its foot, a small garden filled with the rarest flowers. On the other side it overlooked a deep embowered ravine separating the grounds of the Alhambra from those of the Generalife. The interior of the tower was divided into small fairy apartments, beautifully ornamented in the light Arabian style, surrounding a lofty hall, the vaulted roof of which rose almost to the summit of the tower. The walls and the ceilings of the hall were adorned with arabesque and fretwork, sparkling with gold and with brilliant penciling. In the centre of the marble pavement was an alabaster fountain, set round with aromatic shrubs and flowers, and throwing up a jet of water that cooled the whole edifice and had a lulling sound. Round the hall were suspended cages of gold and silver wire, containing singing-birds of the finest plumage or sweetest note.

The princesses had been represented as always cheerful when in the Castle of the Salobreña; the king had expected to see them enraptured with the Alhambra. To his surprise, however, they began to pine, and grow melancholy, and dissatisfied with everything around them. The flowers yielded them no fragrance, the song of the nightingale disturbed their night's rest, and they were out of all patience with the alabaster fountain, with its eternal drop-drop and splash-splash, from morning till night and from night till morning.

The king, who was somewhat of a testy, tyrannical disposition, took this at first in high dudgeon; but he reflected that his daughters had arrived at an age when the female mind expands and its desires augment. "They are no longer children," said he to himself, "they are women grown, and require suitable objects to interest them." He put in requisition, therefore, all the dress-makers, and the jewelers, and the artificers in gold and silver throughout the shops of Granada, and the princesses were overwhelmed with robes of silk, and tissue, and brocade, and cashmere shawls, and necklaces of pearls and diamonds, and rings, and bracelets, and anklets, and all manner of precious things.

All, however, was of no avail; the princesses continued pale and languid in the midst of their finery, and looked like three blighted rose-buds, drooping from one stalk. The king was at his wit's end. He had in general a laudable confidence in his own judgment, and never took advice. "The whims and caprices of three marriageable damsels, however, are sufficient," said he, "to puzzle the shrewdest head." So for once in his life he called in the aid of counsel.

The person to whom he applied was the experienced duenna.

"Kadiga," said the king, "I know you to be one of the most discreet women in the whole world, as well as one of the most trustworthy; for these reasons I have always continued you about the persons of my daughters. I now wish you to find out the secret malady that is preying upon the princesses, and to devise some means of restoring them to health and cheerfulness."

Kadiga promised implicit obedience. In fact she knew more of the malady of the princesses than they themselves. Shutting herself up with them, however, she endeavored to insinuate herself into their confidence.

"My dear children, what is the reason you are so dismal and downcast in so beautiful a place, where you have everything that heart can wish?"

The princesses looked vacantly round the apartment, and sighed.

"What more, then, would you have? Shall I get you the wonderful parrot that talks all languages, and is the delight of Granada?"

"Odious!" exclaimed the princess Zayda. "A horrid, screaming bird, that chatters words without ideas: one must be without brains to tolerate such a pest."

"Shall I send for a monkey from the rock of Gibraltar, to divert you with his antics?"

"A monkey! faugh!" cried Zorayda; "the detestable mimic of man. I hate the nauseous animal."

"What say you to the famous black singer Casem, from Morocco? They say he has a voice as fine as a woman's."

"I am terrified at the sight of these black slaves," said the delicate Zorahayda; "besides, I have lost all relish for music."

"Ah! my child, you would not say so," replied the old woman, slyly, "had you heard the music I heard last evening, from the three Spanish cavaliers whom we met on our journey. But bless me, children! what is the matter that you blush so and are in such a flutter?"

"Nothing, nothing, good mother; pray proceed."

"Well; as I was passing by the Vermilion Towers last evening, I saw the three cavaliers resting after their day's labor. One was playing on the guitar, so gracefully, and the others sang by turns; and they did it in such style, that the very guards seemed like statues, or men enchanted. Allah forgive me! I could not help being moved at hearing the songs of my native country. And then to see three such noble and handsome youths in chains and slavery!"

Here the kind-hearted old woman could not restrain her tears.

"Perhaps, mother, you could manage to procure us a sight of these cavaliers," said Zayda.

"I think," said Zorayda, "a little music would be quite reviving."

The timid Zorahayda said nothing, but threw her arms round the neck of Kadiga.

"Mercy on me!" exclaimed the discreet old woman, "what are you talking of, my children? Your father would be the death of us all if he heard of such a thing. To be sure, these cavaliers are evidently well-bred, and high-minded youths; but what of that? they are the enemies of our faith, and you must not even think of them but with abhorrence."

The princesses hung round their old duenna, and coaxed, and entreated, and declared that a refusal would break their hearts.

What could she do? She was certainly the most discreet old woman in the whole world, and one of the most faithful servants to the king; but was she to see three beautiful princesses break their hearts for the mere tinkling of a guitar? Besides, though she had been so long among the Moors, and changed her faith in imitation of her mistress, like a trusty follower, yet she was a Spaniard born, and had the lingerings of Christianity in her heart. So she set about to contrive how the wish of the princesses might be gratified.

The Christian captives, confined in the Vermilion Towers, were under the charge of a big-whiskered, broad-shouldered renegado, called Hussein Baba, who was reputed to have a most itching palm. She went to him privately, and slipping a broad piece of gold into his hand, "Hussein Baba," said she; "my mistresses the three princesses, who are shut up in the tower, and in sad want of amusement, have heard of the musical talents of the three Spanish cavaliers, and are desirous of hearing a specimen of their skill. I am sure you are too kind-hearted to refuse them so innocent a gratification."

"What! and to have my head set grinning over the gate of my own tower! for that would be the reward, if the king should discover it."

"No danger of anything of the kind; the affair may be managed so that the whim of the princesses may be gratified, and their father be never the wiser. You know the deep ravine outside of the walls which passes immediately below the tower. Put the three Christians to work there, and at the intervals of their labor, let them play and sing, as if for their own recreation. In this way the princesses will be able to hear them from the windows of the tower, and you may be sure of their paying well for your compliance."

As the good old woman concluded her harangue, she kindly pressed the rough hand of the renegado, and left within it another piece of gold.

Her eloquence was irresistible. The very next day the three cavaliers were put to work in the ravine. During the noontide heat, when their fellow-laborers were sleeping in the shade, and the guard nodding drowsily at his post, they seated themselves among the herbage at the foot of the tower, and sang a Spanish roundelay to the accompaniment of the guitar.

The glen was deep, the tower was high, but their voices rose distinctly in the stillness of the summer noon. The princesses listened from their balcony; they had been taught the Spanish language by their duenna, and were moved by the tenderness of the song. The discreet Kadiga, on the contrary, was terribly shocked. "Allah preserve us!" cried she, "they are singing a love-ditty, addressed to yourselves. Did ever mortal hear of such audacity? I will run to the slave-master, and have them soundly bastinadoed."

"What! bastinado such gallant cavaliers, and for singing so charmingly!" The three beautiful princesses were filled with horror at the idea. With all her virtuous indignation, the good old woman was of a placable nature, and easily appeased. Besides, the music seemed to have a beneficial effect upon her young mistresses. A rosy bloom had already come to their cheeks, and their eyes began to sparkle. She made no further objection, therefore, to the love-ditty of the cavaliers.

When it was finished, the princesses remained silent for a time; at length Zorayda took up a lute, and with a sweet, though faint and trembling voice, warbled a little Arabian air, the burden of which was, "The rose is concealed among her leaves, but she listens with delight to the song of the nightingale."

From this time forward the cavaliers worked almost daily in the ravine. The considerate Hussein Baba became more and more indulgent, and daily more prone to sleep at his post. For some time a vague intercourse was kept up by popular songs and romances, which in some measure responded to each other, and breathed the feelings of the parties. By degrees the princesses showed themselves at the balcony, when they could do so without being perceived by the guards. They conversed with the cavaliers also, by means of flowers, with the symbolical language of which they were mutually acquainted; the difficulties of their intercourse added to its charms, for love delights to struggle with difficulties, and thrives the most hardily on the scantiest soil.

The change effected in the looks and spirits of the princesses by this secret intercourse surprised and gratified the left-handed king; but no one was more elated than the discreet Kadiga, who considered it all owing to her able management.

At length there was an interruption in this telegraphic correspondence: for several days the cavaliers ceased to make their appearance in the glen. The princesses looked out from the tower in vain. In vain they stretched their swan-like necks from the balcony; in vain they sang like captive nightingales in their cage: nothing was to be seen of their Christian lovers; not a note responded from the groves. The discreet Kadiga sallied forth in quest of intelligence, and soon returned with a face full of trouble. "Ah, my children!" cried she, "I saw what all this would come to, but you would have your way; you may now hang up your lutes on the willows. The Spanish cavaliers are ransomed by their families; they are down in Granada, and preparing to return to their native country."

The three beautiful princesses were in despair at the tidings. Zayda was indignant at the slight put upon them, in thus being deserted without a parting word. Zorayda wrung her hands and cried, and looked in the glass and wiped away her tears, and cried afresh. The gentle Zorahayda leaned over the balcony and wept in silence, and her tears fell drop by drop among the flowers of the bank, where the faithless cavaliers had so often been seated.

The discreet Kadiga did all in her power to soothe their sorrow. "Take comfort, my children," said she; "this is nothing when you are used it. This is the way of the world. Ah! when you are as old as I am, you will know how to value these men. I'll warrant these cavaliers have their loves among the Spanish beauties of Cordova and Seville, and will soon be serenading under their balconies, and thinking no more of the Moorish beauties in the Alhambra. Take comfort, therefore, my children, and drive them from your hearts."

The comforting words of the discreet Kadiga only redoubled the distress of the three princesses, and for two days they continued inconsolable. On the morning of the third the good old woman entered their apartment, all ruffling with indignation.

"Who would have believed such insolence in mortal man!" exclaimed she, as soon as she could find words to express herself; "but I am rightly served for having connived at this deception of your worthy father. Never talk more to me of your Spanish cavaliers."

"Why, what has happened, good Kadiga?" exclaimed the princesses in breathless anxiety.

"What has happened?—treason has happened! or, what is almost as bad, treason has been proposed; and to me, the most faithful of subjects, the trustiest of duennas! Yes, my children, the Spanish cavaliers have dared to tamper with me, that I should persuade you to fly with them to Cordova, and become their wives!"

Here the excellent old woman covered her face with her hands, and gave way to a violent burst of grief and indignation. The three beautiful princesses turned pale and red, pale and red, and trembled, and looked down, and cast shy looks at each other, but said nothing. Meantime the old woman sat rocking backward and forward in violent agitation, and now and then breaking out into exclamations,—"That ever I should live to be so insulted!—I, the most faithful of servants!"

At length the eldest princess, who had most spirit and always took the lead, approached her, and laying her hand upon her shoulder, "Well, mother," said she, "supposing we were willing to fly with these Christian cavaliers—is such a thing possible?"

The good old woman paused suddenly in her grief, and looking up, "Possible," echoed she; "to be sure it is possible. Have not the cavaliers already bribed Hussein Baba, the renegado captain of the guard, and arranged the whole plan? But, then, to think of deceiving your father! your father, who has placed such confidence in me!" Here the worthy woman gave way to a fresh burst of grief, and began again to rock backward and forward, and to wring her hands.

"But our father has never placed any confidence in us," said the eldest princess, "but has trusted to bolts and bars, and treated us as captives."

"Why, that is true enough," replied the old woman, again pausing in her grief; "he has indeed treated you most unreasonably, keeping you shut up here, to waste your bloom in a moping old tower, like roses left to wither in a flower-jar. But, then, to fly from your native land!"

"And is not the land we fly to the native land of our mother, where we shall live in freedom? And shall we not each have a youthful husband in exchange for a severe old father?"

"Why, that again is all very true; and your father, I must confess, is rather tyrannical; but what then," relapsing into her grief, "would you leave me behind to bear the brunt of his vengeance?"

"By no means, my good Kadiga; cannot you fly with us?"

"Very true, my child; and to tell the truth, when I talked the matter over with Hussein Baba, he promised to take care of me, if I would accompany you in your flight; but then, bethink you, my children, are you willing to renounce the faith of your father?"

"The Christian faith was the original faith of our mother," said the eldest princess; "I am ready to embrace it, and so, I am sure, are my sisters."

"Right again," exclaimed the old woman, brightening up; "it was the original faith of your mother, and bitterly did she lament, on her death-bed, that she had renounced it. Yes, my children, I too was born a Christian, and have remained a Christian in my heart, and am resolved to return to the faith. I have talked on the subject with Hussein Baba, who is a Spaniard by birth, and comes from a place not far from my native town. He is equally anxious to see his own country, and to be reconciled to the Church; and the cavaliers have promised that, if we are disposed to become man and wife, on returning to our native land, they will provide for us handsomely."

In a word, it appeared that this extremely discreet and provident old woman had consulted with the cavaliers and the renegado, and had concerted the whole plan of escape. The eldest princess immediately assented to it; and her example, as usual, determined the conduct of her sisters. It is true the youngest hesitated, for she was gentle and timid of soul, and there was a struggle in her bosom between filial feeling and youthful passion: the latter, however, as usual, gained the victory, and with silent tears and stifled sighs she prepared herself for flight.

The rugged hill on which the Alhambra is built was, in old times, perforated with subterranean passages, cut through the rock, and leading from the fortress to various parts of the city, and to distant sally-ports on the banks of the Darro and the Xenil. They had been constructed at different times by the Moorish kings, as means of escape from sudden insurrections, or of secretly issuing forth on private enterprises. Many of them are now entirely lost, while others remain, partly choked with rubbish, and partly walled up,—monuments of the jealous precautions and warlike stratagems of the Moorish government. By one of these passages Hussein Baba had undertaken to conduct the princesses to a sally-port beyond the walls of the city, where the cavaliers were to be ready with fleet steeds to bear the whole party over the borders.

The appointed night arrived; the tower of the princesses had been locked up as usual, and the Alhambra was buried in deep sleep. Towards midnight the discreet Kadiga listened from the balcony of a window that looked into the garden. Hussein Baba, the renegado, was already below, and gave the appointed signal. The duenna fastened the end of a ladder of ropes to the balcony, lowered it into the garden and descended. The two eldest princesses followed her with beating hearts; but when it came to the turn of the youngest princess, Zorahayda, she hesitated and trembled. Several times she ventured a delicate little foot upon the ladder, and as often drew back, while her poor little heart fluttered more and more the longer she delayed. She cast a wistful look back into the silken chamber; she had lived in it, to be sure, like a bird in a cage; but within it she was secure; who could tell what dangers might beset her, should she flutter forth into the wide world! Now she bethought her of her gallant Christian lover, and her little foot was instantly upon the ladder; and anon she thought of her father, and shrank back. But fruitless is the attempt to describe the conflict in the bosom of one so young and tender and loving, but so timid and so ignorant of the world.

In vain her sisters implored, the duenna scolded, and the renegado blasphemed beneath the balcony: the gentle little Moorish maid stood doubting and wavering on the verge of elopement; tempted by the sweetness of the sin, but terrified at its perils.

Every moment increased the danger of discovery. A distant tramp was heard. "The patrols are walking their rounds," cried the renegado; "if we linger, we perish. Princess, descend instantly, or we leave you."

Zorahayda was for a moment in fearful agitation; then loosening the ladder of ropes, with desperate resolution she flung it from the balcony.

"It is decided!" cried she; "flight is now out of my power! Allah guide and bless ye, my dear sisters!"

The two eldest princesses were shocked at the thoughts of leaving her behind, and would fain have lingered, but the patrol was advancing; the renegado was furious, and they were hurried away to the subterraneous passage. They groped their way through a fearful labyrinth, cut through the heart of the mountain, and succeeded in reaching, undiscovered, an iron gate that opened outside of the walls. The Spanish cavaliers were waiting to receive them, disguised as Moorish soldiers of the guard, commanded by the renegado.

The lover of Zorahayda was frantic when he learned that she had refused to leave the tower; but there was no time to waste in lamentations. The two princesses were placed behind their lovers, the discreet Kadiga mounted behind the renegado, and they all set off at a round pace in the direction of the Pass of Lope, which leads through the mountains towards Cordova.

They had not proceeded far when they heard the noise of drums and trumpets from the battlements of the Alhambra.

"Our flight is discovered!" said the renegado.

"We have fleet steeds, the night is dark, and we may distance all pursuit," replied the cavaliers.

They put spurs to their horses, and scoured across the Vega. They attained the foot of the mountain of Elvira, which stretches like a promontory into the plain. The renegado paused and listened. "As yet," said he, "there is no one on our traces; we shall make good our escape to the mountains." While he spoke a light blaze sprang up on the top of the watch-tower of the Alhambra.

"Confusion!" cried the renegado, "that bale fire will put all the guards of the passes on the alert. Away! away! Spur like mad,—there is no time to be lost."

Away they dashed—the clattering of their horses' hoofs echoed from rock to rook, as they swept along the road that skirts the rocky mountain of Elvira. As they galloped on, the bale fire of the Alhambra was answered in every direction; light after light blazed on the watch-towers of the mountains.

"Forward! forward!" cried the renegado, with many an oath, "to the bridge,—to the bridge, before the alarm has reached there!"

They doubled the promontory of the mountains, and arrived in sight of the famous Bridge of Pinos, that crosses a rushing stream often dyed with Christian and Moslem blood. To their confusion, the tower on the bridge blazed with lights and glittered with armed men. The renegado pulled up his steed, rose in his stirrups and looked about him for a moment; then beckoning to the cavaliers, he struck off from the road, skirted the river for some distance, and dashed into its waters. The cavaliers called upon the princesses to cling to them, and did the same. They were borne for some distance down the rapid current, the surges roared round them, but the beautiful princesses clung to their Christian knights, and never uttered a complaint: The cavaliers attained the opposite bank in safety, and were conducted by the renegado, by rude and unfrequented paths and wild ravines, through the heart of the mountains, so as to avoid all the regular passes. In a word, they succeeded in reaching the ancient city of Cordova; where their restoration to their country and friends was celebrated with great rejoicings, for they were of the noblest families. The beautiful princesses were forthwith received into the Church and were rendered happy wives.

In our hurry to make good the escape of the princesses across the river, and up the mountains, we forgot to mention the fate of the discreet Kadiga. She had clung like a cat to Hussein Baba in the scamper across the Vega, screaming at every bound, and drawing many an oath from the whiskered renegado; but when he prepared to plunge his steed into the river, her terror knew no bounds. "Grasp me not so tightly," cried Hussein Baba; "hold on by my belt and fear nothing." She held firmly with both hands by the leathern belt that girded the broad backed renegado; but when he halted with the cavaliers to take breath on the mountain summit, the duenna was no longer to be seen.

"What has become of Kadiga?" cried the princesses in alarm.

"Allah alone knows!" replied the renegado; "my belt came loose when in the midst of the river, and Kadiga was swept with it down the stream. The will of Allah be done! but it was an embroidered belt, and of great price."

There was no time to waste in idle regrets; yet bitterly did the princesses bewail the loss of their discreet counsellor. That excellent old woman, however, did not lose more than half of her nine lives in the water: a fisherman, who was drawing his nets some distance down the stream, brought her to land, and was not a little astonished at his miraculous draught. What further became of the discreet Kadiga, the legend does not mention; certain it is that she evinced her discretion in never venturing within the reach of Mohamed the Left-handed.

Almost as little is known of the conduct of that sagacious monarch when he discovered the escape of his daughters, and the deceit practised upon him by the most faithful of servants. It was the only instance in which he had called in the aid of counsel, and he was never afterwards known to be guilty of a similar weakness. He took good care, however, to guard his remaining daughter, who had no disposition to elope; it is thought, indeed, that she secretly repented having remained behind: now and then she was seen leaning on the battlements of the tower, and looking mournfully towards the mountains in the direction of Cordova, and sometimes the notes of her lute were heard accompanying plaintive ditties, irk which she was said to lament the loss of her sisters and her lover, and to bewail her solitary life. She died young, and, according to popular rumor, was buried in a vault beneath the tower, and her untimely fate has given rise to more than one traditionary fable.

Legend of the Rose of the Alhambra

For some time after the surrender of Granada by the Moors, that delightful city was a frequent and favorite residence of the Spanish sovereigns, until they were frightened away by successive shocks of earthquakes, which toppled down various houses, and made the old Moslem towers rock to their foundation.

Many, many years then rolled away, during which Granada was rarely honored by a royal guest. The palaces of the nobility remained silent and shut up; and the Alhambra, like a slighted beauty, sat in mournful desolation among her neglected gardens. The Tower of the Princesses, once the residence of the three beautiful Moorish princesses, partook of the general desolation; the spider spun her web athwart the gilded vault, and bats and owls nestled in those chambers that had been graced by the presence of Zayda, Zorayda, and Zorahayda. The neglect of this tower may have been partly owing to some superstitious notions of the neighbors. It was rumored that the spirit of the youthful Zorahayda, who had perished in that tower, was often seen by moonlight seated beside the fountain in the hall, or moaning about the battlements, and that the notes of her silver lute would be heard at midnight by wayfarers passing along the glen.

At length the city of Granada was once more gladdened by the royal presence. All the world knows that Philip V. was the first Bourbon that swayed the Spanish sceptre. All the world knows that he married, in second nuptials, Elizabeth, the beautiful princess of Parma; and all the world knows that by this chain of contingencies a French prince and an Italian princess were seated together on the Spanish throne. For a visit of this illustrious pair, the Alhambra was repaired and fitted up with all possible expedition. The arrival of the court changed the whole aspect of the lately deserted palace. The clangor of drum and trumpet, the tramp of steed about the avenues and outer court, the glitter of arms and display of banners about barbican and battlement, recalled the ancient and warlike glories of the fortress. A softer spirit, however, reigned within the royal palace. There was the rustling of robes and the cautious tread and murmuring voice of reverential courtiers about the ante-chambers; a loitering of pages and maids of honor about the gardens, and the sound of music stealing from open casements.

Among those who attended in the train of the monarchs was a favorite page of the queen, named Ruyz de Alarcon. To say that he was a favorite page of the queen was at once to speak his eulogium, for every one in the suite of the stately Elizabeth was chosen for grace, and beauty, and accomplishments. He was just turned of eighteen, light and lithe of form, and graceful as a young Antinous. To the queen he was all deference and respect, yet he was at heart a roguish stripling, petted and spoiled by the ladies about the court.

This loitering page was one morning rambling about the groves of the Generalife, which overlook the grounds of the Alhambra. He had taken with him for his amusement a favorite ger-falcon of the queen. In the course of his rambles, seeing a bird rising from a thicket, he unhooded the hawk and let him fly. The falcon towered high in the air, made a swoop at his quarry, but missing it, soared away, regardless of the calls of the page. The latter followed the truant bird with his eye, in its capricious flight, until he saw it alight upon the battlements of a remote and lonely tower, in the outer wall of the Alhambra, built on the edge of a ravine that separated the royal fortress from the grounds of the Generalife. It was in fact the "Tower of the Princesses."

The page descended into the ravine and approached the tower, but it had no entrance from the glen, and its lofty height rendered any attempt to scale it fruitless. Seeking one of the gates of the fortress, therefore, he made a wide circuit to that side of the tower facing within the walls.

A small garden, enclosed by a trellis-work of reeds over-hung with myrtle, lay before the tower. Opening a wicket, the page passed between beds of flowers and thickets of roses to the door. It was closed and bolted. A crevice in the door gave him a peep into the interior. There was a small Moorish hall with fretted walls, light marble columns, and an alabaster fountain surrounded with flowers. In the centre hung a gilt cage containing a singing-bird; beneath it, on a chair, lay a tortoise-shell cat among reels of silk and other articles of female labor, and a guitar decorated with ribbons leaned against the fountain.

Ruyz de Alarcon was struck with these traces of female taste and elegance in a lonely, and, as he had supposed, deserted tower. They reminded him of the tales of enchanted halls current in the Alhambra; and the tortoise-shell cat might be some spell-bound princess.

He knocked gently at the door. A beautiful face peeped out from a little window above, but was instantly withdrawn. He waited, expecting that the door would be opened, but he waited in vain; no footstep was to be heard within—all was silent. Had his senses deceived him, or was this beautiful apparition the fairy of the tower? He knocked again, and more loudly. After a little while the beaming face once more peeped forth; it was that of a blooming damsel of fifteen.

The page immediately doffed his plumed bonnet, and entreated in the most courteous accents to be permitted to ascend the tower in pursuit of his falcon.

"I dare not open the door, Señor," replied the little damsel, blushing, "my aunt has forbidden it."

"I do beseech you, fair maid—it is the favorite falcon of the queen: I dare not return to the palace without it."

"Are you then one of the cavaliers of the court?"

"I am, fair maid; but I shall lose the queen's favor and my place, if I lose this hawk."

"It is against you cavaliers of the court my aunt has charged me especially to bar the door."

"Against wicked cavaliers, doubtless, but I am none of these, but a simple, harmless page, who will be ruined and undone if you deny me this small request."

The heart of the little damsel was touched by the distress of the page. It was a thousand pities he should be ruined for the want of so trifling a boon. Surely too he could not be one of those dangerous beings whom her aunt had described as a species of cannibal, ever on the prowl to make prey of thoughtless damsels; he was gentle and modest, and stood so entreatingly with cap in hand, and looked so charming.

The sly page saw that the garrison began to waver, and redoubled his entreaties in such moving terms that it was not in the nature of mortal maiden to deny him; so the blushing little warden of the tower descended, and opened the door with a trembling hand, and if the page had been charmed by a mere glimpse of her countenance from the window, he was ravished by the full-length portrait now revealed to him.

Her Andalusian bodice and trim basquina set off the round but delicate symmetry of her form. Her glossy hair was parted on her forehead with scrupulous exactness, and decorated with a fresh plucked rose, according to the universal custom of the country. It is true her complexion was tinged by the ardor of a southern sun, but it served to give richness to the mantling bloom of her cheek, and to heighten the lustre of her melting eyes.

Ruyz de Alarcon beheld all this with a single glance, for it became him not to tarry; he merely murmured his acknowledgments, and then bounded lightly up the spiral staircase in quest of his falcon.

He soon returned with the truant bird upon his fist. The damsel, in the meantime, had seated herself by the fountain in the hall, and was winding silk; but in her agitation she let fall the reel upon the pavement. The page sprang and picked it up, then dropping gracefully on one knee, presented it to her; but, seizing the hand extended to receive it, imprinted on it a kiss more fervent and devout than he had ever imprinted on the fair hand of his sovereign.

"Señor!" exclaimed the damsel, blushing still deeper with confusion and surprise, for never before had she received such a salutation.

The modest page made a thousand apologies, assuring her it was the way at court of expressing the most profound homage and respect.

Her anger, if anger she felt, was easily pacified, but her agitation and embarrassment continued, and she sat blushing deeper and deeper, with her eyes cast down upon her work, entangling the silk which she attempted to wind.

The cunning page saw the confusion in the opposite camp, and would fain have profited by it, but the fine speeches he would have uttered died upon his lips; his attempts at gallantry were awkward and ineffectual; and to his surprise, the adroit page, who had figured with such grace and effrontery among the most knowing and experienced ladies at court, found himself awed and abashed in the presence of a simple damsel of fifteen.

The diffidence of the page, though genuine, was short-lived, and he was recovering his usual ease and confidence, when a shrill voice was heard at a distance.

"My aunt is returning!" cried the damsel in affright: "I pray you, Señor, depart."

"Not until you grant me that rose from your hair as a remembrance."

She hastily untwisted the rose from her raven locks. "Take it," cried she, agitated and blushing, "but pray begone."

The page took the rose, and at the same time covered with kisses the fair hand that gave it. Then, placing the flower in his bonnet, and taking the falcon upon his fist, he bounded off through the garden, bearing away with him the heart of the gentle Jacinta.

When the vigilant aunt arrived at the tower, she remarked the agitation of her niece, and an air of confusion in the hall; but a word of explanation sufficed. "A ger-falcon had pursued his prey into the hall."

"Mercy on us! to think of a falcon flying into the tower. Did ever one hear of so saucy a hawk? Why, the very bird in the cage is not safe!"

The vigilant Fredegonda was one of the most wary of ancient spinsters. She had a becoming terror and distrust of what she denominated "the opposite sex," which had gradually increased through a long life of celibacy.

The niece was the orphan of an officer who had fallen in the wars. She had been educated in a convent, and had recently been transferred from her sacred asylum to the immediate guardianship of her aunt, under whose over-shadowing care she vegetated in obscurity, like an opening rose blooming beneath a brier. Nor indeed is this comparison entirely accidental; for, to tell the truth, her fresh and dawning beauty had caught the public eye, even in her seclusion, and, with that poetical turn common to the people of Andalusia, the peasantry of the neighborhood had given her the appellation of "the Rose of the Alhambra."

At length King Philip cut short his sojourn at Granada, and suddenly departed with all his train. The vigilant Fredegonda watched the royal pageant as it issued forth from the Gate of justice, and descended the great avenue leading to the city. When the last banner disappeared from her sight, she returned exulting to her tower, for all her cares were over. To her surprise a light Arabian steed pawed the ground at the wicket-gate of the garden;—to her horror she saw through the thicket of roses a youth in gayly embroidered dress, at the feet of her niece. At the sounds of her footsteps he gave a tender adieu, bounded lightly over the barrier of reeds and myrtles, sprang upon his horse, and was out of sight in an instant.

The tender Jacinta, in the agony of her grief, lost all thought of her aunt's displeasure. Throwing herself into her arms, she broke forth into sobs and tears.

"Dear aunt!" cried she, "he's gone!—he's gone!—he's gone! and I shall never see him more'!"

"Gone!—who is gone?—what youth is that I saw at your feet?"

"A queen's page, aunt, who came to bid me farewell."

"A queen's page, child!" echoed the vigilant Fredegonda faintly, "and when did you become acquainted with the queen's page?"

"The morning that the ger-falcon came into the tower. It was the queen's ger-falcon, and he came in pursuit of it."

"Ah, silly, silly girl! know that there are no ger-falcons half so dangerous as these young prankling pages, and it is precisely such simple birds as thee that they pounce upon."

Days, weeks, months elapsed, and nothing more was heard of the page. The pomegranate ripened, the vine yielded up its fruit, the autumnal rains descended in torrents from the mountains; the Sierra Nevada became covered with a snowy mantle, and wintry blasts howled through the halls of the Alhambra—still he came not. The winter passed away. Again the genial spring burst forth with song and blossom and balmy zephyr; the snows melted from the mountains, until none remained but on the lofty summit of Nevada, glistening through the sultry summer air. Still nothing was heard of the forgetful page.

In the meantime the poor little Jacinta grew pale and thoughtful. Her former occupations and amusements were abandoned, her silk lay entangled, her guitar unstrung, her flowers were neglected, the notes of her bird unheeded, and her eyes, once so bright, were dimmed with secret weeping.

"Alas, silly child!" would the staid and immaculate Fredegonda say, when she found her niece in one of her desponding moods—"did I not warn thee against the wiles and deceptions of these men? What couldst thou expect, too, from one of a haughty and aspiring family—thou an orphan, the descendant of a fallen and impoverished line? Be assured, if the youth were true, his father, who is one of the proudest nobles about the court, would prohibit his union with one so humble and portionless as thou. Pluck up thy resolution, therefore, and drive these idle notions from thy mind."

The words of Fredegonda only served to increase the melancholy of her niece, but she sought to indulge it in private. At a late hour one midsummer night, after her aunt had retired to rest, she remained alone in the hall of the tower, seated beside the alabaster fountain. It was here that the faithless page had first knelt and kissed her hand; it was here that he had often vowed eternal fidelity. The poor little damsel's heart was overladen with sad and tender recollections, her tears began to flow, and slowly fell drop by drop into the fountain. By degrees the crystal water became agitated, and—bubble—bubble—bubble—boiled up and was tossed about, until a female figure, richly clad in Moorish robes, slowly rose to view.

Jacinta was so frightened that she fled from the hall, and did not venture to return. The next morning she related what she had seen to her aunt, but the good lady treated it as a fantasy of her troubled mind, or supposed she had fatten asleep and dreamt beside the fountain. "Thou hast been thinking of the story of the three Moorish princesses that once inhabited this tower," continued she, "and it has entered into thy dreams."

"What story, aunt? I know nothing of it."

"Thou hast certainly heard of the three princesses, Zayda, Zorayda, and Zorahayda, who were confined in this tower by the king their father, and agreed to fly with three Christian cavaliers. The two first accomplished their escape, but the third failed in her resolution, and, it is said, died in this tower."

"I now recollect to have heard of it," said Jacinta, "and to have wept over the fate of the gentle Zorahayda."

"Thou mayest well weep over her fate," continued the aunt, "for the lover of Zorahayda was thy ancestor. He long bemoaned his Moorish love: but time cured him of his grief, and he married a Spanish lady, from whom thou art descended."

Jacinta ruminated upon these words. "That what I have seen is no fantasy of the brain," said she to herself, "I am confident. If indeed it be the spirit of the gentle Zorahayda, which I have heard lingers about this tower, of what should I be afraid? I'll watch by the fountain to-night—perhaps the visit will be repeated."

Towards midnight, when everything was quiet, she again took her seat in the hall. As the bell in the distant watch-tower of the Alhambra struck the midnight hour, the fountain was again agitated; and bubble—bubble—bubble—it tossed about the waters until the Moorish female again rose to view. She was young and beautiful; her dress was rich with jewels, and in her hand she held a silver lute. Jacinta trembled and was faint, but was reassured by the soft and plaintive voice of the apparition, and the sweet expression of her pale, melancholy countenance.

"Daughter of mortality," said she, "what aileth thee? Why do thy tears trouble my fountain, and thy sighs and plaints disturb the quiet watches of the night?"

"I weep because of the faithlessness of man, and I bemoan my solitary and forsaken state."

"Take comfort; thy sorrows may yet have an end. Thou beholdest a Moorish princess, who, like thee, was unhappy in her love. A Christian knight, thy ancestor, won my heart, and would have borne me to his native land and to the bosom of his church. I was a convert in my heart, but I lacked courage equal to my faith, and lingered till too late. For this the evil genii are permitted to have power over me, and I remain enchanted in this tower until some pure Christian will deign to break the magic spell. Wilt thou undertake the task?"

"I will," replied the damsel, trembling.

"Come hither then, and fear not; dip thy hand in the fountain, sprinkle the water over me, and baptize me after the manner of thy faith; so shall the enchantment be dispelled, and my troubled spirit have repose."

The damsel advanced with faltering steps, dipped her hand in the fountain, collected water in the palm, and sprinkled it over the pale face of the phantom.

The latter smiled with ineffable benignity. She dropped her silver lute at the feet of Jacinta, crossed her white arms upon her bosom, and melted from sight, so that it seemed merely as if a shower of dewdrops had fallen into the fountain.

Jacinta retired from the hall filled with awe and wonder. She scarcely closed her eyes that night; but when she awoke at daybreak out of a troubled slumber, the whole appeared to her like a distempered dream. On descending into the hall, however, the truth of the vision was established, for beside the fountain she beheld the silver lute glittering in the morning sunshine.

She hastened to her aunt, to relate all that had befallen her, and called her to behold the lute as a testimonial of the reality of her story. If the good lady had any lingering doubts, they were removed when Jacinta touched the instrument, for she drew forth such ravishing tones as to thaw even the frigid bosom of Fredegonda, that region of eternal winter, into a genial flow. Nothing but supernatural melody could have produced such an effect.

The extraordinary power of the lute became every day more and more apparent. The wayfarer passing by the tower was detained, and, as it were, spell-bound in breathless ecstasy. The very birds gathered in the neighboring trees, and hushing their own strains, listened in charmed silence.

Rumor soon spread the news abroad. The inhabitants of Granada thronged to the Alhambra to catch a few notes of the transcendent music that floated about the tower of The Maidens.

The lovely little minstrel was at length drawn forth from her retreat. The rich and powerful of the land contended who should entertain and do honor to her; or, rather, who should secure the charms of her lute to draw fashionable throngs to their saloons. Wherever she went her vigilant aunt kept a dragon watch at her elbow, awing the throngs of impassioned admirers who hung in raptures on her strains. The report of her wonderful powers spread from city to city. Malaga, Seville, Cordova, all became successively mad on the theme; nothing was talked of throughout Andalusia but the beautiful minstrel of the Alhambra. How could it be otherwise among a people so musical and gallant as the Andalusians, when the lute was magical in its powers, and the minstrel inspired by love!

While all Andalusia was thus music mad, a different mood prevailed at the court of Spain. Philip V., as is well known, was a miserable hypochondriac, and subject to all kinds of fancies. Sometimes he would keep to his bed for weeks together, groaning under imaginary complaints. At other times he would insist upon abdicating his throne, to the great annoyance of his royal spouse, who had a strong relish for the splendors of a court and the glories of a crown, and guided the sceptre of her imbecile lord with an expert and steady hand.

Nothing was found to be so efficacious in dispelling the royal megrims as the power of music; the queen took care, therefore, to have the best performers, both vocal and instrumental, at hand, and retained the famous Italian singer, Farinelli, about the court as a kind of royal physician.

At the moment we treat of, however, a freak had come over the mind of this sapient and illustrious Bourbon that surpassed all former vagaries. After a long spell of imaginary illness, which set all the strains of a whole orchestra of court fiddlers at defiance, the monarch fairly, in idea, gave up the ghost, and considered himself absolutely dead.

This would have been harmless enough, and even convenient both to his queen and courtiers, had he been content to remain in the quietude befitting a dead man; but to their annoyance he insisted upon having the funeral ceremonies performed over him, and, to their inexpressible perplexity, began to grow impatient, and to revile bitterly at them for negligence and disrespect, in leaving him unburied. What was to be done? To disobey the king's positive commands was monstrous in the eyes of the obsequious courtiers of a punctilious court—but to obey him, and bury him alive, would be downright regicide!

In the midst of this fearful dilemma a rumor reached the court of the female minstrel who was turning the brains of all Andalusia. The queen dispatched missions in all haste to summon her to St. Ildefonso, where the court at that time resided.

Within a few days, as the queen with her maids of honor was walking in those stately gardens, the far-famed minstrel was conducted into her presence. The imperial Elizabeth gazed with surprise at the youthful and unpretending appearance of the little being that had set the world mad. She was in her picturesque Andalusian dress, her silver lute in hand, and stood with modest and downcast eyes, but with a simplicity and freshness of beauty that still bespoke her "the Rose of the Alhambra."

As usual she was accompanied by the ever-vigilant Fredegonda, who gave the whole history of her parentage and descent to the inquiring queen. If the stately Elizabeth had been interested by the appearance of Jacinta, she was still more pleased when she learnt that she was of a meritorious though impoverished line, and that her father had bravely fallen in the service of the crown. "If thy powers equal thy renown," said she, "and thou canst cast forth this evil spirit that possesses thy sovereign, thy fortunes shall henceforth be my care, and honors and wealth attend thee."

Impatient to make trial of her skill, she led the way at once to the apartment of the moody monarch.

Jacinta followed with downcast eyes through files of guards and crowds of courtiers. They arrived at length at a great chamber hung with black. The windows were closed to exclude the light of day: a number of yellow wax tap? in silver sconces diffused a lugubrious light, and dimly revealed the figures of mutes in mourning dresses, and courtiers who glided about with noiseless step and woe-begone visage. In the midst of a funeral bed or bier, his hands folded on his breast, and the tip of his nose just visible, lay extended this would-be-buried monarch.

The queen entered the chamber in silence, and pointing to a footstool in an obscure corner, beckoned to Jacinta to sit down and commence.

At first she touched her lute with a faltering hand, but gathering confidence and animation as she proceeded, drew forth such soft harmony, that all present could scarce believe it mortal. As to the monarch, who had already considered himself in the world of spirits, he set it down for some angelic melody. By degrees the theme was varied, and the voice of the minstrel accompanied the instrument. She poured forth one of the legendary ballads treating of the ancient glories of the Alhambra and the achievements of the Moors. Her whole soul entered into the theme, for with the recollections of the Alhambra was associated the story of her love. The funeral-chamber resounded with the animating strain. It entered into the gloomy heart of the monarch. He raised his head and gazed around: he sat up on his couch, his eye began to kindle—at length, leaping upon the floor, he called for sword and buckler.

The triumph of music, or rather of the enchanted lute, was complete; the demon of melancholy was cast forth; and, as it were, a dead man brought to life. The windows of the apartment were thrown open; the glorious effulgence of Spanish sunshine burst into the late lugubrious chamber; all eyes sought the lovely enchantress, but the lute had fallen from her hand, she had sunk upon the earth, and the next moment was clasped to the bosom of Ruyz de Alarcon.

The nuptials of the happy couple were celebrated soon afterwards with great splendor, and the Rose of the Alhambra became the ornament and delight of the court. "But hold not so fast "—I hear the reader exclaim; "this is jumping to the end of a story at a furious rate! First let us know how Ruyz de Alarcon managed to account to Jacinta for his long neglect?" Nothing more easy; the venerable, time-honored excuse, the opposition to his wishes by a proud old father: besides, young people who really like one another soon come to an amicable understanding, and bury all past grievances when once they meet.

But how was the proud old father reconciled to the match?

Oh! as to that, his scruples were easily overcome by a word or two from the queen; especially as dignities and rewards were showered upon the blooming favorite of royalty. Besides, the lute of Jacinta, you know, possessed a magic power, and could control the most stubborn head and hardest breast.

And what came of the enchanted lute?

Oh, that is the most curious matter of all, and plainly proves the truth of the whole story. That lute remained for some time in the family, but was purloined and carried off, as was supposed, by the great singer Farinelli, in pure jealousy. At his death it passed into other hands in Italy, who were ignorant of ifs mystic powers, and melting down the silver, transferred the strings to an old Cremona fiddle. The strings still retain something of their magic virtues. A word in the reader's ear, but let it go no further: that fiddle is now bewitching the whole world,—it is the fiddle of Paganini!

The Veteran

Among the curious acquaintances I made in my rambles about the fortress, was a brave and battered old colonel, who was nestled like a hawk in one of the Moorish towers. His history, which he was fond of telling, was a tissue of adventures, mishaps, and vicissitudes.

He was in America at twelve years of age, and reckoned among the most signal and fortunate events of his life, his having seen George Washington. Since then he had taken a part in all the wars of his country; he could speak experimentally of most of the prisons and dungeons of the Peninsula; had been lamed of one leg, crippled in his hands, and so cut up that he was a kind of walking monument of the troubles of Spain, on which there was a scar for every battle and broil, as every year of captivity was notched upon the tree of Robinson Crusoe. The greatest misfortune of the brave old cavalier, however, appeared to have been his having commanded at Malaga during a time of peril and confusion, and been made a general by the inhabitants, to protect them from the invasion of the French. This had entailed upon him a number of just claims upon government, that I feared would employ him until his dying day in writing and printing petitions and memorials, to the great disquiet of his mind, exhaustion of his purse, and penance of his friends; not one of whom could visit him without having to listen to a mortal doc- ument of half an hour in length, and to carry away half a dozen pamphlets in his pocket. This, however, is the case throughout Spain; everywhere you meet with some worthy wight brooding in a corner, and nursing up some pet grievance and cherished wrong. Besides, a Spaniard who has a lawsuit, or a claim upon government, may be considered as furnished with employment for the remainder of his life.

I visited the veteran in his quarters in the upper part of the Wine Tower. His room was small but snug, and commanded a beautiful view of the Vega. It was arranged with a soldier's precision. Three muskets and a brace of pistols, all bright and shining, were suspended against the wall, with a sabre and a cane hanging side by side, and above them two cocked hats, one for parade, and one for ordinary use. A small shelf, containing some half dozen books, formed his library, one of which, a little old mouldy volume of philosophical maxims, was his favorite reading. This he thumbed and pondered over day by day; applying every maxim to his own particular case, provided it had a little tinge of wholesome bitterness, and treated of the injustice of the world.

Yet he was social aid kind-hearted, and, provided he could be diverted from his wrongs and his philosophy, was an entertaining companion. I like these old weather-beaten sons of fortune, and enjoy their rough campaigning anecdotes. In the course of my visits to the one in question, I learnt some curious facts about an old military commander of the fortress; who seems to have resembled him in some respects, and to have had similar fortunes in the wars. These particulars have been augmented by inquiries among some of the old inhabitants of the place, particularly the father of Mateo Ximenes, of whose traditional stories the worthy I am about to introduce to the reader was a favorite hero.

The Governor and the Notary

In former times there ruled, as governor of the Alhambra, a doughty old cavalier, who, from having lost one arm in the wars, was commonly known by the name of Manco, or "The one-armed Governor." He in fact prided himself upon being an old soldier, wore his moustaches curled up to his eyes, a pair of campaigning boots, and a toledo as long as a spit.

He was, moreover, exceedingly proud and punctilious, and tenacious of all his privileges and dignities. Under his sway the immunities of the Alhambra, as a royal residence and domain, were rigidly exacted. No one was permitted to enter the fortress with fire-arms, or even with a sword or staff, unless he were of a certain rank; and every horseman was obliged to dismount at the gate, and lead his horse by the bridle. Now as the hill of the Alhambra rises from the very midst of the city of Granada, it must at all times be somewhat irksome to the captain-general, who commands the province, to have a petty independent post in the very centre of his domains. It was rendered the more galling, in the present instance, from the irritable jealousy of the old governor, that took fire on the least question of authority and jurisdiction; and from the loose vagrant character of the people who had gradually nestled themselves within the fortress, as in a sanctuary, and thence carried on a system of roguery and depredation at the expense of the honest inhabitants of the city.

Thus there was a perpetual feud and heart-burning between the captain-general and the governor, the more virulent on the part of the latter, inasmuch as the smallest of two neighboring potentates is always the most captious about his dignity. The stately palace of the captain-general stood in the Plaza Nueva, immediately at the foot of the hill of the Alhambra; and here was always a bustle and parade of guards, and domestics, and city functionaries. A beetling bastion of the fortress overlooked the palace and public square in front of it; and on this bastion the old governor would occasionally strut backwards and forwards, with his toledo girded by his side, keeping a wary eye down upon his rival, like a hawk reconnoitering his quarry from his nest in a dry tree.

Whenever he descended into the city, it was in grand parade; on horseback, surrounded by his guards; or in his state coach, an ancient and unwieldy Spanish edifice of calved timber and gilt leather, drawn by eight mules, with running footmen, outriders, and lackeys; on which occasions he flattered himself he impressed every beholder with awe and admiration as vicegerent of the king; though the wits of Granada, particularly those who loitered about the palace of the captain-general, were apt to sneer at his petty parade, and, in allusion to the vagrant character of his subjects, to greet him with the appellation of "the king of the beggars." One of the most fruitful sources of dispute between these two doughty rivals was the right claimed by the governor to have all things passed free of duty through the city that were intended for the use of himself or his garrison. By degrees this privilege had given rise to extensive smuggling. A nest of smugglers took up their abode in the hovels of the fortress and the numerous caves in its vicinity, and drove a thriving business under the connivance of the soldiers of the garrison.

The vigilance of the captain-general was aroused. He consulted his legal adviser, a shrewd, meddlesome notary, who rejoiced in an opportunity of perplexing the old potentate of the Alhambra, and involving him in a maze of legal subtleties. He advised the captain-general to insist upon the right of examining every convoy passing through the gates of his city, and penned a long letter for him in vindication of the right. Governor Manco was a straightforward cut-and-thrust old soldier, who hated a notary worse than the devil, and this one in particular worse than all other notaries.

"What!" said he, curling up his moustaches fiercely, "does the captain-general set his man of the pen to practise confusions upon me? I'll let him see an old soldier is not to be baffled by schoolcraft."

He seized his pen and scrawled a short letter, in which, without deigning to enter into argument, he insisted on the right of transit free of search, and denounced vengeance on any custom-house officer who should lay his unhallowed hand on any convoy protected by the flag of the Alhambra. While this question was agitated between the two potentates, it so happened that a mule laden with supplies for the fortress arrived one day at the gate of Xenil, by which it was to traverse a suburb of the city on its way to the Alhambra. The convoy was headed by a testy old corporal, who had long served under the governor, and was a man after his own heart; as trusty and stanch as an old Toledo blade.

As they approached the gate of the city, the corporal placed the banner of the Alhambra on the pack-saddle of the mule, and drawing himself up to a perfect perpendicular, advanced with his head dressed to the front, but with the wary side-glance of a cur passing through hostile ground and ready for a snap and a snarl.

"Who goes there?" said the sentinel at the gate.

"Soldier of the Alhambra!" said the corporal, without turning is head.

"What have you in charge?"

"Provisions for the garrison."

"Proceed."

The corporal marched straight forward, followed by the convoy, but had not advanced many paces before a posse of custom-house officers rushed out of a small toll-house.

"Hallo there!" cried the leader. "Muleteer, halt, and open those packages."

The corporal wheeled round and drew himself up in battle array. "Respect the flag of the Alhambra," said he; "these things are for the governor."

"A fig for the governor and a fig for his flag. Muleteer, halt, I say."

"Stop the convoy at your peril!" cried the corporal, cocking his musket. "Muleteer, proceed."

The muleteer gave his beast a hearty thwack; the custom-house officer sprang forward and seized the halter; whereupon the corporal leveled his piece and shot him dead.

The street was immediately in an uproar.

The old corporal was seized, and after undergoing sundry kicks, and cuffs, and cudgelings, which are generally given impromptu by the mob in Spain as a foretaste of the after penalties of the law, he was loaded with irons and conducted to the city prison, while his comrades were permitted to proceed with the convoy, after it had been well rummaged, to the Alhambra.

The old governor was in a towering passion when he heard of this insult to his flag and capture of his corporal. For a time he stormed about the Moorish halls, and vapored about the bastions, and looked down fire and sword upon the palace of the captain-general. Having vented the first ebullition of his wrath, he despatched a message demanding the surrender of the corporal, as to him alone belonged the right of sitting in judgment on the offences of those under his command. The captain-general, aided by the pen of the delighted notary, replied at great length, arguing, that, as the offence had been committed within the walls of his city, and against one of his civil officers, it was clearly within his proper jurisdiction. The governor rejoined by a repetition of his demand; the captain-general gave a surrejoinder of still greater length and legal acumen; the governor became hotter and more peremptory in his demands, and the captain-general cooler and more copious in his replies; until the old lion-hearted soldier absolutely roared with fury at being thus entangled in the meshes of legal controversy.

While the subtle notary was thus amusing himself at the expense of the governor, he was conducting the trial of the corporal, who, mewed up in a narrow dungeon of the prison, had merely a small grated window at which to show his iron-bound visage and receive the consolations of his friends.

A mountain of written testimony was diligently heaped, up, according to the Spanish form, by the indefatigable notary; the corporal was completely overwhelmed by it. He was convicted of murder, and sentenced to be hanged.

It was in vain the governor sent down remonstrance and menace from the Alhambra. The fatal day was at hand, and the corporal was put in the chapel of the prison, as is always done with culprits the day before execution, that they may meditate on their approaching end and repent them of their sins.

Seeing things drawing to extremity, the old governor determined to attend to the affair in person. For this purpose he ordered out his carriage of state, and, surrounded by his guards, rumbled down the avenue of the Alhambra into the city. Driving to the house of the notary, he summoned him to the portal.

The eye of the old governor gleamed like a coal at beholding the smirking man of the law advancing with an air of exultation.

"What is this I hear," cried he, "that you are about to put to death one of my soldiers?"

"All according to law—all in strict form of justice," said the self-sufficient notary, chuckling and rubbing his hands; "I can show your Excellency the written testimony in the case."

"Fetch it hither,; said the governor. The notary bustled into his office, delighted with having another opportunity of displaying his ingenuity at the expense of the hard-headed veteran. He returned with a satchel full of papers, and began to read a long deposition with professional volubility. By this time a crowd had collected, listening with outstretched necks and gaping mouths.

"Prithee, man, get into the carriage, out of this pestilent throng, that I may the better hear thee," said the governor.

The notary entered the carriage, when, in a twinkling, the door was closed, the coachman smacked his whip,—mules, carriage, guards, and all, dashed off at a thundering rate, leaving the crowd in gaping wonderment; nor did the governor pause until he had lodged his prey in one of the strongest dungeons of the Alhambra.

He then sent down a flag of truce in military style, proposing a cartel, or exchange of prisoners,—the corporal for the notary. The pride of the captain-general was piqued; he returned a contemptuous refusal, and forthwith caused a gallows, tall and strong, to be erected in the centre of the Plaza Nueva for the execution of the corporal.

"Oho! Is that the game?" said Governor Manco. He gave orders, and immediately a gibbet was reared on the verge of the great beetling bastion that overlooked the Plaza. "Now," said he, in a message to the captain-general, "hang my soldier when you please; but at the same time that he is swung off in the square, look up to see your notary dangling against the sky."

The captain-general was inflexible; troops were paraded in the square; the drums beat, the bell tolled. An immense multitude of spectators gathered together to behold the execution. On the other hand, the governor paraded his garrison on the bastion, and tolled the funeral dirge of the notary from the Tower of the Bell.

The notary's wife pressed through the crowd, with a whole progeny of little notaries at her heels, and throwing herself at the feet of the captain-general, implored him not to sacrifice the life of her husband, and the welfare of herself and her numerous little ones, to a point of pride; "for you know the old governor too well," said she, "to doubt that he will put his threat in execution, if you hang the soldier."

The captain-general was overpowered by her tears and lamentations. The corporal was sent up to the Alhambra, under a guard, in his gallows garb, but with head erect and a face of iron. The notary was demanded in exchange, according to the cartel. The once bustling and self-sufficient man of the law was drawn forth from his dungeon more dead than alive. All his flippancy and conceit had evaporated; his hair, it is said, had nearly turned gray with affright, and he had a downcast, dogged look, as if he still felt the halter round his neck.

The old governor stuck his one arm akimbo, and for a moment surveyed him with an iron smile. "Henceforth, my friend," said he, "moderate your zeal in hurrying others to the gallows; be not too certain of your safety, even though you should have the law on your side; and above all, take care how you play off your schoolcraft another time upon an old soldier."

Governor Manco and the Soldier

While Governor Manco, or the "one-armed," kept up a show of military state in the Alhambra, he became nettled at the reproaches continually cast upon his fortress, of being a nestling-place of rogues and smugglers. On a sudden, the old potentate determined to reform, and setting vigorously to work, ejected whole nests of vagabonds out of the fortress and the gypsy caves with which the surrounding hills are honeycombed. He sent out soldiers, also, to patrol the avenues and footpaths, with orders to take up all suspicious persons.

One bright summer morning a patrol, consisting of the testy old corporal who had distinguished himself in the affair of the notary, a trumpeter, and two privates, was seated under the garden-wall of the Generalife, beside the road which leads down from the Mountain of the Sun, when they heard the tramp of a horse, and a male voice singing in rough, though not unmusical tones, an old Castilian campaigning-song.

Presently they beheld a sturdy, sunburnt fellow, clad in the ragged garb of a foot-soldier, leading a powerful Arabian horse caparisoned in the ancient Morisco fashion.

Astonish d at the sight of a strange soldier descending, steed in hand, from that solitary mountain, the corporal stepped forth and challenged him.

Who goes there?"

"A friend."

"Who and what are, you?"

"A poor soldier just from the wars, with a cracked crown and empty purse for a reward."

By this time they were enabled to view him more narrowly. He had a black patch across his forehead, which, with a grizzled beard, added to a certain dare-devil cast of countenance, while a slight squint threw into the whole an occasional gleam of roguish good-humor.

Having answered the questions of the patrol, the soldier seemed to consider himself entitled to make others in return. "May I ask," said he, "what city is that which I see at the foot of the hill?"

"What city!" cried the trumpeter; "come, that's too bad. Here's a fellow lurking about the Mountain of the Sun, and demands the name of the great city of Granada!"

"Granada! can it be possible?"

"Perhaps not!" rejoined the trumpeter; "and perhaps you have no idea that yonder are the towers of the Alhambra."

"Son of a trumpet," replied the stranger, "do not trifle with me; if this be indeed the Alhambra, I have some strange matters to reveal to the governor."

"You will have an opportunity," said the corporal, "for we mean to take you before him." By this time the trumpeter had seized the bridle of the steed, the two privates had each secured an arm of the soldier, the corporal put himself in front, gave the word, "Forward—march!" and away they marched for the Alhambra.

The sight of a ragged foot-soldier and a fine Arabian horse, brought in captive by the patrol, attracted the attention of all the idlers of the fortress, and of those gossip groups that generally assemble about wells and fountains at early dawn. The wheel of the cistern paused in its rotations, and the slip-shod servant-maid stood gaping, with pitcher in hand, as the corporal passed by with his prize. A motley train gradually gathered in the rear of the escort.

Knowing nods and winks and conjectures passed from one to another. "It is a deserter," said one; "A smuggler," said another; "A robber," said a third;—until it was affirmed that a captain of a desperate band of robbers had been captured by the prowess of the corporal and his patrol. "Well, well;" said the old crones, one to another, "captain or not, let him get out of the grasp of old Governor Manco if he can, though he is but one-handed."

Governor Manco was seated in one of the inner halls of the Alhambra, taking his morning's cup of chocolate, a demure, dark-eyed damsel, the daughter of his house-keeper, attending upon him. When word was brought that a suspicious stranger had been taken lurking about the fortress, and was actually in the outer court, in durance of the corporal, waiting the pleasure of his Excellency, the pride and stateliness of office swelled the bosom of the governor. He called for his sword, girded it to his side, twirled up his moustaches, took his seat in a large high-backed chair, assumed a bitter and forbidding aspect, and ordered the prisoner into his presence. The soldier was brought in, still closely pinioned by his captors, and guarded by the corporal. He maintained, however, a resolute, self-confident air, and returned the sharp, scrutinizing look of the governor with an easy squint, which by no means pleased the punctilious old potentate.

"Well, culprit," said the governor, after he had regarded him for a moment in silence, "what have you to say for yourself—who are you?"

"A soldier, just from the wars, who has brought away nothing but scars and bruises."

"A soldier—humph—a foot-soldier by your garb, I understand you have a fine Arabian horse. I presume you brought him too from the wars, besides your scars and bruises."

"May it please your Excellency, I have something strange to tell about that horse. Indeed, I have one of the most wonderful things to relate. Something too that concerns the security of this fortress, indeed of all Granada. It is a matter to be imparted only to your private ear, or in presence of such only as are in your confidence. But I am perfectly willing," said he, "that the damsel should remain."

The governor considered for a moment, and then directed the corporal and his men to withdraw, but to post themselves outside of the door and be ready at a call.

When they had withdrawn, the soldier commenced his story. He was a fluent, smooth-tongued varlet, and had a command of language above his apparent rank.

"May it please your Excellency," said he, "I am, as I before observed, a soldier, and have seen some hard service, but my term of enlistment being expired, I was discharged, not long since, from the army at Valladolid, and set out on foot for my native village in Andalusia. Yesterday evening the sun went down as I was traversing a great dry plain of Old Castile."

"Hold!" cried the governor, "what is this you say? Old Castile is some two or three hundred miles from this."

"Even so," replied the soldier, coolly. "I told your Excellency I had strange things to relate; but not more strange than true, as your Excellency will find, if you will deign me a patient hearing."

"Proceed, culprit," said the governor, twirling up his moustaches.

"As the sun went down," continued the soldier, "I cast my eyes about in search of quarters for the night, but as far as my sight could reach there were no signs of habitation. I saw that I should have to make my bed on the naked plain, with my knapsack for a pillow; but your Excellency is an old soldier, and knows that to one who has been in the wars, such a night's lodging is no great hardship."

The governor nodded assent, as he drew out his pocket-handkerchief to drive away a fly that buzzed about his nose.

"Well, to make a long story short," continued the soldier, "I trudged forward for several miles until I came to a bridge over a deep ravine, through which ran a little dread of water, almost dried up by the summer heat. At one end of the bridge was a Moorish tower, the upper end all in ruins, but a vault in the foundation quite entire. Here, thinks I, is a good place to make a halt; so I went down to the stream, and took a hearty drink, for the water was pure and sweet, and I was parched with thirst; then, opening my wallet, I took out an onion and a few crusts, which were all my provisions, and seating myself on a stone on the margin of the stream, began to make my supper, intending afterwards to quarter myself for the night in the vault of the tower; and capital quarters they would have been for a campaigner just from the wars, as your Excellency, who is an old soldier, may suppose."

"I have put up gladly with worse in my time," said the governor, returning his pocket-handkerchief into the hilt of his sword.

"While I was quietly crunching my crust," pursued the soldier, "I heard something stir within the vault; I listened—it was the tramp of a horse. By and by a man came forth from a door in the foundation of the tower, close by the water's edge, leading a powerful horse by the bridle. I could not well make out what he was, by the starlight. It had a suspicious look to be lurking among the ruins of a tower, in that wild, solitary place. He might be a mere wayfarer, like myself; he might be a smuggler; he might be a robber! what of that? thank heaven and my poverty, I had nothing to lose; so I sat still and crunched my crust.

"He led his horse to the water, close by where I was sitting, so that I had a fair opportunity of reconnoitring him. To my surprise he was dressed in a Moorish garb, with a cuirass of steel, and a polished skull-cap that I distinguished by the reflection of the stars upon it. His horse, too, was harnessed in the Morisco fashion, with great shovel stirrups. He led him, as I said, to the side of the stream, into which the animal plunged his head almost to the eyes, and drank until I thought he would have burst.

"'Comrade,' said I, 'your steed drinks well; it's a good sign when a horse plunges his muzzle bravely into the water.'

"'He may well drink,' said the stranger, speaking with a Moorish accent; 'it is a good year since he had his last draught.'

"'That beats even the camels I have seen in Africa,' said I. 'But come, you seem to be something of a soldier, will you sit down and take part of a soldier's fare?' In fact, I felt the want of a companion in this lonely place, and was willing to put up with an infidel. Besides as your Excellency well knows, a soldier is never very particular about the faith, of his company, and soldiers of all countries are comrades on peaceable ground."

The governor again nodded assent.

"Well, as I was saying, I invited him to share my supper, such as it was, for I could not do less in common hospitality. 'I have no time to pause for meat or drink,' said he, 'I have a long journey to make before morning.'

'In what direction?' said I.

'Andalusia,' said he.

"'Exactly my route,' said I; 'so, as you won't stop and eat with me, perhaps you will let me mount and ride with you. I see your horse is of a powerful frame; I'll warrant he carry double.'

"'Agreed,' said the trooper; and it would not have been civil and soldierlike to refuse, especially as I had offered to share my supper with him. So up he mounted, and up I mounted behind him.

"'Hold fast,' said he, 'my steed goes like the wind.'

"'Never fear me,' said I, and so off we set.

"From a walk the horse soon passed to a trot, from a trot to a gallop, and from a gallop to a harum-scarum scamper. It seemed as if rocks, trees, houses, everything, flew hurry-scurry behind us.

"'What town, is this?' said I.

"'Segovia,' said he; and before the word was out of his mouth, the towers of Segovia were out of sight. We swept up the Guadarama mountains, and down by the Escurial; and we skirted the walls of Madrid, and we scoured away across the plains of La Mancha. In this way we went up hill and down dale, by towers and cities, all buried in deep sleep, and across mountains, and plains, and rivers, just glimmering in the starlight.

"To make a long story short, and not to fatigue your Excellency, the trooper suddenly pulled up on the side of a mountain. 'Here we are,' said he, 'at the end of our journey.' I looked about, but could see no signs of habitation; nothing but the mouth of a cavern. While I looked I saw multitudes of people in Moorish dresses, some on horseback, some on foot, arriving as if borne by the wind from all points of the compass, and hurrying into the mouth of the cavern like bees into a hive. Before I could ask a question, the trooper struck his long Moorish spurs into the horse's flanks, and dashed in with the throng. We passed along a steep winding way, that descended into the very bowels of the mountain. As we pushed on, a light began to glimmer up, by little and little, like the first glimmerings of day, but what caused it I could not discern. It grew stronger and stronger, and enabled me to see everything around. I now noticed, as we passed along, great caverns, opening to the right and left, like halls in an arsenal. In some there were shields, and helmets, and cuirasses, and lances, and cimeters, hanging against the walls; in others there were great heaps of warlike munitions and camp-equipages lying upon the ground.

"It would have done your Excellency's heart good, being an old soldier, to have seen such grand provision for war. Then, in other caverns, there were long rows of horsemen armed to the teeth, with lances raised and banners unfurled, all ready for the field; but they all sat motionless in their saddles, like so many statues. In other halls were warriors sleeping on the ground beside their horses, and foot-soldiers in groups ready to fall into the ranks. All were in old-fashioned Moorish dresses and armor.

"Well, your Excellency, to cut a long story short, we at length entered an immense cavern, or I may say palace, of grotto-work, the walls of which seemed to be veined with gold and silver, and to sparkle with diamonds and sapphires and all kinds of precious stones. At the upper end sat a Moorish king on a golden throne, with his nobles on each side, and a guard of African blacks with drawn cimeters. All the crowd that continued to flock in, and amounted to thousands and thousands, passed one by one before his throne, each paying homage as he passed. Some of the multitude were dressed in magnificent robes, without stain or blemish, and sparkling with jewels; others in burnished and enameled armor; while others were in mouldered and mildewed garments, and in armor all battered and dented and covered with rust.

"I had hitherto held my tongue, for your Excellency well knows it is not for a soldier to ask many questions when on duty, but I could keep silent no longer.

"'Prithee, comrade,' said I, 'what is the meaning of all this?'

"'This,' said the trooper, 'is a great and fearful mystery. Know, O Christian, that you see before you the court and army of Boabdil the last king of Granada.'

"'What is this you tell me?' cried I. 'Boabdil and his court were exiled from the land hundreds of years agone, and all died in Africa.'

"'So it is recorded in your lying chronicles,' replied the Moor; 'but know that Boabdil and the warriors who made the last struggle for Granada were all shut up in the mountain by a powerful enchantment. As for the king and army that marched forth from Granada at the time of the surrender, they were a mere phantom train of spirits and demons, permitted to assume those shapes to deceive the Christian sovereigns. And furthermore let me tell you, friend, that all Spain is a country under the power of enchantment. There is not a mountain cave, not a lonely watch-tower in the plains, nor ruined castle on the hills, but has some spellbound warriors sleeping from age to age within its vaults, until the sins are expiated for which Allah permitted the dominion to pass for a time out of the hands of the faithful. Once every year, on the eve of St. John, they are released from enchantment, from sunset to sunrise, and permitted to repair here to pay homage to their sovereign! and the crowds which you beheld swarming into the cavern are Moslem warriors from their haunts in all parts of Spain. For my own part, you saw the ruined tower of the bridge in Old Castile, where I have now wintered and summered for many hundred years, and where I must be back again by daybreak. As to the battalions of horse and foot which you beheld drawn up in array in the neighboring caverns, they are the spellbound warriors of Granada. It is written in the book of fate, that when the enchantment is broken, Boabdil will descend from the mountain at the head of this army, resume his throne in the Alhambra and his sway of Granada, and gathering together the enchanted warriors from all parts of Spain, will reconquer the Peninsula and restore it to Moslem rule.'

"'And when shall this happen?' said I.

" "Allah alone knows: we had hoped the day of deliverance was at hand; but there reigns at present a vigilant governor in the Alhambra, a stanch old soldier, well known as Governor Manco. While such a warrior holds command of the very outpost, and stands ready to check the first irruption from the mountain, I fear Boabdil and his soldiery must be content to rest upon their arms.'"

Here the governor raised himself somewhat perpendicularly, adjusted his sword, and twirled up his moustaches.

"To make a long story short, and not to fatigue your Excellency, the trooper, having given me this account, dismounted from his steed.

"'Tarry here,' said he, 'and guard my steed while I go and bow the knee to Boabdil.' So saying, he strode away among the throng that pressed forward to the throne.

"'What's to be done?' thought I, when thus left to myself; 'shall I wait here until this infidel returns to whisk me on his goblin steed, the Lord knows where; or shall I make the most of my time and beat a retreat from this hobgoblin community?' A soldier's mind is soon made up, as your Excellency well knows. As to the horse, he belonged to an avowed enemy of the faith and the realm, and was a fair prize according to the rules of war. So hoisting myself from the crupper into the saddle, I turned the reins, struck the Moorish stirrups into the sides of the steed, and put him to make the best of his way out of the passage by which he had entered. As we scoured by the halls where the Moslem horsemen sat in motionless battalions, I thought I heard the clang of armor and a hollow murmur of voices. I gave the steed another taste of the stirrups and doubled my speed. There was now a sound behind me like a rushing blast; I heard the clatter of a thousand hoofs; a countless throng overtook me. I was borne along in the press, and hurled forth from the mouth of the cavern, while thousands of shadowy forms were swept off in every direction by the four winds of heaven.

"In the whirl and confusion of the scene I was thrown senseless to the earth. When I came to myself, I was lying on the brow of a hill, with the Arabian steed standing beside me; for in falling, my arm had slipped within the bridle, which, I presume, prevented his whisking off to Old Castile.

"Your Excellency may easily judge of my surprise, on looking round, to behold hedges of aloes and Indian figs and other proofs of a southern climate, and to see a great city below me, with towers, and palaces, and a grand cathedral.

"I descended the hill cautiously, leading my steed, for I was afraid to mount him again, lest he should play me some slippery trick. As I descended I met with your patrol, who let me into the secret that it was Granada that lay before me, and that I was actually under the walls of the Alhambra, the fortress of the redoubted Governor Manco, the terror of all enchanted Moslems. When I heard this, I determined at once to seek your Excellency, to inform you of all that I had seen, and to warn you of the perils that surround and undermine you, that you may take measures in time to guard your fortress, and the kingdom itself, from this army that lurks in the very bowels of the land."

"And prithee, friend, you who are a veteran campaigner, and have seen so much service," said the governor, "how would you advise me to proceed, in order to prevent this evil?"

"It is not for a humble private of the ranks," said the soldier, modestly, "to pretend to instruct a commander of your Excellency's sagacity, but it appears to me that your Excellency might cause all the caves and entrances into the mountains to be walled up with solid mason-work, so that Boabdil and his army might be completely corked up in their subterranean habitation."

The governor now placed his arm akimbo, with his hand resting on the hilt of his toledo, fixed his eye upon the soldier, and gently wagging his head from one side to the other,—

"So, friend," said he, "then you really suppose I am to be gulled with this cock-and-bull story about enchanted mountains and enchanted Moors? Hark ye, culprit!—not another word. An old soldier you may be, but you'll find you have an older soldier to deal with, and one not easily outgeneralled. Ho! guards there! put this fellow in irons."

As they were pinioning the soldier, one of the guards felt something of bulk in his pocket, and drawing it forth, found a long leathern purse that appeared to be well filled. Holding it by one corner, he turned out the contents upon the table before the governor, and never did freebooter's bag make more gorgeous delivery. Out tumbled rings, and jewels, and rosaries of pearls, and sparkling diamond crosses, and a profusion of ancient golden coin, some of which fell jingling to the floor, and rolled away to the uttermost parts of the chamber. For a time the functions of justice were suspended; there was a universal scramble after the glittering fugitives. The governor alone, who was imbued with true Spanish pride, maintained his stately decorum, though his eye betrayed a little anxiety until the last coin and jewel-was restored to the sack.

"I was just going to tell your Excellency when you interrupted me," said the stranger, "that, on taking possession of the trooper's horse, I unhooked a leathern sack which hung at the saddle-bow, and which I presume contained the plunder of his campaignings in days of old, when the Moors overran the country."

"Mighty well; at present you will make up your mind to take up your quarters in a chamber of the Vermilion Towers, which, though not under a magic spell, will hold you as safe as any cave of your enchanted Moors."

"Your Excellency will do as you think proper," said the prisoner, coolly. "I shall be thankful to your Excellency for any accommodation in the fortress. A soldier who has been in the wars, as your Excellency well knows, is not particular about his lodgings. Provided I have a snug dungeon and regular rations, I shall manage to make myself comfortable. I would only entreat that while your Excellency is so careful about me, you would have an eye to your fortress, and think on the hint I dropped about stopping up the entrances to the mountain."

Here ended the scene. The prisoner was conducted to a strong dungeon in the Vermilion Towers, the Arabian steed was led to his Excellency's stable, and the trooper's sack was deposited in his Excellency's strong box.

To explain these prompt and rigid measures on the part of old Governor Manco, it is proper to observe, that about this time the Alpuxarra mountains in the neighborhood of Granada were terribly infested by a gang of robbers, under the command of-a daring chief named Manuel Borasco, who were accustomed to prowl about the country, and even to enter the city in various-disguises, to gain intelligence of the departure of convoys of merchandise, or travellers with well-lined purses, whom they took care to waylay in distant and solitary passes of the road. These repeated and daring outrages had awakened the attention of the government, and the commanders of the various posts had received instructions to be on the alert, and to take up all suspicious stragglers. Governor Manco was particularly zealous in consequence of the stigma that had been cast upon his fortress, and he now doubted not he had entrapped some formidable desperado of this gang.

In the meantime the story took wind, and became the talk, not merely of the fortress, but of the whole city of Granada. It was said that the noted robber Manuel Borasco, the terror of the Alpuxarras, had fallen into the clutches of old Governor Manco, and been cooped up by him in a dungeon of the Vermilion Towers; and every one who had been robbed by him flocked to recognize the marauder. The Vermilion Towers, as is well known, stand apart from the Alhambra on a sister hill, separated from the main fortress by the ravine down which passes, the main avenue. There were no outer walls, but a sentinel patrolled before the tower. The window of the chamber in which the soldier was confined was strongly grated, and looked upon a small esplanade. Here the good folks of Granada repaired to gaze at him, as they would at a laughing hyena, grinning through the cage of a menagerie. Nobody, however, recognized him for Manuel Borasco, for that terrible robber was noted for a ferocious physiognomy, and had by no means the good-humored squint of the prisoner. Visitors came not merely from the city, but from all parts of the country; but nobody knew him, and there began to be doubts in the minds of the common people whether there might not be some truth in his story. That Boabdil and his army were shut up in the mountain; as an old tradition which many of the ancient inhabitants had heard from their fathers. Numbers went up to the Mountain of the Sun, in search of the cave mentioned by the soldier; and saw and peeped into the deep dark pit, descending, no one knows how far, into the mountain, and which remains there to this day—the fabled entrance to the subterranean abode of Boabdil.

By degrees the soldier became popular with the common people. A freebooter of the mountains is by no means the opprobrious character in Spain that a robber is in any other country: on the contrary, he is a kind of chivalrous personage in the eyes of the lower classes. There is always a disposition, also, to cavil at the conduct of those in command; and many began to murmur at the high-handed measures of old Governor Manco, and to look upon the prisoner in the light of a martyr.

The soldier, moreover, was a merry, waggish fellow, that had a joke for every one who came near his window, and a soft speech for every female. He had procured an old guitar also, and would sit by his window and sing ballads and love-ditties to the delight of the women of the neighborhood, who would assemble on the esplanade in the evening and dance to his music. Having trimmed off his rough beard, his sunburnt face found favor in the eyes of the fair, and the demure handmaid of the governor declared that his squint was perfectly irresistible. This kind-hearted damsel had from the first evinced a deep sympathy in his fortunes, and having in vain tried to mollify the governor, had set to work privately to mitigate the rigor of his dispensations. Every day she brought the prisoner some crumbs of comfort which had fallen from the governor's table, or been abstracted from his larder, together with, now and then, a consoling bottle of choice wine.

While this petty treason was going on in the very centre of the old governor's citadel, a storm of open war was brewing up among his external foes. The circumstance of a bag of gold and jewels having been found upon the person of the supposed robber, had been reported, with many exaggerations in Granada. A question of territorial jurisdiction was immediately started by the governor's inveterate rival, the captain-general. He insisted that the prisoner had been captured without the precincts of the Alhambra, and within the rules of his authority. He demanded his body therefore, and the spoils taken with him. The feud ran high; the governor was furious, and swore; rather than surrender his captive, he would hang him up within the Alhambra, as a spy caught within the fortress.

The captain-general threatened to send a body of soldiers to transfer the prisoner from the Vermilion Towers to the city. Word was brought late at night to the governor of this intention. "Let them come," said he, "they'll find me beforehand with them; he must rise bright and early who would take in an old soldier." He accordingly issued orders to have the prisoner removed, at daybreak, to the donjon-keep within the walls of the Alhambra. "And d'ye hear, child," said he to his demure handmaid, "tap at my door, and wake me before cock-crowing, that I may see to the matter myself."

The day dawned, the cock crowed, but nobody tapped at the door of the governor. The sun rose high above the mountain-tops, and glittered in at his casement, ere the governor was awakened from his morning dreams by his veteran corporal, who stood before him with terror stamped upon his iron visage.

"He's off! he's gone!" cried the corporal, gasping for breath.

"Who's off—who's gone?"

"The soldier—the robber—the devil, for aught I know; his dungeon is empty, but the door locked: no one knows how he has escaped out of it."

The old governor had scarce time to wince at this news, when fresh misfortune broke upon his view. On going into his cabinet he found his strong box open, the leather purse of the trooper abstracted, and with it a couple of corpulent bags of doubloons.

But how, and which way had the fugitive escaped? An old peasant who lived in a cottage by the road-side leading up into the Sierra, declared that he had heard the tramp of a powerful steed just before daybreak, passing up into the mountains; he had looked out at his casement and could just distinguish a horseman with a maiden seated before him.

"Search the stables!" cried Governor Manco. The stables were searched; all the horses were in their stalls; excepting the Arabian steed. In his place was a stout cudgel, tied to the manger, and on it a label bearing these words, "A Gift to Governor Manco, from an Old Soldier."

The Crusade of the Grand Master
of Alcántara

In the course of a morning's research among the old chronicles in the Library of the University, I came upon a little episode in the history of Granada, so strongly characteristic of the bigot zeal which sometimes inflamed the Christian enterprises against this splendid but devoted city, that I was tempted to draw it forth from the parchment-bound volume in which it lay entombed, and submit it to the reader.

In the year 1394, there was a valiant and devout grand master of Alcántara, named Martin Yanez de Barbudo, who was inflamed with a vehement desire to serve God and fight the Moors. Unfortunately for this brave and pious cavalier, a profound peace existed between the Christian and Moslem powers. Henry III. had just ascended the throne of Castile, and Yusef ben Mohammed had succeeded to the throne of Granada, and both were disposed to continue the peace which had prevailed between their fathers. The grand master looked with repining at Moorish banners and weapons, which decorated his castle-hall, trophies of the exploits of his predecessors; and repined at his fate to exist in a period of such inglorious tranquillity.

At length his impatience broke through all bounds, and seeing that he could find no public war in which to engage, he resolved to carve out a little war for himself. Such at least is the account given by some ancient chronicles, though others give the following as the motive for this sudden resolution to go campaigning.

As the grand master was one day seated at table with several of his cavaliers, a man suddenly entered the hall,—tall, meagre, and bony, with haggard countenance and fiery eyes. All recognized him for a hermit, who had been a soldier in his youth, but now led a life of penitence in a cave. He advanced to the table and struck upon it with a fist that seemed of iron. "Cavaliers," said he, "why sit ye here idly, with your weapons resting against the wall, while the enemies of the faith lord it over the fairest portion of the land?"

"Holy father, what wouldst thou have us do," asked the grand master, "seeing the wars are over and our swords bound up by treaties of peace?"

"Listen to my words," replied the hermit. "As I was seated late at night at the entrance of my cave, contemplating the heavens, I fell into a reverie, and a wonderful vision was presented to me. I beheld the moon, a mere crescent, yet luminous as the brightest silver, and it hung in the heavens over the kingdom of Granada. While I was looking at it, behold there shot forth from the, firmament a blazing star, which, as it went, drew after it all the stars of heaven; and they assailed the moon and drove it from the skies; and the whole firmament was filled with the glory of that blazing star. While mine eyes were yet dazzled by this wondrous sight, some one stood by me with snowy wings and a shining countenance. 'Oh man of prayer,' said he, 'get thee to the grand master of Alcántara and tell him of the vision thou hast beheld. He is the blazing star, destined to drive the crescent, the Moslem emblem, from the land. Let him boldly draw the sword and victory will assuredly attend his banner.'"

The grand master listened to the hermit as to a messenger from heaven, and followed his counsel in all things. By his advice he despatched two of his stoutest warriors on an embassy to the Moorish king. They entered the gates of Granada without molestation, as the nations were at peace; and made their way to the Alhambra, where they were promptly admitted to the king, who received them in the Hall of Ambassadors. They delivered their message roundly and hardly. "We come, O King, from Don Martin Yañez de Barbudo, grand master of Alcántara; who affirms the faith of Jesus Christ to be true and holy, and that of Mahomet false and detestable, and he challenges thee to maintain the contrary, hand to hand, in single combat. Shouldst thou refuse, he offers the combat with one hundred cavaliers against two hundred; or, in like proportion to the number of one thousand, always allowing thy faith a double number of champions. Remember, O King, that thou canst not refuse this challenge; since thy prophet, knowing the impossibility of maintaining his doctrines by argument, has commanded his followers to enforce them with the sword."

The beard of King Yusef trembled with indignation. "The master of Alcántara," said he, "is a madman to send such a message, and ye are saucy knaves to bring it."

So saying, he ordered the ambassadors to be thrown into a dungeon, by way of giving them a lesson in diplomacy; and they were roughly treated on their way thither by the populace, who were exasperated at this insult to their sovereign and their faith.

The grand master of Alcántara could scarcely credit the tidings of the maltreatment of his messengers; but the hermit rejoiced when they were repeated to him. "God," said he, "has blinded this infidel king for his downfall. Since he has sent no reply to thy defiance, consider it accepted.

Marshal thy forces, therefore; march forward to Granada; pause not until thou seest the gate of Elvira. A miracle will be wrought in thy favor. There will be a great battle; the enemy will be overthrown; but not one of thy soldiers will be slain."

The grand master called upon every warrior zealous in the Christian cause to aid him in this crusade. In a little while three hundred horsemen and a thousand foot-soldiers rallied under his standard. The horsemen were veterans, seasoned to battle and well armed; but the infantry were raw and undisciplined. The victory, however, was to be miraculous; the grand master was a man of surpassing faith, and knew that the weaker the means the greater the miracle. He sallied forth confidently, therefore, with his little army, and the hermit strode ahead, bearing a cross on the end of a long pole, and beneath it the pennon of the order of Alcántara.

As they approached the city of Cordova they were overtaken by messengers, spurring in all haste, bearing missives from the Castilian monarch, forbidding the enterprise. The grand master was a man of a single mind and a single will; in other words, a man of one idea. "Were I on any other errand," said he, "I should obey these letters as coming from my lord the king; but I am sent by a higher power than the king. In compliance with its commands I, have advanced the cross thus far against the infidels; and it would be treason to the standard of Christ to turn back without achieving my errand."

So the trumpets were sounded; the cross was again reared aloft, and the band of zealots resumed their march. As they passed through the streets of Cordova the people were amazed at beholding a hermit bearing a cross at the head of a warlike multitude; but when they learnt that a miraculous victory was to be effected and Granada destroyed, laborers and artisans threw by the implements of their handicrafts and joined in the crusade; while a mercenary rabble followed on with a view to plunder.

A number of cavaliers of rank who lacked faith in the promised miracle, and dreaded the consequences of this unprovoked irruption into the country of the Moor, assembled at the bridge of the Guadalquivir and endeavored to dissuade the grand master from crossing. He was deaf to prayers, expostulations, or menaces; his followers were enraged at this opposition to the cause of the faith; they put an end to the parley by their clamors; the cross was again reared and borne triumphantly across the bridge.

The multitude increased as it proceeded; by the time the grand master had reached Alcala, which stands on a mountain overlooking the Vega of Granada, upwards of five thousand men on foot had joined his standard.

At Alcala came forth Alonzo Fernandez de Cordova, Lord of Aguilar, his brother Diego Fernandez, Marshal of Castile, and other cavaliers of valor and experience. Placing themselves in the way of the grand master, "What madness is this, Don Martin?" said they; "the Moorish king has two hundred thousand foot-soldiers and five thousand horse within his walls; what can you and your handful of cavaliers and your noisy rabble do against such force? Bethink you of the disasters which have befallen other Christian commanders, who have crossed these rocky borders with ten times your force. Think, too, of the mischief that, will be brought upon this kingdom by an outrage of the kind committed by a man of your rank and importance, a grand master of Alcántara. Pause, we entreat you, while the truce is yet unbroken. Await within the borders the reply of the king of Granada to your challenge. If he agree to meet you singly, or with champions two or three, it will be your individual contest, and fight it out in God's name; if he refuse, you may return home with great honor and the disgrace will fall upon the Moors."

Several cavaliers, who had hitherto followed the grand master with devoted zeal, were moved by these expostulations, and suggested to him the policy of listening to this, advice.

"Cavaliers," said he, addressing himself to Alonzo Fernandez de Cordova and his companions, "I thank you for the counsel you have so kindly bestowed upon me, and if I were merely in pursuit of individual glory I might be swayed by it. But I am engaged to achieve a great triumph of the faith, which God is to effect by miracle through my means. As to you, cavaliers," turning to those of his followers who had wavered, "if your hearts fail you, or you repent of having put your hands to this good work, return, in God's name, and my blessing go with you. For myself, though I have none to stand by me but this holy hermit, yet will I assuredly proceed, until I have planted this sacred standard on the walls of Granada, or perished in the attempt."

"Don Martin Yañez de Barbudo," replied the cavaliers, "we are not men to turn our backs upon our commander, however rash his enterprise. We spoke but in caution. Lead on, therefore, and if it be to the death, be assured to the death we will follow thee."

By this time the common soldiers became impatient. "Forward! forward!" shouted they. "Forward in the cause of faith." So the grand master gave signal, the, hermit again reared the cross aloft, and they poured down a defile of the mountain, with solemn chants of triumph.

That night they encamped at the river of Azores, and the next morning, which was Sunday, crossed the borders. Their first pause was at a solitary tower, built upon a rock; a frontier post to keep a watch upon the border, and give notice of invasion. It was thence called the Tower of the Spy. The grand master halted before it and summoned its petty garrison to surrender. He was answered by a shower of stones and arrows, which wounded him in the hand and killed three of his men.

"How is this, father?" said he to the hermit; "you assured me that not one of my followers would be slain!"

"True, my son; but I meant in the great battle of the infidel king; what need is there of miracle to aid in the capture of a petty tower?"

The grand master was satisfied. He ordered wood to be piled against the door of the tower to burn it down. In the meantime provisions were unloaded from the sumpter-mules, and the crusaders, withdrawing beyond bow-shot, sat down on the grass to a repast to strengthen them for the arduous day's work before them. While thus engaged, they were startled by the sudden appearance of a great Moorish host. The watch towers had given the alarm by fire and smoke from the mountain-tops of "an enemy across the border," and the king of Granada had sallied forth with a great force to the encounter.

The crusaders, nearly taken by surprise, flew to arms and prepared for battle. The grand master ordered his three hundred horsemen to dismount and fight on foot in support of the infantry. The Moors, however, charged so suddenly that they separated the cavaliers from the foot-soldiers and prevented their uniting. The grand master gave the old war-cry, Santiago! Santiago! and close Spain!" He and his knights breasted the fury of the battle, but were surrounded by a countless host and assailed with arrows, stones, darts, and arquebuses. Still they fought fearlessly and made prodigious slaughter. The hermit mingled in the hottest of the fight. In one hand he bore the cross, in the other he brandished a sword, with which he dealt about him like a maniac, slaying several of the enemy, until he sank to the ground covered with wounds. The grand master saw him fall, and saw too late the fallacies of his prophecies. Despair, however, only made him fight the more fiercely, until he also fell overpowered by numbers. His devoted cavaliers emulated his holy zeal. Not one turned his back nor asked for mercy; all fought until they fell. As to the foot-soldiers, many were killed, many taken prisoners; the residue escaped to Alcala. When the Moors came to strip the slain, the wounds of the cavaliers were all found to be in front.

Such was the catastrophe of this fanatic enterprise. The Moors vaunted it as a decisive proof of the superior sanctity of their faith, and extolled their king to the skies when he returned in triumph to Granada.

As it was satisfactorily shown that this crusade was the enterprise of an individual, and contrary to the express orders of the king of Castile, the peace of the two kingdoms was not interrupted. Nay, the Moors evinced a feeling of respect for the valor of the unfortunate grand master, and readily gave up his body to Don Alonzo Fernandez de Cordova, who came from Alcala to seek it. The Christians of the frontier united in paying the last sad honors to his memory. His body was placed upon a bier, covered with the pennon of the order of Alcántara; and the broken cross, the emblem of his confident hopes and fatal disappointment, was borne before it. In this way his remains were carried back in funeral procession, through the mountain tract which he had traversed so resolutely. Wherever it passed, through a town or village, the populace followed, with tears and lamentations, bewailing him as a valiant knight and a martyr to the faith. His body was interred in the chapel of the convent of Santa Maria de Almocovara, and on his sepulchre may still be seen engraven in quaint and antique Spanish the following testimonial to his bravery:— HERE LIES ONE WHOSE HEART NEVER KNEW FEAR.

Spanish Romance

In the latter part of my sojourn in the Alhambra, I made frequent descents into the Library of the University; and relished more and more the old Spanish chronicles, which I found there bound in parchment. I delight in those quaint histories which treat of the times when the Moslems maintained a foothold in the Peninsula. With all their bigotry and occasional intolerance, they are full of noble acts and generous sentiments, and have a high, spicy, Oriental flavor, not to be found in other records of the times, which were merely European. In fact, Spain, even at the present day, is a country apart; severed in history, habits, manners, and modes of thinking, from all the rest of Europe. It is a romantic country; but its romance has none of the sentimentality of modern European romance; it is chiefly derived from the brilliant regions of the East, and from the high-minded school of Saracenic chivalry.

The Arab invasion and conquest brought a higher civilization, and a nobler style of thinking, into Gothic Spain. The Arabs were a quick-witted, sagacious, proud-spirited, and poetical people, and were imbued with Oriental science and literature. Wherever they established a seat of power, it became a rallying-place for the learned and ingenious; and they softened and refined the people whom they conquered. By degrees, occupancy seemed to give them an hereditary right to their foothold in the land; they ceased to be looked upon as invaders, and were regarded as rival neighbors. The Peninsula, broken up into a variety of states, both Christian and Moslem, became, for centuries, a great campaigning-ground, where the art of war seemed to be the principal business of man, and was carried to the highest pitch of romantic chivalry. The original ground of hostility, a difference of faith, gradually lost its rancor. Neighboring states, of opposite creeds, were occasionally linked together in alliances, offensive and defensive; so that the cross and crescent were to be seen side by side, fighting against some common enemy. In times of peace, too, the noble youth of either faith resorted to the same cities, Christian or Moslem, to school themselves in military science. Even in the temporary truces of sanguinary wars, the warriors who had recently striven together in the deadly conflicts of the field, laid aside their animosity, met at tournaments, jousts, and other military festivities, and exchanged the courtesies of gentle and generous spirits. Thus the opposite races became frequently mingled together in peaceful intercourse, or if any rivalry took place, it was in those high courtesies and nobler acts, which bespeak the accomplished cavalier. Warriors, of opposite creeds, became ambitious of transcending each other in magnanimity as well as valor. Indeed the chivalric virtues were refined upon to a degree sometimes fastidious and constrained, but at other times noble and affecting. The annals of the times teem with illustrious instances of high-wrought courtesy, romantic generosity, lofty disinterestedness, and punctilious honor, that warm the very soul to read them. These have furnished themes for national plays and poems, or have been celebrated in those all-pervading ballads, which are as the life-breath of the people, and thus have continued to exercise an influence on the national character, which centuries of vicissitudes and decline have not been able to destroy; so that, with all their faults, and they are many, the Spaniards, even at the present day, are, on many points, the most high-minded and proud-spirited people of Europe. It is true, the romance of feeling derived from the sources I have mentioned, has, like all other romance, its affectations and extremes. It renders the Spaniard at times pompous and grandiloquent; prone to carry the point of honor, beyond the bounds of sober sense and sound morality; disposed, in the midst of poverty, to affect the "grand gentleman," and to look down with sovereign disdain upon "arts mechanical," and all the gainful pursuits of plebeian life; but this very inflation of spirit, while it fills his brain with vapors, lifts him above a thousand meannesses; and though it often keeps him in indigence, ever protects him from vulgarity.

In the present day, when popular literature is running into the low levels of life, and luxuriating on the vices and follies of mankind; and when the universal pursuit of gain is trampling down the early growth of poetic feeling, and wearing out the verdure of the soul, I question whether it would not be of service for the reader occasionally to turn to these records of prouder times and loftier modes of thinking; and to steep himself to the very lips in old Spanish romance.

With these preliminary suggestions, the fruit of a morning's reading and rumination in the old library of the University, I will give him a legend in point, drawn forth from one of the venerable chronicles alluded to.

Legend of Don Munio
Sancho de Hinojosa

In the cloisters of the ancient Benedictine convent of San Domingo, at Silos, in Castile, are the mouldering yet magnificent monuments of the once powerful and chivalrous family of Hinojosa. Among these reclines the marble figure of a knight, in complete armor, with the hands pressed together, as if in prayer. On one side of his tomb is sculptured in relief a band of Christian cavaliers, capturing a cavalcade of male and female Moors; on the other side, the same cavaliers are represented kneeling before an altar. The tomb, like most of the neighboring monuments, is almost in ruins, and the sculpture is nearly unintelligible, excepting to the keen eye of the antiquary. The story connected with the sepulchre, however, is still preserved in the old Spanish chronicles, and is to the following purport.

I n old times, several hundred years ago, there was a noble Castilian cavalier, named Don Munio Sancho de Hinojosa, lord of a border castle, which had stood the brunt of many a Moorish foray. He had seventy horsemen as his household troops, all of the ancient Castilian proof; stark warriors, hard riders, and men of iron; with these he scoured the Moorish lands, and made his name terrible throughout the borders. His castle-hall was covered with banners, cimeters, and Moslem helms, the trophies of his prowess. Don Munio was, moreover, a keen huntsman, and rejoiced in hounds of all kinds, steeds for the chase, and hawks for the towering sport of falconry. When not engaged in warfare his delight was to beat up the neighboring forests; and scarcely ever did he ride forth without hound and horn, a boar-spear in his hand, or a hawk upon his fist, and an attendant train of huntsmen.

His wife, Doña Maria Palacin, was of a gentle and timid nature, little fitted to be the spouse of so hardy and adventurous a knight; and many a tear did the poor lady shed, when he sallied forth upon his daring enterprises, and many a prayer did she offer up for his safety.

As this doughty cavalier was one day hunting, he stationed himself in a thicket, on the borders of a green glade of the forest, and dispersed his followers to rouse, the game, and drive it toward his stand. He had not been here long, when a cavalcade of Moors of both sexes, came pranking over the forest-lawn. They were unarmed, and magnificently dressed in robes of tissue and embroidery, rich shawls of India, bracelets and anklets of gold, and jewels that sparkled in the sun.

At the head of this gay cavalcade rode a youthful cavalier, superior to the rest in dignity and loftiness of demeanor, and in splendor of attire: beside him was a damsel, whose veil, blown aside by the breeze, displayed a face of surpassing beauty, and eyes cast down in maiden modesty, yet beaming with tenderness and joy.

Don Munio thanked his stars for sending him such a prize, and exulted at the thought of bearing home to his wife the glittering spoils of these infidels. Putting his hunting-horn to his lips, he gave a blast that rung through the forest. His huntsmen came running from all quarters, and the astonished Moors were surrounded and made captives.

The beautiful Moor wrung her hands in despair, and her female attendants uttered the most piercing cries. The young Moorish cavalier alone retained self-possession. He inquired the name of the Christian knight who commanded this troop of horsemen. When told that it was Don Munio Sancho de Hinojosa, his countenance lighted up. Approaching that cavalier, and kissing his hand, "Don Munio Sancho," said he, "I have heard of your fame as a true and valiant knight, terrible in arms, but schooled in the noble virtues of chivalry. Such do I trust to find you. In me you behold Abadil, son of a Moorish official of rank. I am on the way to celebrate my nuptials with this lady; chance has thrown us in your power, but I confide in your magnanimity. Take all our treasure and jewels; demand what ransom you think proper for our persons, but suffer us not to be insulted nor dishonored."

When the good knight heard this appeal, and beheld the beauty of the youthful pair, his heart was touched with tenderness and courtesy. "God forbid," said he, "that I should disturb such happy nuptials. My prisoners in troth shall ye be, for fifteen days, and immured within my castle, where I claim, as conqueror, the right of celebrating your espousals."

So saying, he despatched one of his fleetest horsemen in advance, to notify Doña Maria Palacin of the coming of this bridal party; while he and his huntsmen escorted the cavalcade, not as captors, but as a guard of honor. As they drew near to the castle, the banners were hung out, and the trumpets sounded from the battlements; and on their nearer approach, the drawbridge was lowered, and Doña Maria came forth to meet them, attended by her ladies and knights, her pages and her minstrels. She took the young bride, Allifra, in her arms, kissed her with the tenderness of a sister, and conducted her into the castle. In the meantime, Don Munio sent forth missives in every direction, and had viands and dainties of all kinds collected from the country round; and the wedding of the Moorish lovers was celebrated with all possible state and festivity. For fifteen days the castle was given up to joy and revelry. There were tiltings and jousts at the ring, and bull-fights, and banquets, and dances to the sound of minstrelsy. When the fifteen days were at an end, he made the bride and bridegroom magnificent presents, and conducted them and their attendants safely beyond the borders. Such, in old times, were the courtesy and generosity of a Spanish cavalier.

Several years after this event, the king of Castile summoned his nobles to assist him in a campaign against the Moors. Don Munio Sancho was among the first to answer to the call, with seventy horsemen, all stanch and well-tried warriors. His wife, Doña Maria, hung about his neck. "Alas, my lord!" exclaimed she, "how often wilt thou tempt thy fate, and when will thy thirst for glory be appeased!"

"One battle more," replied Don Munio, "one battle more, for the honor of Castile, and I here make a vow, that when this is over, I will lay by my sword, and repair with my cavaliers in pilgrimage to the sepulchre of our Lord at Jerusalem." The cavaliers all joined with him in the vow, and Doña Maria felt in some degree soothed in spirit; still, she saw with a heavy heart the departure of her husband, and watched his banner with wistful eyes, until it disappeared among the trees of the forest.

The king of Castile led his army to the plains of Almanara, where they encountered the Moorish host. The battle was long and bloody; the Christians repeatedly wavered and were as often rallied by the energy of their commanders. Don Munio was covered with wounds, but refused to leave the field. The Christians at length gave way, and the king was hardly pressed, and in danger of being captured.

Don Munio called upon his cavaliers to follow him to the rescue. "Now is the time," cried he, "to prove your loyalty. Fall to, like brave men! We fight for the true faith, and if we lose our lives here, we gain a better life hereafter."

Rushing with his men between the king and his pursuers, they checked the latter in their career, and gave time for their monarch to escape; but they fell victims to their loyalty. They all fought to the last gasp. Don Munio was singled out by a powerful Moorish knight, but having been wounded in the right arm, he fought to disadvantage, and was slain. The battle being over, the Moor paused to possess himself of the spoils of this redoubtable Christian warrior. When he unlaced the helmet, however, and beheld the countenance of Don Munio, he gave a great cry and smote his breast. "Woe is me!" cried he,

"I have slain my benefactor! The flower of knightly virtue! the most magnanimous of cavaliers!"

While the battle had been raging on the plains of Almanara, Doña Maria Palacin remained in her castle, a prey to the keenest anxiety. Her eyes were ever fixed on the road that led from the country of the Moors, and often she asked the watchman of the tower, "What seest thou?"

One evening, at the shadowy hour of twilight, the warden sounded his horn. "I see," cried he, "a numerous train winding up the valley. They are mingled Moors and Christians. The banner of my lord is in the advance. Joyful tidings!" exclaimed the old seneschal; "my lord returns in triumph, and brings captives!" Then the castle courts rang with shouts of joy; and the standard was displayed, and the trumpets were sounded, and the drawbridge was lowered, and Doña Maria went forth with her ladies, and her knights, and her pages, and her minstrels, to welcome her lord from the wars. But as the train drew nigh, she beheld a sumptuous bier, covered with black velvet, and on it lay a warrior, as if taking his repose: he lay in his armor, with his helmet on his head, and his sword in his hand, as one who had never been conquered, and around the bier were the escutcheons of the house of Hinojosa.

A number of Moorish cavaliers attended the bier, with emblems of mourning, and with dejected countenances; and their leader cast himself at the feet of Doña Maria, and hid his face in his hands. She beheld in him the gallant Abadil, whom she had once welcomed with his bride to her castle; but who now came with the body of her lord, whom he had unknowingly slain in battle!

The sepulchre erected in the cloisters of the convent of San Domingo, was achieved at the expense of the Moor, Abadil, as a feeble testimony of his grief for the death of the good knights Don Munio, and his reverence for his memory. The tender and faithful Doña Maria soon followed her lord to the tomb. On one of the stones of a small arch, beside his sepulchre, is the following simple inscription: "Here lies Maria Palacin, wife of Munio Sancho de Hinojosa."

The legend of Don Munio Sancho does not conclude with his death. On the same day on which the battle took place on the plains of Almanara, a chaplain of the Holy Temple at Jerusalem, while standing at the outer gate, beheld a train of Christian cavaliers advancing, as if in pilgrimage. The chaplain was a native of Spain, and as the pilgrims approached, he knew the foremost to be Don Munio Sancho de Hinojosa, with whom he had been well acquainted in former times. Hastening to the patriarch, he told him of the honorable rank of the pilgrims at the gate. The patriarch, therefore, went forth with a grand procession of priests and monks, and received the pilgrims with all due honor. There were seventy cavaliers beside their leader,—all stark and lofty warriors. They carried their helmets in their hands, and their faces were deadly pale. They greeted no one, nor looked either to the right or to the left, but entered the chapel, and kneeling before the sepulchre of our Saviour, performed their orisons in silence. When they had concluded, they rose as if to depart, and the patriarch and his attendants advanced to speak to them, but they were no more to be seen. Every one marvelled what could be the meaning of this prodigy. The patriarch carefully noted down the day, and sent to Castile to learn tidings of Don Munio Sancho de Hinojosa. He received for reply, that on the very day specified, that worthy knight, with seventy of his followers, had been slain in battle. These, therefore, must have been the blessed spirits of those Christian warriors, come to fulfil their vow of pilgrimage to the Holy Sepulchre at Jerusalem. Such was Castilian faith in the olden time, which kept its word, even beyond the grave.

The Author's Farewell to Granada

My serene and happy reign in the Alhambra was suddenly brought to a close by letters which reached me, while indulging in Oriental luxury in the cool hall of the baths, summoning me away from my Moslem elysium, to mingle once more in the bustle and business of the dusty world. How was I to encounter its toils and turmoils, after such a life of repose and reverie! How was I to endure its commonplace, after the poetry of the Alhambra!

But little preparation was necessary for my departure. A two-wheeled vehicle, called a tartana, very much resembling a covered cart, was to be the traveling equipage of a young Englishman and myself through Murcia, to Alicant and Valencia, on our way to France; and a long-limbed varlet, who had been a smuggler, and, for aught I knew, a robber, was to be our guide and guard. The preparations were soon made, but the departure was the difficulty. Day after day it was postponed; day after day was spent lingering about my favorite haunts, and day after day they appeared more delightful in my eyes.

The social and domestic little world also, in which I had been moving, had become singularly endeared to me; and the concern evinced by them at my intended departure, convinced me that my kind feelings were reciprocated. Indeed, when at length the day arrived, I did not dare venture upon a leave-taking at the good dame Antonia's; I saw the soft heart of little Dolores, at least, was brim full and ready for an overflow. So I bade a silent adieu to the palace and its inmates, and descended into the city as if intending to return. There, however, the tartana and the guide were ready; so, after taking a noon-day's repast with my fellow-traveler at the inn, I set out with him on our journey.

Manuel, the nephew of Tia Antonia, Mateo, my officious but now disconsolate squire, and two or three old invalids of the Alhambra with whom I had grown into gossiping companionship, had come down to see me off; for it is one of the good old customs of Spain, to sally forth several miles to meet a coming friend, and to accompany him as far on his departure. Thus then we set out, our long-legged guard striding ahead, with his gun on his shoulder; Manuel and Mateo on each side of the tartana, and the old invalids behind.

At some little distance to the north of Granada, the road gradually ascends the hills; here I alighted and walked up slowly with Manuel, who took this occasion to confide to me the secret of his heart and of all those tender concerns between himself and Dolores, with which I had been already informed by the all-knowing and all-revealing Mateo Ximenes. His doctor's diploma had prepared the way for their union, and if he could get the post of physician of the fortress, his happiness would be complete! I congratulated him on the judgment and good taste he had shown in his choice of a helpmate and invoked all possible felicity on their union.

It was indeed a sorrowful parting when I took leave of these good people and saw them slowly descend the hills; now and then turning round to wave me a last adieu. Manuel, it is true, had cheerful prospects to console him, but poor Mateo seemed perfectly cast down. It was to him a grievous fall from the station of prime minister and historiographer, to his old brown cloak and his starveling mystery of ribbon-weaving; and the poor devil, notwithstanding his occasional officiousness, had, somehow or other, acquired a stronger hold on my sympathies than I was aware of. It would have really been a consolation in parting, could I have anticipated the good fortune in store for him, and to which I had contributed; for the importance I had appeared to give to his tales and gossip and local knowledge, and the frequent companionship in which I had indulged him in the course of my strolls, had elevated his idea of his own qualifications and opened a new career to him; and the son of the Alhambra has since become its regular and well-paid cicerone; insomuch that I am told he has never been obliged to resume the ragged old brown cloak in which I first found him.

Towards sunset I came to where the road wound into the mountains, and here I paused to take a last look at Granada. The hill on which I stood commanded a glorious view of the city, the Vega, and the surrounding mountains. I now could realize something of the feelings of poor Boabdil when he bade adieu to the paradise he was leaving behind, and beheld before him a rugged and sterile road conducting him to exile.

The setting sun as usual shed a melancholy effulgence on the ruddy towers of the Alhambra. I could faintly discern the balconied window of the tower of Comares, where I had indulged in so many delightful reveries. The bosky groves and gardens about the city were richly gilded with the sunshine, the purple haze of a summer evening was gathering over the Vega; everything was lovely, but tenderly and sadly so, to my parting gaze.

"I will hasten from this prospect," thought I, "before the sun is set. I will carry away a recollection of it clothed in all its beauty."

With these thoughts I pursued my way among the mountains. A little further and Granada, the Vega, and the Alhambra, were shut from my view; and thus ended one of the pleasantest dreams of a life, which the reader perhaps may think has been but too much made up of dreams. THE END.

Notes

Note 1.

In 711 the peninsula of Spain was invaded by the Saracens or Moors, who were Mohammedans from the northern part of Africa. At first the invasion was intended by their governor, Musa, as a raid for plunder, but under the leadership of his general, Taric, and through the treachery of the Spanish governor of Ceuta, a fortress on the African coast, overlooking the straits of Gibraltar, a horde of Moslem soldiers poured into Spain, and most unexpected conquest followed.

Within the next four years the whole southern part of the Peninsula had been subdued, and the Spanish people driven into the northern mountainous districts.

Elated by their success the Moors hoped for the conquest of Western Europe, and invaded France, where they were for a time victorious; but in 732 they were so completely routed by the French king, Charles Martel, at the battle of Tours that they made no further attempts to enter the country.

For over seven hundred years they remained in Spain, though a constant warfare was kept up between them and the different kingdoms into which the northern part of the peninsula was divided.

In the thirteenth century they had been so far conquered that their rule was restricted to the beautiful and fertile province of Granada, and as a condition of peace they were obliged to pay a yearly tribute of 12,000 gold ducats to their Christian foes.

Here they made a final stand for another two hundred and fifty years, but towards the latter part of the fifteenth century the Moorish king, Muly Abel Hassan, a most cruel and warlike monarch, refused to pay the tribute any longer. He led his army out of Granada and made a raid upon the Christian city of Zahara, which he surprised in the midst of a stormy winter's night. Having overcome the garrison, he plundered the city, laid it waste, slaughtered many of the people, and treated the unfortunate captives whom he brought back with the utmost cruelty. So shocking were his deeds that many of his own people cried: "Woe to Granada! the hour of its destruction is at band." This act so aroused the Christians that from this time the warfare was almost incessant, and in 1491 Boabdil, the last of the Moorish kings, the weak and vacillating son of Muly Abel Hassan, delivered up the keys of Granada to Ferdinand and Isabella.

Those who enjoy the recital of the deeds of these stirring times are recommended to read Irving's Conquest of Granada and Lockhart's Spanish Ballads.

Note 2.

The bull fight, the chief pastime of the Spanish people, is a most cruel and revolting sport. It takes place in a large circular arena, surrounded by raised seats. The circus at Madrid is capable of holding 12,000 people and the spectacle is patronized by all classes. The combat is between bulls and men trained to the profession, some of whom fight on foot and others on horseback. Human life is rarely sacrificed, but many bulls, and often horses, are killed at each exhibition.

Note 3.

Don Quixote is the hero of a famous Spanish romance of the same name, by Cervantes (1547-1616). He is represented as a country gentleman, who spends his money in buying, and his time in reading, tales of chivalry, to the neglect of his domestic affairs. Having "his imagination full of all that he had read; of enchantments, contests, battles, challenges, tortures, and impossible absurdities," he determines to set forth, like a wandering knight, to do battle against all sorts of wrongs. He is accompanied by his squire, Sancho Panza, and the two meet with many amusing adventures. The tale was written not only to show the absurdities into which writers on chivalry had been led, but it was also a protest against the prejudice, common to Spain and other countries at that time, against any sort of useful labor, whether of brains or of hands.

Note 4.

About the beginning of the seventh century an Arabian prophet, called Mohammed, began to preach the religion of Islam, or entire submission to the will of God, to his idolatrous countrymen. The Hebrew religion had been carried into Arabia by Jewish colonists, who established themselves in the northern part of the Peninsula, after the destruction of Jerusalem; and Christianity also had its disciples in the country.

The new religion was built upon the teachings of the Old Testament, with additions and alterations. Of the Christian religion Mohammed knew but little; he had, however, reverence for its founder, whom he ranked as the greatest prophet next to himself. He recognized six persons as especially commissioned to proclaim new laws and dispensations, each of which had in time taken the place of the preceding one. These teachers were Adam, Noah, Abraham, Moses, Jesus, and Mohammed—the last and greatest of them all.

He set forth his doctrines in a series of writings called the Koran—the sacred book of the Moslems or Mohammedans. The two principal articles of belief are contained in the oft-repeated words "There is no God but Allah, and Mohammed is his prophet."

He was born at Mecca, a city some forty miles from the Red Sea, to which numbers of the Arab tribes resorted at that time, on the pilgrimages prescribed by their ancient idolatrous creed. In this city was the Caaba, or Kaaba, an ancient building, in which was set a black stone, said to have fallen with Adam from Paradise. The belief in the sacredness of the Kaaba and the ceremonies of the pilgrimage were incorporated in the new belief; but all former idolatrous practices were strictly forbidden, and fasting, prayer, and almsgiving were enjoined.

For some time after Mohammed began to preach, but little attention was paid to his doctrines by the people of Mecca, but they finally became alarmed, as the number of his disciples increased, and they rose in anger against the prophet who "called their ancient gods idols, and their ancestors fools." Mohammed accordingly fled with his followers from the city, and sought refuge in Medina, and from this flight, or Hegira, the Mohammedan era is dated.

In this city he was better appreciated, and soon rose to the position of law-giver and judge. He drew to himself many disciples and sent his missionaries all over Arabia and into neighboring countries. He then proclaimed a holy war against the enemies of Islam, at first confining himself to attacking caravans of merchants on their way to Syria. As his forces became more numerous, and his power increased, he engaged in many battles, and at last he besieged Mecca at the head of ten thousand men, took the city, and was publicly recognized as its chief and prophet.

Before Mohammed's time the Arabs had been a collection of rival tribes, but he consolidated them into the Moslem people and made himself the master of Arabia.

His followers carried their conquest over Syria, Persia, and as far as Spain, and finally placed the crescent, the emblem of their religion, on the spires of the great Christian cathedral of St. Sophia at Constantinople, where it still remains. To-day about thirty millions of people profess the faith of Islam.

Note 5.

Spain in the time of the Greeks and Romans was known as Iberia or Hispania. Its people were made up from many different races, some of whom had colonized its coasts, and others had from time to time overrun the country and made themselves its masters.

At the time of the Saracen or Moorish invasion, the Goths, the last conquerors of Spain after the fall of the Roman Empire, held the governing power, though the Peninsula was subdivided into many petty kingdoms.

In 1469 Arragon and Castile, two of the most powerful states, were united by the marriage of their sovereigns, Ferdinand and Isabella, names of great interest to Americans, as it was under their patronage, especially that of the queen, that Christopher Columbus sailed forth to the discovery of the New World.

It was to them also that the Moorish King Boabdil surrendered his stronghold, and they rode into Granada the masters of united Spain.

Their grandson Charles V. (1500-1558) was the ablest and most powerful monarch of the sixteenth century. From his father he inherited the archduchy of Austria and the kingdom of the Netherlands; from his grandparents all Spain, increased by the addition of the Two Sicilies (1504) and by the annexation of the southern part of Navarre. In his reign Mexico and Peru were added to Spain's possessions, and his power was further augmented by his election as Emperor of Germany. This was the period of Spain's greatest glory.

Under succeeding monarchs of lesser ability, and after many wars, the power of the country waned, but a fresh period of activity was entered upon when in 1700 the kingdom came to Philip V. , a prince of the house of Bourbon.

After the French Revolution Napoleon invaded the country, deposed the king, Ferdinand VII., and placed his own brother on the throne. The Spaniards revolted, and, aided by the armies of Great Britain, expelled the French from the Peninsula in 1814.

Note 6.

In the Middle Ages emblems or devices were pictured on the shields of knights, and afterwards embroidered on the surcoat or garment worn over the coat of mail—from this came the designation coat of arms. These devices were of practical use, since they identified the wearer, whose face, when in battle, was concealed by the visor of his helmet.

At first every knight chose his emblem according to his fancy, and all sorts of animals, imaginary monsters, plants, and forms of many other objects were used. When possible, the symbol suggested the name, title, or some distinguishing quality of its bearer,—a custom which has its counterpart among the American Indians,

As these coats-of-arms became numerous, great confusion arose, for the same emblem was often taken by different knights. In the course of time it was found necessary to regulate the bearing of coats-of-arms, as they were made hereditary, and descended from their original bearer to his heirs.

This regulation respecting coats-of-arms was intrusted to heralds, who were officers appointed by their sovereigns, and who had various other duties to perform, such as to marshal processions, superintend public ceremonies, hear messages of courtesy or defiance between princes or knights, and to take charge of tournaments, jousts, and all other exercises of chivalry.

An escutcheon represents an old knightly shield, with a coat-of-arms depicted upon it.

Where a family is entitled by inheritance to bear several coats-of-arms, the escutcheon is divided into parts called quarterings, upon each of which the different emblems are emblazoned.

Glossary

THE JOURNEY battlements:
Notched walls on the top of buildings, originally used only on fortifications. freebooters:
Robbers, highwaymen. blunderbuss:
A short gun of large bore, capable of discharging many bullets, and intended to do much execution without accurate aim. stiletto:
A small, round, pointed dagger. banditti:
Robbers, a band of outlaws. gentlemen of the road:
Highwaymen. rib-roasting:
A hard beating. valet:
A gentleman's personal servant. saws:
Wise sayings. wiseacre:
A pretender to wisdom. grandiloquence:
High-sounding language. señors:
Sirs, gentlemen. castanet:
An instrument of hard wood or ivory, shaped like a pair of chestnuts attached by a string. It is fastened to the thumb, held inside the hand, and beaten with the middle finger as an accompaniment to dances and to the guitar, used particularly by the Moors and Spaniards. amateur:
One who is a lover of any pursuit, art, or science, but is not engaged in it professionally. Orpheus:
A famous ancient poet of Thrace, who was said by the Greeks to have enchanted wild beasts, and also trees and rocks, by the music of his lyre, a stringed instrument resembling the harp. fandango:
A favorite and lively dance of the Spaniards. buxom:
Gay, lively. dragoon:
A soldier taught and armed to fight on horseback or on foot, as circumstances may require. siesta:
A, short nap taken about the middle of the day, or after dinner. sombrero:
A broad-brimmed hat. cockade:
A knot of ribbon worn on the hat, generally as a military badge. mantilla:
Head-covering for women, made of silk, lace, or other stuff. basquina:
Upper petticoat worn by Spanish women. heterogeneous:
Dissimilar, differing in kind. hidalgo:
A Spanish nobleman of the lower class. curate:

Parish priest. notary:

An officer authorized to attest writings of any kind. Boabdil:

The last of the Moorish kings of Spain. See also note 1. orison:

Prayer. dramatis personae:

The Latin for persons represented in the play. sabre:

Cavalry sword. Don:

Mr., Sir, a Spanish title. guerilla exploits:

Petty or irregular warfare. Vega:

The great plain of Granada, over a hundred miles in circumference and surrounded by lofty mountains. This was so carefully cultivated that the whole territory appeared like a vast garden. Here the Moors made their last stand against their conquerors.

PALACE OF THE ALHAMBRA Moslems:

Followers of the prophet Mahomet or Mohammed. See note 4. royal demesne:

Property under the immediate control of the crown. parochial:

belonging to a parish. varlet:

rascal or rogue. cicerone:

A guide who shows strangers places of interest, and explains them in a loquacious manner. Phœnicians:

natives of Phœnicia, a country of Asia, on the coast of Syria. At a very early time they excelled in the fine arts. They were regarded by the Greeks as the inventors of the alphabet, and much knowledge of arts and science is ascribed to them. Their voyages and colonies extended to the coasts of Africa and Spain, and even to Great Britain. barbican:

Watch-tower at the entrance of a castle or on the walls of a town. jousts and tournaments:

Sports or exercises, common in the Middle Ages, in which a number of combatants, or knights, engaged for the purpose of exhibiting their courage and skill at arms. esplanade:

A level ground within a fortified place used for exercise, etc. Dolores:

"The Sorrowful". escutcheon:

A shield adorned with coat of arms. See note 6. cipher:

A secret character or mark, invented for a special purpose. Cufic:

A species of characters anciently used in the sacred books of the Mohammedans. alabaster:

A white stone used for ornamental purposes. arcade:

A series of arches supported on pillars. filigree work:

Delicately wrought ornamental work. fretwork:

A sort of ornamental raised work formed of small interlaced bands or fillets. cavalier:

knight, horseman. wicket:

A small door made in a gate. cuirass:

A piece of armor, covering the body from neck to thighs, before and behind. cimeter:

A short sword with curved point. poniard:

A small pointed dagger for stabbing. apocryphal:

Of doubtful authority. Orientalist:

A native or inhabitant of the East. parterres:

A system of flower beds of different shapes and sizes, with walks of gravel or turf between. ardent:

Hot, burning.

IMPORTANT NEGOTIATIONS bivouac:

A military term meaning to pass the night in the open air, without encamping, ready for action. Here it means to sleep without a regular bed. perquisite:

Something received in addition to, or in place of, regular wages. wight:

Person, creature. historiographic:

Professing historical knowledge. shopboard:

A board or bench on which any work is done.

INHABITANTS OF THE ALHAMBRA tatterdemalion:

ragamuffin, Scheherezade:

The fictitious relater of the stories in the Arabian Nights' Entertainments. bottle-nose:

A large, bottle-shaped nose. cocked hat:

A hat with the brim turned up at one or more sides. marker of a fives-court:

One who keeps the score for a game of ball called fives. maravetdi:

A small Spanish copper coin of less value than a cent; — now disused. litigious:

Fond of contending in lawsuits. grandiose:

Characterized by self-display; pompous. bastion:

A projecting mass of earth or masonry at the angles of a fortification.

THE HALL OF AMBASSADORS stuccoed:
Covered with decorations moulded in fine plaster. Morisco:
Moorish. pensile:
Hanging, pendent. anomalous:
Irregular, deviating from the regular rule. Crescent:
The figure of the new moon used for the symbol of Mohometanism, as the cross is that of the Christian religion. fanes:
Temples. Allah:
The Arabic name for God.

ALHAMAR, THE FOUNDER OF THE ALHAMBRA alchemy:
An ancient science which aimed to turn baser metals into gold, to find a universal remedy for sickness, etc. Hegira:
The flight of Mahomet from Mecca; the epoch from which the Mahometan era is reckoned. astrologer:
A person who in former times studied the stars and pre-tended to foretell events by their aspects and situations. horoscope:
An observation of the stars made at the time of a person's birth, by which his future was foretold. auspicious:
Favorable. santon:
A Moslem saint or hermit. prognosticated:
Predicted, foretold. vassal:
One who holds his possessions subject to the will of a superior or lord. feudal tenure:
The right which a vassal had in the Middle Ages to land or they property, by the payment of some tax or service to his superior lord or sovereign. Cortes:
The assembly of the states or legislative body of Spain. prowess:
Bravery.

THE MYSTERIOUS CHAMBERS damask:
Cloth made of a mixture of silk and flax, and woven with flowers or figures. It was originally brought from Damascus. fresco:
A method of painting upon walls covered with a freshly laid coat of plaster, into which the colors sink and become durable. belvedere:
A small building on the top of an edifice, open on one or more sides. It means literally beautiful view, and is constructed as an outlook over some fine prospect. pristine:
Former. mope and mow:

To make mouths, wry faces. colonnade:
A range or row of columns placed at regular intervals. pavilion:
A small insulated building. parapet:
A wall, breast high, to prevent people from falling over.

PANORAMA FROM THE TOWER OF COMARES environs:
Places which surround or lie in the neighborhood of an-other place.
rendezvous:
A place for meeting. grange:
A farm with its house, stables, etc. regent:
One who governs a kingdom in the minority, absence or disability of the
sovereign. van:
The front of an army.

THE BALCONY panvier:
A wicker basket for carrying fruit and vegetables on a horse or mule. matin
bell:
The bell for morning prayer. vesper bell:
The bell for evening prayer. votive:
given by vow.

THE ADVENTURE OF THE MASON cadaverous:
Pale, ghastly, having the appearance of a dead body. matins:
Morning prayers. curmudgeon:
A miserly, churlish fellow. ducat:
A coin of gold or silver, of several countries of Europe, issued in the
dominions of a duke.

THE COURT OF THE LIONS phantasmagoria:
An exhibition of shadows thrown upon a flat surface by a magic lantern;
hence an illusive image or fancy. armorial ensigns:
Flags bearing coats of arms. See note 7. pageant:
A pompous show or spectacle of entertainment. Te Deum:
An ancient and celebrated Christian hymn, often sung on occasions of
special thanksgiving. turban:
The usual headdress of Orientals. It consists of a close-fitting cap, with a
scarf or shawl wound about it. stanza:

A number of lines or verses regularly adjusted to each other, and properly ending in a full point or pause. couplet:

Two lines that rhyme. Pacha:

(Also Pasha) A Moslem governor of a province. lineage:

Descent in a line from a common ancestor. crusader:

One who took part in the military expeditions sent out by the different Christian nations, during the Middle Ages, for the purpose of rescuing the Holy Land, Palestine, from its Mohammedan possessors.

LOCAL TRADITIONS charm:

Enchantment. amulet:

An object supposed to protect its possessor from evil. occult:

Secret, hidden. talisman:

A charm; something that produces extraordinary effects. effigy:

An image or figure of a person.

THE HOUSE OF THE WEATHERCOCK faquir:

A Mohammedan begging monk. Mosque:

A Mohammedan temple or place of worship.

LEGEND OF THE ARABIAN ASTROLOGER foray:

Any irregular incursion for warfare or spoils. invest:

To surround with troops so as to prevent succor or escape. hieroglyphic:

The picture-writing of the ancient Egyptian priests. magic:

Enchantment; a pretended science of Eastern nations, by which it is claimed that the power of spirits is brought into action. cabalistic:

Having a hidden meaning or possessing secret powers. ecstasy:

Excessive joy; delight. mummy:

A dead body preserved from putrefaction, especially by the Egyptian art of embalming. labyrinth:

A passage full of intricate turnings and windings, out of which one would find it exceedingly difficult to extricate himself. genii:

(pl. of genius) good or evil spirits, supposed to have charge over particular places or things. belabor:

To beat soundly. hermitage:

The dwelling-place of a hermit, or one who lives apart from his fellows. ottoman:

A stuffed seat without a back, originally used in Turkey. divan:

A cushioned seat or couch, especially one fixed to its place, and not movable. garish:

gaudy; glaring. sorceress:

A woman who is supposed to exercise magical powers by the aid of evil spirits. Koran:

The Mohammedan Bible. dervise:

The name of a class of religious persons among the Mohammedans, who affect great austerity, living partly in monasteries, and partly leading a solitary life. incantation:

A form of words used in connection with certain ceremonies for the purpose of enchantment. palfrey:

A gentle horse for ladies. juggle:

To play tricks upon. primeval:

Of the earliest ages. elysium:

Any place exquisitely pleasant.

LEGEND OF PRINCE AHMEND AL KAMEL; OR, THE PILGRIM OF LOVE amorous:

Fond; affectionate. sage:

A learned and venerable philosopher. abstruse lore:

Learning that is difficult to acquire. rapine and carnage:

Plundering and slaughter. votary:

One who is consecrated to any object by vow or promise. topography:

The exact and minute knowledge of any place or region. elopement:

Secret or unauthorized flight. specter:

An apparition, a ghost. palmistry:

The pretended art of telling fortunes by the lines in the palm of the hand. mentor:

A wise and faithful monitor or guide. soothsayer:

One who undertakes to foretell events. conjurer:

One who practises magical arts. black art:

A name given in the Middle Ages to magic, or the performance of difficult acts, by the supposed aid of evil spirits or supernatural power. a bird of parts:

A bird possessing great talents. sinecure:

An office or position without active service. erudition:

Learning. savant:

A learned person. antiquarian:

Pertaining to ancient things. metaphysics:

A science exclusively occupied with mind, as contrasted with physics, which is the science of nature or of natural objects. bon-mot:

A witty reply, a jest. casement:

A window opening on hinges like a door. ambassador:

A representative of the highest rank, sent by one prince or government to another for the management of affairs. coronet:

An inferior crown worn by noble lords and ladies. to enter the lists:

The ground or field inclosed for combat between knights was called the lists. To enter the lists is to accept a challenge or engage in a contest. arbitrament of arms:

A decision arrived at by a personal combat between candidates for honors or special favors. tourney:

Tournament, a public combat between knights. buckler:

A kind of shield anciently used in warfare. pastoral reed:

Shepherd's pipe, a musical instrument made from the joint of a reed. harbinger:

Forerunner. oracle:

One whose opinion is considered to be of great authority. caparison:

The decorative harness or trappings of a horse. punctilio:

Most careful observance of nice points of etiquette, or ceremony.

LEGEND OF THE MOOR'S LEGACY esplanade:

A clear space between a citadel or fortress and the nearest houses of the town. bandy-legged:

Having crooked legs. aids de camp:

A military term signifying an officer selected by a general to carry orders. Here it means merely an assistant. slattern:

A woman who is negligent of her dress or house. sandal-wood:

The highly perfumed yellowish heart-wood of an East Indian and Polynesian, tree. cadence:

A rhythmical modulation of the voice or of any sound. provender:

Provisions. quidnunc:

Latin, what now? One who is curious to know all that is going on. insignia:

Mark or sign; badge of authority. parchment:

The skin of a lamb, calf, or other animal prepared for writing on. scroll:

A roll of parchment or paper. egregious:

Extraordinary, surpassing, usually joined with words of a bad sense, as an egregious rascal. incantation:

The act or process of using certain formulas for the purpose of raising spirits or producing enchantments. myrrh, frankincense, storax:

Fragrant, aromatic gums, burned as incense in religious or other rites. aigrette:

A plume or tuft for the head, composed of feathers or gems. coffer:

A casket or chest, especially one used for holding money or jewels.

LEGEND OF THE THREE BEAUTIFUL PRINCESSES sinister:

Disastrous, evil. The left being usually regarded as the unlucky side; the left hand is frequently called the sinister hand. dexter hand:

The right hand. This is generally the more skilful hand, hence dexterous, active or expert in the use of body and limbs. duenna:

An elderly woman who is appointed to keep guard over a younger one. cogency:

Conclusiveness, force. to cast one's nativity:

To find out and represent the position of the heavenly bodies at the time of one's birth. This was formerly practised by astrologers, or men who studied the stars, and pretended to foretell events by their positions. The same thing as to cast one's horoscope. fates:

Fabled beings who were supposed to control human destinies. galley:

A vessel propelled by oars, whether having sails or not. jalousie:

An inside window-blind with slats. renegado:

One faithless to principle or party, especially one who for-sakes one religious faith for another. roundelay:

A tune in which a simple strain is often repeated. bastinado:

To beat with a stick or cudgel, especially on the soles of the feet. An Eastern punishment. sally-port:

A back gate or door in the outer works of a fortification, reached by an underground passage. bale fire:

A signal or alarm fire.

LEGEND OF THE ROSE OF ALHAMBRA eulogium:

Highest praise. Antinous:

A youth of extraordinary beauty, who was the favorite companion of the Roman emperor Hadrian. He was drowned in the Nile, and the emperor enrolled him among the gods, and caused a temple to be erected to him at Mantinea. ger-falcon:

A large species of falcon, or hawk, a bird with a short-hooked beak, strong claws, and rapid flight. It was formerly trained to the pursuit of other birds and game, When at rest its eyes were kept covered by a hood, which was removed when it was let loose upon its quarry or prey. tortoise-shell cat:

A cat with markings and color resembling a tortoise shell. bonnet:

This name was formerly applied to a soft cap for men or boys. prankling:

Frolicsome; full of pranks. hypochondriac:

One affected with extreme melancholy. megrims:

Lowness of spirits; whims. regicide:

The crime of killing a king. sconce:

A fixed hanging or projecting candlestick. lugubrious:

Mournful. Paganini:

A famous Italian violinist.

THE GOVERNOR AND THE NOTARY doughty:

Valiant; strong. toledo:

A sword made at Toledo in Spain, a city famous for the excellence of its weapons. jurisdiction:

The power or right of exercising authority. sanctuary:

A sacred spot; a place of refuge and protection. virulent:

Very bitter in enmity; actuated by a desire to injure. beetling:

Overhanging. vicegerent:

An officer who is deputed to exercise the powers of another. connivance:

Intentional failure or forbearance to discover a fault. convoy:

A guard or escort to protect provisions or other stores in their transit from one place to another. posse:

A throng. impromptu:

Off-hand; without previous thought. to vapor:

To bluster. surrejoinder:

A legal term, meaning to reply to a rejoinder, or reply. acumen:

Quickness of perception; acuteness. akimbo:

The arms are akimbo when the hands are on the hips, and the elbows turned outwards. deposition:

The testimony of a witness reduced to writing and signed, as given under oath before a judicial officer in answer to questioning and cross-questioning.

GOVERNOR MANCO AND THE SOLDIER stigma:

Slur or disgrace. physiognomy:

Face; countenance.

THE CRUSADE OF THE GRAND MASTER OF ALCANTARA Grand Master of Alcántara:

The head of one of the religious orders of Spanish knighthood, which was founded in 1156 as a military fraternity for defence against the Moors. pennon:

A flag or streamer. zealot:

One who is absorbed in devotion to any cause; an enthusiast. Santiago: St. James. arquebuse:

A sort of hand gun used before the invention of the musket. vicissitude: Irregular change; revolution. indigence:

Poverty.

THE LEGEND OF DON MUNIO SANCHO DE HINOJOSA helm:

Helmet; a defensive covering for the head when knights were clothed in armor. nuptials:

Marriage. ransom:

The price paid for the redemption of a prisoner, or for goods captured by an enemy. espousals:

The marriage ceremony. drawbridge:

A bridge which could be drawn up or let down at pleasure before the gate of a town or castle. viands:

Food; provisions. pilgrimage:

A journey to some sacred place. seneschal:

An officer in the houses of princes and dignitaries in the Middle Ages, who had the charge of feasts and domestic ceremonies.

AUTHORS FAREWELL TO GRANADA elysium:

In Greek and Roman mythology, the place of happy souls' after death; any delightful place. bosky:

Woody.

CPSIA information can be obtained at www.ICGtesting.com
Printed in the USA
BVOW01s1640230716

456570BV00002BA/141/P

The Alhambra : a series of tales and
sketches of the Moors and Spaniards
was published in May 1832, Consisting of a series of essays and short fic-
tion pieces, it was referred to as his
"Spanish Sketch Book." In 1851
Irving wrote the "Author's Revised
Edition", also titled Tales of the Alhambra. Tales of the Alhambra is a
collection of essays, verbal sketches,
and stories.

ISBN 978-1-61720-462-3

90000

9 781617 204623